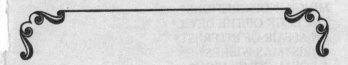
He swung her up and onto the stool so their eyes met at the same level. Lisanne was about to protest that she wasn't a girl, wasn't to be treated like a child, when he pressed a cool, soft kiss on her lips that deepened to a warm, hard embrace. He knew.

"About those sons . . . "

"I have to start packing." Lisanne jumped off the stool and ran toward the house, leaving her hat, her hair net, and her bemused husband. Her cheeks were burning with embarrassment, but her lips were burning with something else altogether. . . .

By Barbara Metzger:

CUPBOARD KISSES*
BETHING'S FOLLY
THE EARL AND THE HEIRESS
RAKE'S RANSOM
MINOR INDISCRETIONS*
THE LUCK OF THE DEVIL*
AN AFFAIR OF INTEREST*
CHRISTMAS WISHES*
A LOYAL COMPANION*
LADY IN GREEN*
AUTUMN LOVES: An Anthology*
AN ANGEL FOR THE EARL*
A SUSPICIOUS AFFAIR*
LADY WHILTON'S WEDDING*
FATHER CHRISTMAS*
VALENTINES: A Trio of Regency Love Stories for
  Sweethearts' Day*
MY LADY INNKEEPER
  and AN EARLY ENGAGEMENT*
AN ENCHANTED AFFAIR*

Published by Fawcett Books

AN ENCHANTED AFFAIR

Barbara Metzger

FAWCETT CREST • NEW YORK

A Fawcett Crest Book
Published by Ballantine Books
Copyright © 1996 by Barbara Metzger

All rights reserved under International and Pan-American Copyright Conventions. Published in the United States by Ballantine Books, a division of Random House, Inc., New York, and simultaneously in Canada by Random House of Canada Limited, Toronto.

http://www.randomhouse.com

Library of Congress Catalog Card Number: 95-96167

ISBN 0-449-22353-1

Manufactured in the United States of America

First Edition: August 1996

10 9 8 7 6 5 4 3 2 1

To Stacy Seiden and Mark Siegal
in honor of your marriage.

May you be as happy
as any fairy-tale lovers,
forever after.

Happy First Anniversary.

AN
ENCHANTED
AFFAIR

Chapter One

*L*isanne Neville was six years old before she realized no one else could talk to the fairies. No one else cared, either, so Lisanne was not concerned. She simply felt more special.

Her nanny was an old Cornishwoman, with superstitions bred into her blood since the Celts fled the mainland. Nanny Murtagh blamed the piskis for stealing her thimbles, for making holes in her stockings, and for causing her frequent bilious attacks. The medicinal tot of rum she added to her tea at night couldn't be contributing to her sore head and her upset stomach, ah, no. Didn't she leave a saucer of the brew on the windowsill every night to appease the wee folk, and didn't they drink it up by morning? If, by chance, an inordinate amount of pigeons fell off the roof at night, well, the pixies were a mischievous race indeed.

Nanny saw nothing unusual in her darling girl's knowing which herbs and meadow flowers made the most soothing tisane for a maudled digestion, or knowing how to bind a pigeon's broken wing. The Neville estate bordered on Sevrin Woods, didn't it?

Everyone knew the woods were bewitched. They were

1

not as dangerous as demon-filled Dartmoor, at Devonshire's other end, but bad enough that the locals wouldn't set foot under the ancient oaks and wide-spreading hollies. Not even Devon's intrepid smugglers used the forest's winding paths, nor did poachers follow its deer tracks. Neither group feared the Duke of St. Sevrin or his minions, for His Grace was away in London dissipating what little remained of the family's fortune, and St. Sevrin Priory was going to wrack and ruin without benefit of housekeeper, gatekeeper, or gamekeeper. What would-be trespassers feared was magic, witchcraft, sorcery. A bit of venison or a tickled trout wasn't worth the risk of being turned into a toad or getting elf-led off the paths to wander for enchanted eternity.

The vicar's harangues against paganism didn't open a single closed mind, nor did the fact that Lord Neville's little girl played in the woods all the time without coming to harm. The housemaids and stable boys at Neville Hall simply crossed themselves when Lisanne claimed the forest folk weren't evil, that they'd never hurt anybody.

As for Lisanne's parents, Lord Neville had married late in life, and his wife had conceived even later in their marriage. After Lisanne's difficult birth, the physicians had warned the baron that there would be no more children. Lord Neville was content. His barony was one of those archaic land grants by which title and property could pass through the female line if necessary. The papers were drawn, the succession was secure, and the baron could return to his translations of the early Greeks and Romans.

To say that Lisanne was the apple of her father's eye would be an understatement. She was the whole orchard, with nary a blight or a blemish to spoil his satisfaction. So when his little golden-haired cherub climbed on her papa's knee and babbled about her friends in the forest, Tug and Moss, Alon and baby Rimtim, Lord Neville was delighted. What a bright puss she was, his precious poppet, creative and clever. She was already learning the

2

Greek alphabet along with her ABC's. Best of all, she was happy to play for hours at the far side of Neville Hall's sloping lawns, past the formal gardens and the maze. She did not interfere with her papa's concentration on a difficult passage, but was right there when he looked up and out his library's windows. The baron could always spot his jewel of a daughter, laughing and dancing and skipping around while Nanny sat with her knitting on a nearby bench, there at the edge of Sevrin Woods. As Nanny Murtagh would have said, the sight warmed the cockles of his heart.

Lady Neville's cockles were not quite so contented, although she loved her daughter none the less. It was a lonely child who created imaginary playmates, the baroness believed, an only child. Whenever she saw Lisanne frolicking with sunbeams at the edge of the forest, Lady Neville's heart ached. When she heard Lisanne's bedtime recital of her day's adventures with her little friends, the baroness nodded and smiled and agreed that the forest people were the happiest, wisest, most amusing companions a child could have, and wasn't Lisanne lucky they'd chosen her. Inside, Lady Neville grieved for the sisters and brothers Lisanne would never have.

There were no wellborn children of an age with Lisanne in the neighborhood, and the tenants' children were too busy with chores, the village youngsters too rough. Neither Lady Neville nor the baron, of course, would ever entertain the notion of sending their treasure away to school with other daughters of the nobility. Perhaps when she got older, they'd tell each other, never intending to part with their dearest joy.

Of frail constitution herself, the baroness never considered joining her daughter for rambles through the woods. She also never considered how such a little girl seemed to know the name of every wildflower, which berries were safe to eat, or when a storm was coming. Perhaps old

Nanny Murtagh was teaching her, or the gardeners. The gardeners? Heaven forfend the future Lady Neville was reduced to befriending the servants. Imaginary playmates were better, even if they were fairies.

So Lady Neville took matters into her own frail hands. It wasn't what she would have wished, but for her daughter's sake the baroness was willing to make the sacrifice. She invited her brother and his hopeful family to spend the summer at Neville Hall.

Sir Alfred Findley was hopeful of separating his scholarly brother-in-law from a portion of the Neville fortune. Findley was a baronet of very minor gentry as was his father before him, and as his son Nigel would be after him, with a barely adequate competence. Sir Alfred's baroness sister, however, had risen to the nobility—the wealthy, landed, idle, and inbred nobility. Sir Alfred bitterly resented this fact, which was one reason traffic between the two families was so infrequent. The other was that Lord Neville considered his in-laws nothing but a clump of ignorant mushrooms.

Still, the invitation went out and was accepted. The Findley *familia* arrived and settled in.

"Why don't you show your cousins around, dearest," her mother directed Lisanne the next morning. "They might enjoy the maze and the gardens. Nigel can roll his hoop on the lawns, and you and Esmé can have a tea party in the gazebo."

Nigel was a year older than Lisanne and didn't want to play with girls. Esmeralda, Esmé as she was called, was a year younger than Lisanne and didn't want to get her slippers wet in the damp grass. They went anyway, following the stern direction of their father and the nervous cautions of their city-bred mother. Lisanne promptly lost them in the woods.

She didn't mean to, of course. She merely intended to introduce her cousins to her other playmates. The cousins couldn't see them, of course.

4

"I don't understand," Lisanne complained to her friend Moss, who was reclining beneath a dandelion.

Moss stood and puffed out his cheeks and blew until the dandelion fuzz drifted away. "That's what they have between their ears, your cousins, nothing but fluff. A toadstool has more imagination. Who wants to talk to lumpish, loutish children like them?"

Lisanne turned back to her guests. Nigel was tossing stones at the crows jabbering above them. "This is boring," he whined when he didn't hit any.

Esmé was brushing a smudge off her pinafore and sniveling, "I want to go home."

"See?" Moss asked. "You're not like them. You're special. Now, come, the vixen just had her babies in the meadow."

Lisanne politely invited her guests along to see the new fox kits.

"Mama said we weren't to get out of sight of the house," Esmé dutifully reminded, "and it's nearly time for tea."

Nigel sneered at his cousin. "You can't know there's any such thing in the meadow. And no fox is going to let you play with her babies. We should go find the head huntsman, anyway, so he can drown the vermin or take the young hounds cubbing."

Moss just laughed, shaking the tiny bells on his cap. Lisanne looked from her glum-faced cousins to her smiling friend. There was no competition. She waved to Nigel and Esmé and ran laughing after the tinkling chimes. "Wait for me!"

Esmé would have been happy to go back to the house, but Nigel was having none of it. What, get shown up by a mere girl? He grabbed his sister's hand and pulled her along the faint path Lisanne had taken. Then he dragged her through briars and brambles and a stream. It was the stream that did it. Esmé set up such a howling that Nigel relented. "Very well, you sissy, we'll go home." Except that Nigel had no idea of where home was.

Lady Findley lay prostrate on the sofa while her maid burned feathers under her nose. Sir Alfred was all for calling out the stable hands, the tenant farmers, the militia. Even Lisanne's fond papa was a tad concerned when his poppet ambled out of the woods some hours later, leaves in her braids, mud on her skirts, and berry juice on her chin, sans cousins.

Matters were not helped any when Lisanne was able to lead the searchers through the woods on a direct route to the missing children. Nigel and Esmé were huddled under a juniper bush, damp, cold, and frightened out of what wits they possessed. Sobbing, Nigel shoved his sister aside to be first into his father's arms. Then he remembered he was a boy.

"She did it," he screamed, pointing at Lisanne, the cause of his shameful tears. "She led us into the woods saying we'd see wonderful things. Then she left us alone so we couldn't get back. She pretended to talk to someone who wasn't there, just to frighten us."

"No, Papa, I never did. They didn't want to come with Moss and me, so I left them in the gardens."

"Moss? Who's this Moss?" Uncle Alfred demanded. "Nigel said there was no one else around."

Lord Neville could only shrug, but Nigel hopped up and down. "There wasn't, Pa, I swear. She was talking to a dandelion. Lisanne's a loony, Pa. Addled Annie, they should call her."

And Esmé, now that she was safe in her father's arms, chanted, "Addled Annie, Addled Annie," all the way home.

Suddenly, being special wasn't quite so much fun.

Sir Alfred raged at his sister while his wife saw to the packing. "You always were a weakling, Elizabeth. And now you're raising a mooncalf because you're too feeble to do anything about it. You are letting some half-mad Cornishwoman raise your daughter, and look what it's gotten you. Why, the woman didn't even know the children had wandered off. Drunk, I don't doubt."

Lady Neville wiped at her eyes with a delicate scrap of lace. "Nanny Murtagh? Never."

"Hah! That's how much attention you pay to your household. I could smell Blue Ruin on her breath the instant I arrived."

Since Lady Neville would not have recognized Blue Ruin from a blue moon, she could only sniff some more.

"And what's she teaching the chit, that's what I want to know," Alfred ranted on. "Dash it, the gel could snabble a duke if she's reared properly. My girl's younger, and she's had a governess for two years, not a cloth-headed nanny. Of course Nigel has a tutor, but that's irrelevant. Watercolors, your girl needs, and pianoforte lessons, dance instruction. She should be sewing samplers instead of wandering around in haunted woods."

Lady Neville did not think this was the time to inform her brother that Lisanne had already read every book in the nursery and was starting on her father's library, Greek and Latin volumes included. Not when they'd all had to suffer through an hour the previous afternoon watching Esmé blot her way through signing her name, and listen to Nigel stutter over a short paragraph in his primer. Perhaps Alfred was right, though, that parts of Lisanne's education were being neglected. Heaven knew Elizabeth had endured hours with a backboard, and she'd won herself a baron. Lady Neville promised to consider hiring a governess for her daughter.

"What, some down-at-heels parson's daughter from the next village? Your gel's a hoyden, a dreamer, a scheming liar, if she's not knocked-in-the-cradle altogether. Are you sure that Murtagh woman didn't drop her on her head? For certain she filled Lisanne's mind with all that fairy-tale tripe. What the little baggage needs now is a firm hand on the reins. Someone who's up to every rig and row, and knows her way around the ton besides. I'll look into it on my way through London. The chit has to be ready to take her place where she belongs, in Town, not in a benighted blueberry patch."

Someone had to plan for the girl's glorious future, Alfred told himself. A well-bred, titled heiress would have the eligibles buzzing around her like flies on fruit. And he meant for his Esmeralda to be at Lisanne's side, and his Nigel at her feet. "It's never too early to start," Alfred told his sister as he climbed into the baron's luxurious coach for the ride back to his own pawky property. Alfred lovingly rubbed his hand over the bright lacquerwork of the carriage door. No, it was never too early to start.

"Nice holiday, what?" Lord Neville asked his wife, putting his arm around her thin shoulders as the coach pulled away. "Just the way I like visits from your family. Short."

Chapter Two

The new governess arrived. Sir Alfred had done his job well. Miss Armbruster was the most widely recommended instructress of young females in all of London. Her blood was the bluest, with an earl for an uncle, albeit said earl was currently languishing in the Fleet debtors' prison. Miss Armbruster was also intelligent, reliable, and the highest paid governess currently on the market, which iced Sir Alfred's cake, since her wages were coming out of Lord Neville's deep pockets, not his own.

Miss Armbruster was a female of a certain age who was certain in her notions. When Sir Alfred cautiously mentioned that the nearby woods were said to be haunted, Miss Armbruster replied, "Bosh. There is no such thing." Warned that her charge was considered fey in the neighborhood, she answered, "Nonsense. The child simply needs discipline." A difficult charge? Miss Armbruster hadn't met one yet.

Nanny Murtagh was pensioned off to a cottage back in Lostwithiel, and Miss Armbruster took over Lisanne's education. She tried, anyway.

Lessons. That was the key, Miss Armbruster declared to Lady Neville. Prayers before breakfast, then grammar,

9

composition, and mathematics, with history and geography on alternate days. After luncheon, healthful exercise: nature walks in the formal gardens on pleasant days, to be combined with science and sketching, or laps around the portrait gallery on inclement afternoons for more history and heritage. French before tea, etiquette and elocution during. The interval between tea and supper would be reserved for music instruction, voice and instrument, with dance to be added later. Needlework could be accomplished after the meal, in the hour before the child's bedtime. If not, they could rise earlier in the mornings.

Sunday afternoons, Miss Armbruster continued, were to be her half days, and she had one full-day holiday per month; but, the governess assured Lady Neville, she would leave enough assignments behind that Lady Lisanne would not have a moment free to get into any trouble.

Lady Neville took to her bed.

Lisanne took to the new regime the way a crocodile waltzes, which is to say not at all. No time for her friends? No time for her books? No time for the wonders of Sevrin Woods? No way. Being a polite, obedient, cheerful child, Lisanne did not throw herself on the floor in a tantrum, run away from home, or hold her breath until she turned blue. She merely cried. She didn't even cry on her papa's waistcoat or, worse, on his translation of Ovid. She simply sobbed in her bed at night and came to breakfast with red, swollen eyes. Then she silently wept through luncheon. If ever there was a doting father who could see his little girl's misery and not be moved to rehang the moon for her, it was not Lord Neville. He took another look at the new governess.

Sir Alfred had outsmarted himself in finding such an intelligent, competent, expensive female to bear-lead his peculiar niece onto a more conventional path. Miss Armbruster was intelligent enough to see which way the wind blew. She was most definitely competent to recognize precisely who it was who paid that exorbitant salary—the same quiet and bookish gentleman who wouldn't hesitate to throw her out on her aristocratic ear if his little darling was unhappy.

So there was a compromise. In the mornings Lisanne was expected in the schoolroom with completed assignments. In the afternoons, well, in the afternoons Miss Armbruster suddenly found it necessary to work on the reference book she was compiling for the education of young females. Lisanne was to return for tea, dinner at the very latest, having practiced at least one ladylike skill to show off to her proud parents. And she was never, not in public, not in private, to mention fairies, little people, pixies, or elves.

Miss Armbruster was happy. This was the easiest position she had ever held, and the child was bright, inquisitive, and quite endearing, so long as one didn't inquire too closely as to where she went of an afternoon. Since that involved forbidden topics, Miss Armbruster was able to ignore what she considered the odd kick in Lisanne's gallop. Over the years of her tenure, she was able to complete three volumes of her textbook, which were very well received in academic circles.

Lisanne was happy. She had friends, freedom, her parents' affection, and her governess's approval.

Lord Neville was happy, too, until he died.

The doctors would not let Lisanne near the sickroom. They wouldn't listen to her rantings about willow bark tea and foxglove infusions. The Honorable Lisanne Neville had all of twelve years in her dish by now. She had no business with possets and potions.

What did a child, a feebleminded one at that, if rumor was to be believed, know about the healing arts? the consulting London surgeons asked each other. Herbal quackery, that was all she proposed, likely from some ancient crone who lived in a hollow tree stump and stole pennies

11

from the poor with a handful of dried weeds. Next the chit would be bringing the learned physicians eye of newt or some such thing from an old household book of simples.

The medical scientists cupped the baron, bled the baron, and purged the baron. They killed the baron.

Lady Neville could not survive on her own. The grief, the details of the estate, the uncertainty of her future were too much for the baroness. She never had been strong in will or in body, but without the baron, Lady Neville was too weak to get out of bed. Then she was too weak to keep waking up in the morning. One morning she didn't.

No one was going to see Lisanne's tears and make things right. Not even her friends in the woods could make this right. What did they know of death? They lived forever. So Lisanne stopped crying. Miss Armbruster was concerned: a child needed to grieve instead of wandering alone through the corridors of an empty manor house. But nothing in all of the governess's book learning or learning books could change matters, either.

And then Lisanne wasn't quite so alone. Uncle Alfred and his family came. To stay.

Since the nearest Neville relation was so distant that the baron had never met the chap, Lord Neville had reluctantly named his wife's brother as guardian for his daughter and heiress. Alfred Findley might be family, but the baron made sure to appoint his own London solicitor as trustee of Lisanne's vast estate.

Sometimes no family was better than the family one had. Uncle Alfred's first order of business, after moving himself and his vaporish wife, Cherise, into the master suite, was to get rid of Miss Armbruster. Now that Sir Alfred was paying the household bills—and pocketing what he could scrape off the accountings—he saw no need to keep the pricey dragoness. Esmé's governess was good enough for Annie, too. Mrs. Graybow wouldn't stand for any of this wandering off alone, playing in forbidden woods like some savage or grubbing about in the dirt for roots and stuff. Widow of an infantry sergeant, built like a cavalry horse, Mrs. Graybow would shape the new baroness into a proper lady, one way or another.

Miss Armbruster had amassed a tidy sum from her years at Neville Hall, both from her generous salary, frequent bonuses, and profits from her books. She had enough money put by that she could either live quietly at a respectable boardinghouse for the rest of her days, or she could use her savings to found a school for young ladies. One look at Sir Alfred's unprepossessing daughter convinced her on the boardinghouse. Too bad they couldn't all be like Lisanne.

Lisanne didn't cry when Miss Armbruster left, promising frequent letters. Nor did she weep when her uncle and Mrs. Graybow forbade her the woods. There were no more tears in her. Lisanne simply disobeyed and disappeared into her beloved woods for hours on end. So Mrs. Graybow boxed her ears. Then she rapped her knuckles with a ruler. Then she whipped her with a switch.

Lisanne wouldn't cry, and she wouldn't promise not to go off again.

So Uncle Alfred beat her. Years of bitter rancor went into every stroke: anger at his dead sister's elevating marriage, anger at the terms of the dead baron's will, and anger at fate, that put such a fortune into the hands of a city shyster instead of the much worthier ones of the brat's uncle. The exercise might have relieved some of the baronet's ingrained resentment, but it had no effect on Annie, as the family now called her, beyond the obvious. As soon as she recovered, Lisanne left the house and stayed away for two days and a night.

When she returned, Sir Alfred had Mrs. Graybow lock her in her bedroom. Lisanne climbed out the window onto the trellised vines. They locked her in the butler's pantry. The Hall's old butler would never have stood for seeing his mistress so abused, but the Findleys' own major domo held sway now. Sir Alfred had given all the Neville staff the sack, saying he preferred his own loyal retainers. These servants just happened to be used to more niggardly wages—not that Alfred needed to mention that fact to Lisanne's London solicitor. Alfred rented out his own small property near London, preferring to put up at a hotel when visiting the City on his niece's business—and on her expense account.

No one, therefore, protested as Lisanne spent hour after hour in the small dark room. She was hauled out three times a day for meals, Mrs. Graybow deeming tea unnecessary for a disobedient child. At those meals Lisanne was given the chance to swear on her honor not to leave the property. Now she not only stopped crying, she stopped talking, and stopped eating.

Rescue came from an unexpected source. Aunt Cherise was having palpitations. Not only was she forced into the country away from the shops and entertainments of the City, but she was too embarrassed to venture into local society. "The child is going to die if you keep this up, Alfred. Look at her, she's skin and bones already." And bruises, but Aunt Cherise turned her eyes. "I can not accept invitations because we are in mourning, but what will people say?"

Sir Alfred didn't care what a parcel of country nobodies said. He did care what that blasted will said. If she died, the little baroness, that distant Neville cousin inherited everything, all those trust-fund earnings, all those rent rolls. Findley wasn't about to let his meal ticket waste away over a bit of hoydenish behavior the chit would likely outgrow anyway.

The baronet rubbed his weak chin. After all, there was no chance his own daughter would be contaminated with Annie's disobedience. Esmé treated her cousin as a *grande dame* would a noxious puddle, pulling her skirts aside and ignoring the mess. Esmeralda would never set foot in those bothersome woods again if her life depended on it, even if she was assured her slippers wouldn't get soiled. Nigel tried once when they first arrived, taking his gun into the woods after a deer. He got lost again, which had to have been Annie's fault, he swore, since she eventually came to lead him home.

Although he never mentioned it to anyone, Sir Alfred went into the forest one day, determined to drag Annie back by her hair if necessary. But under the great trees he found a dark, forbidding atmosphere with odd, earthy scents. The baronet even thought he heard voices laughing at him where no one was. He'd turned around while he could still see the chimneys of Neville Hall.

"It's not as if any of the neighbors are going to spot her outside without an escort or a bonnet," Aunt Cherise urged, to get the impossible child out of the house.

No, none of the neighbors were about to spy on his niece whatever the brat did in those woods. Annie could take her clothes off and dance naked in a Black Sabbath. No one would know, because no one ever ventured a toe into Sevrin Woods. And she was still only a little girl.

So there was another compromise, of sorts. Sir Alfred and his family lived in Lisanne's house, off her income, and ignored her presence as well as her absence. This suited the young baroness just fine.

Lisanne kept away from the house and away from its surly servants as much as she could. When she was at home, she read in her papa's library, where there was small chance of encountering any of her relations. She also kept up with her studies in the woods, the stillroom, and the herb gardens. And she still nursed the injured birds and orphaned rabbits that came her way.

One other duty kept her from the forest on occasion: her responsibility to the Neville tenants. Sir Alfred wasn't able to replace the bailiff, so those dependent on the barony were not subject to his penny-pinching ways. Neither were they well served by him or his wife. The Findleys made frequent trips to London, nary a one to the thatch-roofed cottages. It was Annie, remembering her father's gentle teachings, who brought baskets of food when the crops were meager, blankets when the winter was severe. She had an elixir for old man Jenkins's rheumatics, and a syrup for Neddy Broome's cough. Soon the household servants started coming to her with toothaches and such. For sure Sir Alfred wouldn't pay out the fee for a doctor's visit. They might make the sign to ward off the evil eye when Annie was through, but they brought her their sniffles and spasms.

Annie could doctor simple ailments, but she was better with animals. Soon the tenants were asking her to look at a sow that wouldn't farrow, a cow that gave no milk. And gardens, why, the slip of a girl could sniff at a handful of dirt and tell why the roses didn't bloom or when the peas should be planted.

Lisanne's reputation grew, despite all of her uncle's efforts to curb it. While there was respect for the child's learning, there was suspicion, too. That was a powerful lot of knowledge for such a young head, the rumors went. And where did she come by guessing whether Rob Fleck's next babe was a boy or a girl—and getting it right year after year? No one could have taught her, for the servants said she had no schooling. The Devonshire folks shook their heads. They never let any of *their* children play in Sevrin Woods. Whispers of Addled Annie followed Lady Lisanne's visits.

Uncle Alfred was furious. His fortune, his plans, his dreams of having Esmé and Nigel marry fortunes and titles, were all going up in smoke with one of Annie's reeking concoctions. The girl wasn't outgrowing that claptrap about fairy friends; she just wasn't talking about it. Her silence, in turn, made the locals wonder all the more how she came by her knowledge. It wasn't normal, they said, crossing themselves. It wasn't natural. And wasn't there a peculiar vagueness behind the girl's blue-eyed stare, almost as if she were seeing other sights, hearing other voices?

Sir Alfred decided to send Annie away to school, away from the gossip, away from those thrice-cursed woods. One of those strict seminaries would know what to do about making a lady out of a chit who constantly looked as if she'd been pulled through a thicket backward. Esmé could go along as companion. On Annie's account, of course.

When informed of the treat in store for her, Lisanne stared down at the hands correctly folded in her lap, not seeing the dirt under her fingernails that made Aunt Cherise wince. She quietly, politely, ever so assuredly, informed her guardian that she would find a way to run away from whatever school he chose. She'd live in the woods, and he'd never see her again . . . or a groat more of her income. Lisanne wasn't half as vague as everyone thought. She'd managed to read her father's will as well as most of the communications from the London solicitor. She knew her worth to the ha'penny, and knew how much of it was going into Uncle Alfred's pockets.

Sir Alfred believed the little witch would do what she said, disappear forever just to spite him. So he bit his lip and let her be. As she turned fourteen, then fifteen, and neared sixteen—almost of an age for a presentation—he gnawed on his own frustrations.

How could he bring Annie to London to make a grand match that would benefit him and his children? Even if he could get her there, Annie wouldn't take. She never cared about her clothes, wearing whatever she found in her closet. Since these were usually the taller, plumper Esmé's castoffs, Sir Alfred hadn't complained at Annie's dowdiness, not in light of the expenses saved. The chit still wore her hair in braids down her back, while Esmé was already nagging her mother to have hers put up. Annie's skin was browned from the sun, she ran barefoot half the time, and to his knowledge she had no drawing-room skills or conversation. Wouldn't the Almack's patronesses just love to chat about Farmer Goode's infected thumb? What man of means would look twice at a filthy, dreamy, waiflike female? What nobleman would chance begetting an heir with attics to let? None.

Chapter Three

*N*o man in his right mind was going to marry a woman who wasn't in her right mind. Sir Alfred slowly repeated that obvious fact to himself, in wonder. It was almost as if the skies had opened up and the heavenly host presented him with a divine revelation. No one was ever going to marry Lisanne Neville, not even the most desperate fortune hunter. All these years Alfred had been thinking of the grand marriage he'd arrange for Annie—and for his own advancement. But if she never married, he didn't have to relinquish her guardianship for ten more years, not until she turned five and twenty. If, by some happenstance, he could then show that the poor, unfortunate lackwit needed a keeper, well, perhaps he could spend the rest of his days in clover.

Yes, Sir Alfred liked this new idea very much indeed. He let Annie go her own way, higgledy-piggledy adding to her reputation as an eccentric or worse. He encouraged the local gossip, and even added some of his own when in Town, laying the groundwork with the deceased baron's old acquaintances.

"Dreadful news about Neville's daughter." Sir Alfred sighed. "Why, the poor dear is as queer as Dick's hatband, don't you know. The death of both parents was too much for her, such a fragile little thing. Her mind must have snapped."

He gravely accepted the condolences of Lord Harrington, the biggest rattle in Town. "Sad fate for a noble family to end that way. Nothing to be done, eh?"

Findley shook his head. "Unfortunately not. She lives in a fantasy world, dabbling in herbalism and woodlore so she doesn't have to face the harsh reality of her loss. It's all harmless, you understand, but not the thing for a proper young female. She simply cannot be taught any of the usual accomplishments."

"You've had her to the sawbones, of course. Don't suppose they did her any good. Can't cure the king, after all."

Another sigh. "The professionals have given up. It's a hopeless case. Besides, all they advised was to bleed her or put her in restraints, or drill holes in her head. We couldn't put the dear child through that."

Harrington shuddered. "Nothing left but to send her to Bethlehem Hospital."

"What, declare my own sister's child a bedlamite? I couldn't betray the baron's trust in me that way. No, we'll keep her safe at home." Alfred put his hand over where his heart would be, if he had one. "Her loving family will stand by her."

Of course they would.

"Pa, I don't see why you can't make Annie show me the way through Sevrin Woods. It ain't as if it's hers or anything."

Nigel had been sent down from school again. This was the last time, for Sir Alfred knew better than to send good money after bad. They were at the breakfast table on a gloomy, rainy day. The eggs were runny and the rashers were greasy. Sir Alfred had the newspaper propped in front of him in hopes of avoiding the morning brangling between his children and the carping demands of his wife. He looked over the newspaper and said, "Why don't you ask her yourself? She's sitting across the table from you."

Lisanne was taking one of her infrequent meals with the family because it was raining too hard to venture out, and the current cook refused to permit any hell-born babe in her kitchens lest her bread stop rising. As usual, the family ignored Lisanne's presence in their midst, except for Aunt Cherise's calling for her sal volatile when she saw her niece's apparel. Tired of Esmé's billowy castoffs that snagged on every bush and briar, Lisanne had taken to wearing Nigel's.

"Tell her she must not appear in the public rooms in such attire, Alfred. I have a hard enough time holding my head up in this neighborhood as is."

Alfred pointedly nodded to where Lisanne was placidly nibbling at a sweet roll, and went back to his paper.

Esmé took up the complaint: "Well, I don't see why I have to have lessons anymore when Annie doesn't. She's only a year older than me, and she's been out of the classroom forever."

"Than I, Esmé," Sir Alfred wearily corrected without looking up. "And if you knew that, perhaps you wouldn't need schooling any longer, either."

Nigel reached across the table for the jam pot. "But, Pa, I have to hunt in Sevrin Woods. You know the bailiff won't let me shoot on Neville grounds."

"That's because you shot two goats and a chicken last time." Esmé snickered before returning to her claims of injustice. "I think you should make Annie practice the pianoforte at least, Papa. It's not fair that I have to play when the church ladies come visit and Annie doesn't."

"What, have her in the parlor when company comes?" Lady Cherise screeched before falling back in her seat, clutching her chest. "Tell her she cannot, Alfred."

Sir Alfred tossed down his papers. He couldn't recall the last occasion he'd been able to tell his niece anything but the time of day.

Lessons? Hah! Even Mrs. Graybow had confessed years ago that there wasn't a blessed thing she could teach the chit, and a lot she could learn from her. Trust that fusty old Neville to spawn a brilliant child, while Alfred's two progenies hadn't a brain to share between them. It suited the baronet's purposes to have everyone consider Annie an unlettered wantwit, however, so he kept mum about her abilities, although a bluestocking was nearly as unmarkable as an imbecile on the marriage block. As for music, heaven only knew what language the chit would sing if she ever opened her mouth. Annie must know six or seven languages by now, the governess reported after spying in her room. Chances were the gel had the voice of an angel, too, to show up Esmé's cater-wauling. The devil knew she understood farming better than Alfred did, and horses, too.

As for making Annie do what she didn't choose, such as taking Nigel hunting, or wearing proper dress, or practicing some mind-numbing set piece, well, Findley might as soon whistle for the wind. And Alfred hated to whistle; it was common. The deuced chit was like a thorn in his side, though, going her own quiet way. Nigel could be kept on a short lead by threatening his allowance or a caning, and Esmé would jump through burning hoops for some new gewgaw or other. It was only Annie that Findley couldn't control. The very thought gave Sir Alfred dyspepsia. He pushed his chair back and stood up. "Dash it all, can't a man have any peace at his own breakfast table?"

"I believe it is *my* breakfast table, sir."

Six pairs of eyes turned to stare at Lisanne: four Findleys and two servants. It was the first time in ages any of them had heard her voluntarily enter a dialogue. She spoke to the tenants, she made requests of the servants, but Lisanne did not often speak to her family.

Sir Alfred sat down again. "What, you've blessed us with your presence and now you're going to extend us the gift of your conversation?"

Lisanne sipped at her chocolate.

"Come now, Annie, surely you have more to say than to claim a piece of mahogany."

"Yes, sir. I wish to tell Nigel that he must not hunt in Sevrin Woods."

"Dash it all, Annie, it's not yours to say me aye or nay. Is it, Pa?"

Lisanne stared at her cup. "The animals and birds there have never been hunted. They're tame."

Giggling, Esmé taunted, "Then maybe he can hit something."

Nigel's face got red, but he spat back, "Shut up, brat. And what's the difference, I say. A deer's a deer, no matter where it lives."

"It wouldn't be sportsmanlike" was all Lisanne said, finally staring Nigel in the eyes, daring her cousin to admit he was less than a gentleman. His adolescent amour propre could not let him confess to such a thing in front of his disdainful father or his sniggling sister. He might feel that there was nothing wrong with shooting ducks in a barrel, either, as long as you managed to hit one, but he knew better than to admit it. Nigel looked away first.

Lisanne nodded. "Besides, you would be poaching on Lord St. Sevrin's preserves. His Grace might be in London, but he is still the owner of the property."

"Then how come you get to wander on his land free and clear?" Nigel wanted to know, his voice cracking in his agitation.

"I never harm anything," Lisanne answered in her quiet way.

Esmé couldn't resist adding: "Neither would Nigel, the way he shoots."

Ignoring his sister, Nigel tried to shake Lisanne's composure. The fact that his cousin was so poised and confident when she was the one dicked in the nob infuriated him. "Harm, my foot! What's that to the matter? It's still trespassing! You've never met St. Sevrin. For sure the duke never gave permission for no loony to ramble around his estate."

"I did meet His Grace once, when I was very small. He put some of the Priory's furnishings up for auction. Papa took me when he went to look at the books."

"I daresay the man was run off his feet even then," Aunt Cherise put in, addressing the table at large. She knew everything about everyone in the ton, being an avid reader of the gossip pages and a faithful correspondent to her like-minded London acquaintances. "They say he took to drink right after his wife died, well before Annie could have been born, and started gambling away his fortune. I'd always heard he was a dirty dish."

"He was pleasant to me," Lisanne said, smiling at the memory. "I told him he had the loveliest wildflowers growing in his wood, and he said I may as well pick all I wanted, for he couldn't make any profit off them." She turned to Nigel. "So you see, I do have His Grace's permission to be on the property."

"Not anymore you don't, missy." Uncle Alfred tapped the newspaper that was next to his plate. "The old duke is dead. Shot in a duel over a Covent Garden whore."

"Sir Alfred!" Aunt Cherise nodded in Esmé's direction. "Little pitchers."

The baronet shrugged. "You're the one who said the chit was almost ready for a London come-out. She'll hear a lot worse there."

Lisanne was burning to snatch up the newspaper and run to her room with it, but her uncle still held the folded pages. "The article says the heir is being notified. He's with the army in the Peninsula. I suppose he'll have to resign his commission and settle the estate, what there is left of it."

Aunt Cherise sniffed. "It's more likely Viscount Shearingham will take up where his father left off. The young man already has a reputation for wildness. There were rumors of his being turned away from various clubs before he purchased his colors." Aunt Cherise had to stop and think. "Money from his mother's side, I believe. There was not enough left of his patrimony to purchase a corncob pipe, much less a coronetcy."

Lisanne excused herself, although no one noticed when she left. The footman did not even pull her seat back, she got up in such a hurry, eager to get to the bundle of old newspapers that was always stored in the polishing room. Yes, there he was, Major Lord Shearingham, mentioned in the dispatches. The viscount was on Wellesley's own staff, and it seemed, from the tittle-tattle columns, that he'd made a career of equal parts daring and debauchery.

From that day on, Lisanne made sure she saw the daily newspapers, even if they were two days late from London. She skimmed the war news, the political reporting, and the financial sections, but she studied the *on dits* with as much intensity as her father had studied his Greek tomes. She even paid attention to Aunt Cherise's gleanings from her gabble-grinding correspondents.

The new Duke of St. Sevrin was frequently mentioned for his acts of bravery, his commendations and medals. It was duly noted that he refused to sell out in the middle of the war. According to Aunt Cherise's informants, from whom Wellesley could have learned a thing or two, His Grace hired a London man of business to engage a new bailiff, to handle the income, and to make investments until St. Sevrin was good and ready to take up the domestic reins.

An infected saber wound wasn't good, but it made St. Sevrin ready to leave the front a year or so later. Lisanne read the papers even more avidly. Now the news was of the swath St. Sevrin was cutting through London's *demi monde*, instead of through the French forces. He seemed to favor opera dancers, from all she could gather. If Aunt Cherise and the budding debutante Esmé were examples of the females in Society, Lisanne didn't blame him. Weighed against the rest of the gossip she read, Sloane St. Sevrin didn't seem much worse than any other London profligate—certainly no worse than his own father. No better, either.

Tongues wagged and turbaned heads shook in disapproval, but not Lisanne's. She didn't care a jot about St. Sevrin's morals. In fact, she wished him joy of his birds of paradise, his gaming hells, his dockside brawls, whatever it took to keep him happy in London—and away from St. Sevrin Priory.

Chapter Four

Sloane Shearingham, late of Her Majesty's First Hussars, only son of the late fifth Duke of St. Sevrin, and perpetually late with the rent, was not happy in London. Not at all. The gossip mills might lump him with the other idle pleasure-seekers of his class, but the sixth Duke of St. Sevrin was getting deuced little pleasure out of the constant rounds of gambling, drinking, and wenching.

It wasn't that he missed the army. Zeus knew he'd hated the bloody war. Sloane still woke in the middle of the night bathed in sweat from the memories of cannons and fallen comrades, screaming horses and the stench of blood. He still ached where the Frenchie's saber had sliced across his chest and under his left arm, which the sawbones warned would always be weak. If Sloane's right arm hadn't been so strong around the surgeon's neck, the medico would have removed the left one altogether, so Sloane should have considered himself lucky.

Lucky, hah! He'd come home to find that his man of business had played ducks and drakes with whatever income the swindling bailiff had sent on to London. There was nothing left of his inheritance but bills. The estates had been bled dry and weren't about to see a profit

27

without a major investment of capital that His Grace simply did not possess. St. Sevrin would have broken the entail in an instant, sold off half the property to maintain the other half, or at least let himself live in comfort. Half the time he was shivering with the return of the fevers just because there wasn't enough blunt to waste on coal.

But the new duke couldn't break the entail. His cousin and presumed heir Humbert Shearingham had made sure of that. Bertie didn't need the unprofitable Priory acres; he didn't even need the blunt the sale would bring. He wanted the title. He sat like a spider that had built its web, waiting for the unwary bug. Bertie had agreed to pay off the mortgages, Sloane's new solicitor reported, and to restore the estate. He'd even make Sloane a handsome annuity. All St. Sevrin had to do was renounce the title in his cousin's favor.

Well, Napoleon Bonaparte hadn't succeeded in giving Humbert the dukedom. Be damned if Sloane would, either.

So the former officer was living on his wits and luck, and feeling more every day that both had gone begging. He lived in three rooms of St. Sevrin House in Berkeley Square with his retired batman Kelly as his only servant. He paid his expenses, when he managed to pay at all, with his gaming winnings.

Unfortunately the men he gambled with—not always gentlemen, either—were heavy drinkers. Anyone more sober than themselves was suspected of being a Captain Sharp, as was anyone who won too often or too much. The drink kept St. Sevrin from being distrusted—and from being a successful gamester.

It was easier to stay drunk than to face the piles of bills, as well as the pity and disdain on his fellow peers' faces. Soon the doors of polite Society were closing in his face, except for a few that remained open on account of his war record. St. Sevrin didn't give a rap for the

Quality, save that they were easier to pry loose from their blunt.

A good cardplayer, though no wizard with the pasteboards, St. Sevrin managed to keep his head above water, barely. There was nothing left to sink back into the estates, so there was no hope, therefore, of His Grace's seeing a shilling from his fine inheritance.

There was nothing his father hadn't mortgaged, nothing unentailed that the old rip hadn't sold. Sloane was desperate, and the vultures knew it. A man on the edge couldn't wager recklessly because he couldn't afford to lose. Time and again Sloane had warned his young recruits not to play where they couldn't pay. Now he was doing the same thing, finding himself deeper in debt every day.

The war may have been a nightmare, but at least Sloane had felt he was getting a job done. Here in London he was accomplishing nothing, and it was taking all day and night to do it. He was exhausted and dejected, but not yet ready to admit defeat.

"I have a new plan," he announced to his valet-butler-groom one morning. It was actually more like late afternoon when St. Sevrin opened his eyes for the second time that day. The first time he'd seen nothing but the walls swaying, so he'd shut them again. Now the pounding headache was almost endurable.

"What, are we going to go on the high toby? Might be more profitable holding up coaches. And hanging might be quicker'n freezing to death in this place." Kelly placed a cup of coffee near his master's hand, his right hand. Kelly was tired of mopping up when the major, what was now His Grace if Kelly could only remember, tried to use that left arm. The old infantryman's joints were too sore for all that bending.

"Freezing be damned. It's spring. We don't need fires."

"Then why are you sleeping under your greatcoat?" Kelly had been with the major through Coruña, Oporto,

29

and Cifuente. He'd dragged him off the fields of Talavera to the hospital tents. With all the gray hairs Kelly'd sprouted on the major's behalf, he could deuced well complain about the conditions in Berkeley Square, and frequently did.

St. Sevrin as frequently ignored the older man's grousing. He'd promised Kelly a glowing recommendation if the batman wanted to find other employment, but Kelly chose to stay on, for which the duke felt grateful, and guilty as hell. "You can borrow my greatcoat tonight," he offered now, taking a gulp of the coffee to help clear his mind. The coffee had been sitting on the stove all day for just that eventuality, though. Now it was scalding, bitter, and thick as boot polish. In fact, it could have been boot polish. The duke spit out the brew and fell back on his pillows. "Thunderation, what does it take to get a decent cup of coffee?"

"Let me think . . . some fresh beans, 'haps a grinder what works, a pot without rust, one of them modern stoves. Oh, and maybe a real cook what gets paid. Yessir, Yer Grace, that ought to do the trick."

So the duke threw one of his pillows at his longtime, long-suffering servant and companion. "Stubble it. I know you're doing the best you can."

Kelly picked up the pillow and His Grace's discarded clothes from the evening before. "A'course, I could go out to the coffeehouse and bring you back some fresh-brewed and a meat pasty or such, was the dibs in tune." He shook the duke's coat, hoping to hear the rustle of paper money and the jingle of coins. All he heard was his own stomach grumbling that they'd have to eat his own cooking again. "So what's the new idea?"

"We're going to Devon, Kelly, that's what." St. Sevrin felt better just thinking of getting out of the stinking City, especially with the weather turning toward spring. In London all one noticed was a warmer fog.

"Devon, eh? We taking up smuggling, then?"

"Dash it all, I know you don't approve of my making a living at the baize table, but it's not as if I've been shaving the deck or anything. And this plan is strictly legitimate." The coffee was cool enough to drink now. St. Sevrin tried to make it more palatable by pouring in a dollop of brandy from the bottle at his bedside. "We're going home, if you can call St. Sevrin Priory my home."

"You usually dub the place the millstone around your neck."

"Yes, well, it is the ducal seat, even if I've only been back there a handful of times since I was out of short pants."

His Grace did not have fond memories of those visits, either. He'd been sent off to boarding school when he was six, unfazed at the petty cruelties there. The schoolyard brawls were as nothing compared to the arguments between his parents. Theirs had been an arranged match, the old story of the groom's title and the bride's wealth. Fiona's father was an Irish shipbuilder who'd amassed a fortune that he left to his daughter, so pleased was he that his little lassie was to be a duchess.

Sloane's mother died after his seventh birthday, and his father began a quick descent into dissipation. It wasn't grief that sent the fifth duke into his decline; it was the freedom from his duchess's shrewish tongue and her hand controlling the purse strings.

· The heir was sent to relatives during vacations at first, when his father remembered to make arrangements. The few times the young viscount did return to his birthplace, he found the ancient building depressingly run-down, ill-staffed, and damp. His father was usually passed out from drink, or entertaining the kitchen wenches in the ducal suite. The duke's bed must have been the only warm thing in the house; surely the food never arrived hot. After that, Viscount Shearingham managed to sidestep Devon and the duke as much as possible. He planned walking tours or tutorials during school breaks, and accepted friends' invitations for the long holidays.

Upon graduation, when his classmates were eager to acquire a veneer of Town bronze, Sloane was only eager to avoid his father's dissolute presence. He purchased his colors as soon as he came down from university, and hadn't been back to the Priory since. He wasn't looking forward to this trip, either.

Kelly knew the major never spoke of home or family, so the batman wasn't ready to commit himself to an opinion. He hadn't heard the rest of the plan. He did move the bottle of spirits farther out of reach, making room on the bedside table for His Grace's shaving lather. "I hear Devon's pretty countryside. Good farmland. Cows and sheep."

"Pretty be damned. And if there was a cow or a sheep on the property, the thieving bastard I had as bailiff would have eaten it by now."

"Then what? We're going on a repairing lease to St. Sevrin Priory? The footman next door says as how it's in the guidebooks."

"As a location to avoid, I'm sure. The house is not worth saving for dry rot and termites, the staff decamped ages ago, and the whole pile is supposed to be haunted. This place is a regular palace compared to what we might find there."

"And I was just telling myself a tent in the mud and dust of Portugal would look good about now. So why are we going to Devon?"

Sloane was happy to hear the "we." Despite his complaints, Kelly was the best forager St. Sevrin had ever known. And the most loyal. The duke tipped his cup in salute—without spilling any when he saw Kelly wince. "We are going to the ancestral abode," he declared after a swallow and a cough, "because we are at *point non plus* here. We'll be reduced to burning the banisters for the cookstove, which will only bring my cousin Humbert breathing down my neck. Every rung and railing is part of the entail. I checked. If they weren't, the pater would have sold them for kindling the way he did the Hepplewhite chairs."

"Maybe the gudgeon's hot air would keep us warm." Kelly didn't think much of Humbert's Corinthian set: wealthy, active, sportive young men who'd be better employed facing Boney's artillery like honest Englishmen. He started to strop the razor in angry swipes that had St. Sevrin's bloodshot eyes blinking rapidly.

"We'll be warm, I swear. For there is one thing at St. Sevrin Priory that my esteemed parent didn't manage to sell. If I can get a decent price, it might just see us through the next winter at least. I'd have a stake to bet with, or I could buy back my commission."

"Can't say as I'd rather face the frogs again, iffen I had my druthers."

"Yes, well, I doubt Whitehall would let me go, with this confounded weak arm of mine, although old Humbert would take the medical exam for me if he could."

Kelly approached with the razor and lather and a sour expression. The duke thought he'd better have another sip of fortification first. "They reminded me over at Horse Guards that Prinny didn't approve of his nobles going over as cannon fodder until they've ensured their successions. I don't count Humbert, so we're likely stuck in England anyway."

"In a moldering heap what's been deserted by everyone except the rats and the ghosts of them long-gone monks?"

"Only temporarily. And we'll be warm, remember? Because the one thing the old man left intact is the home woods."

Kelly was not impressed by his master's pronouncement. "I thought all the land was entailed. That's why an officer and a gentleman is living worse off than a coal heaver. Leastways that's how you explained it."

"And it's true. I can't sell off the land because it's actually held in trust for my heirs and their heirs, ad infinitum. But what's on it isn't. I checked with the solicitor. He says I can go ahead with the sale. There's I don't know how many acres of prime timber in the home woods. I'd have to check the estate maps to be sure. And it's never been cut, as far as I know. The lumber is bound to bring in a pretty penny, the solicitor thinks. Maybe I'll invest in turnip seeds and become a farmer. What do you think?"

Kelly'd been a farmer's son before he became a duke's batman. He'd eaten better then. Spreading lather on the duke's cheeks, he asked, "When do we leave?"

Chapter Five

"*Y*our uncle wants to see you, miss," the maid said when she brought Lisanne's hot water in the morning, an hour earlier than usual. "In a huff, he is. Says he looked for you all day yesterday. Made me get up before I'd had my sleep out, he did, to make sure you didn't leave the house without seeing him." The maid wasn't best pleased, either, it sounded.

Lisanne didn't listen. Birds were singing, trees were budding. It was spring. There was no reason to stay in the house and every reason to be gone, not the least of which was that it was warmer out-of-doors than in. Uncle Alfred was another who subscribed to the notion that fires were not necessary after the first of March. His belief stemmed from parsimony rather than need, and did not, of course, extend to his own bedchamber or the parlor, where he sat of an evening.

But it was the birthing season, the planting season, a time when everything burst into new life. That was outside. Inside Neville Hall, the Findleys stagnated in the same fetid pool of their discontent, only louder than ever, like bullfrogs with the colic.

Esmé wanted to be a lady now that she was seventeen.

She demanded a social life, a London Season, and every new whim that whistled on fashion's fickle breeze. She also wanted that stable boy, Diccon. Tears and tantrums erupted at each meal or family gathering.

Nigel saw no reason he shouldn't have digs of his own in Town now that he was done with schooling. He was nineteen, a real man. Since Nigel found ways aplenty to overspend his allowance, overturn the carriages, and overset his mama's notions of propriety right here in Devon, Uncle Alfred wasn't about to loose such an expensive piece of goods on the metropolis. Nigel pouted and pounded the table and flicked peas at his sister. A real man.

Aunt Cherise still resorted to her smelling salts at every raised voice. Most mealtimes were interrupted for the burning of feathers or the waving of a vinaigrette. The family should invest in the apothecary business, Lisanne thought, but not even that windfall would be enough to satisfy her greedy, grasping relations.

Lisanne usually ate in the kitchens, where she'd come to terms with the latest cook after curing the old woman's asthma. Curing the ailment was simple: Lisanne had merely ordered the kitchen cats outside and the room aired. Winning Cook's trust was another matter. The woman still made the sign of the cross when Lisanne entered her precincts. Lisanne shrugged. So what if everyone thought she was a witch, a wantwit, a lunatic? She was free to come and go as she pleased, to live her life without the constant nerve-gnawing that passed for family feeling among the Findleys.

But not this morning. Of course Lisanne could disobey her uncle's demand for her presence. She could go down the back stairs and not return till the candle in the master bedroom was snuffed at night. But years of experience had taught her that Uncle Alfred would only take his ire out on the servants. The poor maid who brought the message would be blamed. She might even lose her position, lowly as it was. Besides, Lisanne was curious to find what was so important that her uncle deigned to tell her. He never mentioned how her income was being invested—she had to find that out from the solicitor's letters on his desk—or what plans were afoot for the farms and fields of the Neville holdings. The bailiff gave her that information, being one of the few retainers who still respected the Neville barony, if not the current bizarre baroness.

Lisanne donned the dress the maid laid out for her. It was another of Esmé's castoffs, but since that spoiled miss was notoriously fussy and hard to please, the gowns in Lisanne's closet were nearly new, not that she cared. Rid of all the bows and lace frills, taken up six inches in the hem, the dresses were not half bad, especially since a sash at the high waist could gather in the extra material. Besides, Nigel's outgrown clothes were instantly burned. Those were Aunt Cherise's orders, so Lisanne had no choice unless she wanted to shop with her cousin for fabric, ponder fashion magazines for the perfect designs, then stand for hours being pinned. Esmé's muslins were good enough. And they'd soon have spots and stains on them, anyway, from the days Lisanne spent in the fields and forest, the garden and the stillroom.

The maid didn't bother with a hat or gloves or reticule, for everyone knew Miss Annie would only lose them by lunchtime, poor thing. At least she wore shoes now, most times, anyway.

Lisanne twisted her long hair into a braid that hung neatly down her back. It wouldn't stay that way, of course, so she crammed a ribbon into her pocket for later. A knife followed, and scissors, a needle and thread, a handful of handkerchiefs, that jar with the butterfly larva, the packet of seeds from the wild orchid, a book with the spiderweb from the windowsill pressed between its pages, and a small, meticulously carved flute. The maid rolled her eyes behind Lisanne's back.

Sir Alfred cleared his throat. The footmen serving the breakfast snapped to attention, but of the family only Lisanne looked up from her muffin and chocolate. Esmé and Nigel continued their bickering over the last rasher of bacon.

"I have news," Sir Alfred pronounced. When that gained him no more notice, he slammed his fist on the table and shouted, "Dash it, I will have your silence when I speak."

Aunt Cherise, picking at her invalid's fare of weak tea and dry toast, cringed. "Not so loud, Sir Alfred. My nerves, you know."

The baronet didn't apologize, he just forged on, now that the small group in the morning room, family and servants alike, was listening. "I want all of you to pay close heed. I heard some important news in the village yesterday. I wanted to mention it sooner." At this point he glared at Lisanne for not being where he could issue his orders. "At any rate, the news was confirmed by Squire Pemberton last night. St. Sevrin is in residence."

Lisanne's cup shook in her hand, spilling a trail of chocolate down her badly altered gown. Lisanne didn't notice. For once, neither did Aunt Cherise.

"That awful Sloane Shearingham? Why, he's not received anywhere anymore. All the important houses have been closed to him since the duns started knocking on his door. Now, why didn't my cousin write and tell me that knave was coming to Devon on a repairing lease? We could have been long gone on our way elsewhere."

"What, madam, should we run away from our home?" her husband asked, amazed.

"But what if he comes to church?" Lady Findley was in a fidge of indecision. "Should we recognize him or give him the cut? He's a rakehell, for sure, but a duke still and all. Oh, how I wish I knew what the ladies of London had decided about the dratted man. One wouldn't want to be blamed for lending countenance to such licentious behavior, but neither should one be behind times in courtesy to our noble neighbor."

Her husband had no patience for such niceties. "He isn't coming to church, you can be certain of that. I doubt His Grace St. Sevrin could even recognize the inside of one. Besides, sots like him are never out of bed in time for services."

"Can we go call on him, then, Pa?" Nigel wanted to know. "Can we? I hear he's a regular Trojan, a real hero."

"He's a wastrel." The last thing Sir Alfred needed was for his gudgeon of a son to pattern himself after a cardsharp and a basket scrambler. "He most likely plucks green pigeons like you as an appetizer before he gets down to serious wagering. Pray you stay out of his clutches."

Esmé wasn't listening. "*I* think it's the most romantic thing in the world, a real live hero right on our doorstep. Perhaps the duke drinks to forget a lost love who wouldn't wait for him to come home from the wars. Or some injury that makes their marriage impossible."

Nigel groaned. "Just like you to make a Cheltenham tragedy out of a chap's tossing back a few. Next you'll be offering to bathe his fevered brow. Now, if that ain't what every soldier dreams of, some plump little schoolgirl's pity."

Before Esmé could retaliate, their father pounded the table again. "The man is a libertine, I say. You will not make him out to be any kind of Minerva Press hero. Heroes are just bloody fools who don't care about their own hides anyhow. This one is a dashed loose screw drowning on River Tick. Not even rich cits will look at him for a son-in-law, that's how low he's fallen. The father was a rakehell; the son's a rakehell."

But he was Esmé's first rakehell and, like the first taste of champagne, irresistible. She had every intention of trotting her old mare back and forth in front of the

Priory's gates in case the duke rode out. "Do you think he'll attend the assembly at Honiton? You said I could go, remember, Pa?"

"I think he'd attend his own funeral before doing the pretty with a hall full of provincials. But that's no matter. You are not going to meet him, you are not going to speak to him if you do see him, and you are not going to go out of the house while he's here. It's just a day or two, according to the squire, while St. Sevrin transacts some business."

Lady Findley was nodding vigorously. "A girl can't be too careful of her reputation, Esmé. You wouldn't want to be tarred with the same brush."

"And that goes for you, too, missy," Uncle Alfred told Lisanne, as usual not minding his tongue in front of the servants. "I don't want you in his woods or on his land. I don't want you anywhere St. Sevrin might happen to be." He took a look at his niece's suntanned face, the childish braid, the bunched-up and besmirched gown, whose neckline fell much lower on her than it had on the more rounded Esmé. Damn, but the chit was turning into a tempting morsel. "He's liable to mistake you for a dairy-maid and tumble you in the grass. And I'm not about to call him out over your honor. They say he hasn't got any, when it comes to wenches."

Aunt Cherise was near to swooning. The well-practiced footmen stood on either side of her chair ready to catch her. "Oh, my word, the scandal."

"Precisely. And it's the last thing we need just when we're going to be bringing Esmé out next fall. Everything has to be perfect. I don't want word getting back to London that my niece is fast, chasing after a rank libertine on his own grounds."

No, Lisanne thought, it was all right for people to think she was a lunatic, but not immoral. She wouldn't set foot in the London marriage mart for anything, which suited her uncle's plans to a cow's thumb. She knew he intended to claim she was supposed to share Esmé's Season. Actually Esmé was supposed to share Lisanne's; that's how Uncle Alfred could justify opening Neville House, which was much larger and more fashionably situated than the Findleys' own leased town house. Then he'd tell everyone that his poor niece had come down with something. That's what he wrote to her London trustee last year, explaining why she was not making her come-out with other girls her age. A sickly child, don't you know. This year he might bruit it about that she was too emotionally unstable to handle the pressure of curtsying at a court presentation, undergoing the scrutiny of the Almack's patronesses, or having to impress the eligible *partis*. Since those were the last things Lisanne wanted or desired, she didn't mind not going to London with her relations.

The Findleys would all be leaving, and their servants with them. That was enough. For once Lisanne could have her home to herself. She didn't need London when everything that mattered was here. The problem was that half of what mattered to her was on St. Sevrin property.

"Thunderation, girl, stop your air-dreaming for once and pay attention! It's for your own safety, too. The man might go out hunting and never know you're about."

Nigel was muttering about the unfairness that St. Sevrin should get to hunt those well-stocked woods, when he'd never been allowed.

"They're his woods, you nodcock," Sir Alfred ground out before turning back to Lisanne. "I don't want you out of the house, Annie, and I mean it. You've always been the most stubborn, disobedient child I've ever known, and I can't imagine you're any different now that you are eighteen. But that's not too old to beat, I swear."

Lisanne just looked at him with that clear blue gaze that seemed to read Alfred's soul, and to know how much guilty pleasure he'd get from laying his hands on her. Findley flushed and looked away. They both also knew a beating wouldn't gain him one iota of respect—or obedience. Lisanne didn't even respect him enough to be afraid.

"I'll lock you up," he blustered. "I swear I'll . . . I'll . . ." Sir Alfred looked around for inspiration, something that might make her comply with his orders, for once. "I'll burn the library. That's what I'll do. I'll have all your precious books taken out and burned if you put one foot out of this door."

"They are part of the estate," Lisanne reminded her uncle in the usual composed, reasonable way she had that aggravated the baronet to no end. "How will you explain such wanton destruction to the trustees?"

Thunderation, the blasted chit was too smart for Alfred's liking. "I'll go ask St. Sevrin's permission, then, to go out hunting with him. I'll shoot down every animal in those cursed woods of his."

Nigel's mouth was open, and Lady Cherise was mopping her forehead with lavender water, but Lisanne knew Uncle Alfred wouldn't dare step an inch into the forest. She asked the footman for more chocolate, effectively showing the baronet what she thought of his tirade.

Findley knew his niece recognized him for a coward and hated her the more. "Then I'll take my gun and shoot that deuced dog of yours." He smiled when he finally saw the stricken look on her face. So the chit wasn't made entirely of ice water after all. "Yes, that's what I'll do."

Lisanne knew her uncle just might, out of meanness alone, if he could find Becka. She got up to take her pet into the woods. Since Aunt Cherise did not allow animals in the house, Becka was used to being out alone. The big dog was used to the woods, too, and would stay there until Lisanne came for her. Before she left the breakfast parlor, Lisanne thought to ask: "Did the squire happen to say what business St. Sevrin has at the Priory?"

"Oh, did I forget to mention it?" Sir Alfred smiled, showing his yellowed teeth. Almost ten years of aggrava-

42

tion were about to be repaid. Satisfaction sat sweetly on his lips. "Why, the duke is here to get bids from various lumber mills. He's selling off your precious forest."

Chapter Six

The old ways were dying. No one believed, no one cared. Without that ancient forest, so full of history, so full of mystery, a bit more of the world's magic would be lost. And a lot more of Lisanne Neville's world. Wealth and title, fame and social standing, reputation and the respect of those around her—none mattered to Lisanne as much as Sevrin Woods. She didn't count her personal safety or her personal appearance, only the woods.

Now the forest was threatened, to pay some scapegrace's gambling debts. It just couldn't happen. Lisanne couldn't let it happen. She was the one who understood, the special one, so she had to do something. But what?

She stayed in her room that day, thinking. Uncle Alfred had footmen stationed in the hall outside her room, and groundskeepers working close to the house. Lisanne wondered what they would do if she just strolled past them and kept going. Most of the staff was afraid of her, she knew. They wouldn't be too anxious to chase her down and bring her back by force, for fear she'd lay a curse on them or contaminate them with her strangeness. Most likely they would simply send for Uncle Alfred.

Becka was safe enough. Lisanne had gone to the stables

after breakfast and taken the animal out for exercise. She managed to "lose" the dog at the edge of the Neville lawns where they met the forest. After that she'd had all day to pace the confines of her room, making plans. If the squire knew of the duke's intentions, everyone in the countryside knew, so Lisanne didn't have to hurry to give warning. No harm could be done immediately, anyway, not if the dastard was first sending for lumbermen.

How could he? Such arrant waste and disregard for a place of beauty was appalling. Lisanne knew how the foresters operated, for she'd seen it often enough on Neville property under Sir Alfred's care. The men would come in with their huge wagons and teams of heavy workhorses, their ropes and saws and axes, and they'd begin chopping away. They wouldn't take only the fallen, diseased, or overcrowded trees, giving the others more room to grow. No, that took too long, required too many men, didn't yield enough profit. Instead they'd cut everything in sight, leaving nothing but ugly stumps as a mark of shame and greed on the landscape.

All the animals, the precious wildflowers, the secrets in the soil—those things could never survive, could never be replaced. There wouldn't even be birdsong if the sparrows had nowhere to nest.

And then there were the trees themselves. Despite his current low tide, the duke was likely some high-nosed blue blood, claiming his family came over with William the Conqueror. But the trees would have been here to greet the invaders, to give them shelter, firewood, and fruit. The trees had blood and life, too, besides nurturing the souls of other ancient races.

The forest would die, and everything with it. Oh, some creatures could find other roosts, other dens, but not those whose very spirits were tied to Sevrin Woods. There was no place else for them to go.

Lisanne couldn't let it happen. Neither could she buy the woods or offer to pay the dreadful duke's bills. She didn't control her own income and wouldn't until she was five and twenty, if she managed to wrest the guardianship from Uncle Alfred's grasping fingers then. For the first time Lisanne wished that she'd cared more about worldly matters, that she'd written to her solicitors herself to tell them what was happening. Now it was too late. Her pocket money wouldn't keep a mare in oats, much less a spendthrift sot in London, where he belonged.

Uncle Alfred finally went to sleep. His valet had crept down the silent hall ages ago, but candlelight still shone under the baronet's door. Lisanne waited another half hour after the light went out.

She knew one of the gardeners still patrolled the grounds, because she could see him and his lantern pass under her room every fifteen minutes or so. That was enough time for Lisanne to lift her window and scurry down the trellis, then scamper across the lawns to the boxwood maze. She could have made her escape in pitch darkness, so many times had she taken the same route, but tonight, when she didn't need it, the moon lit up her path through the ornamental gardens. Still wearing Esmé's light-colored muslin, with an old woolen shawl hurriedly tied around her shoulders against the chill night air, she'd stick out like a lighthouse at sea. She pulled the shawl over her blond hair and waited behind a topiary unicorn for the guard to pass by again before entering the maze. Then, racing through its twists and turns past the fountain at the center, she exited at the opposite side, where the maze's high hedges would block her flight across the lawns and into Sevrin Woods.

Only Becka greeted Lisanne, joyous to see her mistress and the rolls she had stuffed in her pockets. Everything else was hushed except for the mist that dripped steadily off just-budded branches. 'Twas almost as if the trees themselves were weeping.

No one answered Lisanne's call, or came tumbling out of the mist when she played a tune on her little flute. They knew. She could already feel their pain.

"No!" she shouted into the empty night, and "No!" again. Becka set up a howl that had the Neville Hall groundsman dropping his staff and his lantern and heading for the next county.

Sloane Shearingham was drunk. There was nothing unusual in that except for the location. Tonight he was castaway in three barely habitable rooms of St. Sevrin Priory in Devon instead of three barely habitable rooms of St. Sevrin House in London.

He and Kelly had arrived the afternoon before, enough time, thank goodness, for a hasty inspection of the centuries-old building to see if it was liable to fall down around their ears as they slept. While Kelly unpacked and tried to find chimneys that weren't blocked by squirrel nests and mattresses that weren't burrowed through by mice, Sloane had made a quick trip to the village to arrange for a delivery of fodder for the horses. If Kelly couldn't find them reasonably comfortable billets in the house, at least they'd have fresh hay to sleep on in the nearly intact stables. It wouldn't be the first time Sloane and his batman had bedded down with their mounts.

When Sloane returned, pockets slightly emptier since the liveryman wouldn't extend credit to any St. Sevrin, he rubbed the tired horses down himself, and discovered where some chickens had taken up housekeeping in one of the stalls. He relieved the hens of a clutch of eggs, helped Kelly fire the antique stove in the kitchen, and sat down to a halfway decent omelette. Theirs was such a hand-to-mouth existence, he thought, that those chickens should be making out their wills.

At least they wouldn't be cold. There was firewood lying all over the place from fallen trees, broken shutters, wrecked carriages. Better yet, the duke unearthed a case

47

of old brandy in a far corner of the wine cellar that the servants or squatters or his sire had overlooked. 'Twas better to stay drunk, His Grace decided, for St. Sevrin Priory was indeed haunted, if only with the ghosts of the past. A mass of murdered monks would have been good company by comparison.

Asleep Sloane had nightmares of battle, of fallen comrades he couldn't raise, of devastated Spanish villages after the French had been through. He saw the eyes of the children there, beseeching him, accusing him. By day, he had the shambles of his life to torment him. This morning he'd made inquiries about lumber mills, then he'd ridden across parts of his estate to see firsthand what years of neglect and avarice had wrought. He'd seen the bare fields, the tumbled cottages, the abandoned gristmill. The children of his own tenants—the ones who'd remained at St. Sevrin because they had nowhere else to go—had those same pleading eyes.

When Sloane returned from his inspection, he'd started drinking the brandy. Now it was well after dinner— chicken, as expected—and he wasn't done yet. No, he was still sober enough to see the damp spots on the ceilings of the Priory, the warped floors where priceless Aubusson carpets used to lie, the empty gallery walls, the boarded windows. Worse, he could hear his mother crying.

Hell and damnation, he'd hated everything his father was. Now he was his father.

Two hours later the Duke of St. Sevrin was propped against one of the windows that still had glass in it, in one of the parlors of the Priory's modern section. This addition was only one century old instead of two or three, and it overlooked the rear of the Priory, toward the home woods. He could just make out the distant trees in the hazy moonlight, spreading as far as he could see in either direction. The next duke, he told himself, Humbert or whoever, would likely be looking out this very window right at Neville Hall. The two estates weren't all that close, but the land was flat. 'Twould be just like Humbert to purchase a telescope to peek in his neighbor's bedrooms.

Sloane had long since dispensed with the glass; but the bottle of brandy, the second bottle of brandy, dangled from his right hand. He wouldn't trust his unreliable left arm with such a fine vintage, such a fine, mind-numbing companion. When he saw the ghost walk from the woods, the bottle slid, unnoticed, to the floor anyway.

St. Sevrin blinked to try to clear his eyes, but the figure didn't disappear. It was definitely a woman, her light-colored skirts billowing around her in the breeze. She couldn't be real, of course. Women did not float out of forests in the middle of the night, not even in Devon. The Priory ghosts were all said to be monks, so those old stories of the woods being enchanted must be correct after all. A fairy creature was coming to visit. Either that or he'd finally had too much to drink. Sloane rather hoped it was the brandy.

The woman held neither lantern nor torch, yet she was walking directly toward him across the unscythed lawns. Her hair looked silvery by the moonlight, and his experienced eye told him she must be small-boned and thin, perhaps still a girl.

She kept coming closer until she stood just outside his window. St. Sevrin did the only thing possible, of course, for a gentleman so deep in his cups. He opened the window, not without a struggle with the rusted latch. " 'Well met by moonlight, proud Titania,' " he greeted her.

"That's 'Ill met,' " she corrected automatically, worried lest the real quote prove true.

Sloane held out his hand. "Won't you join me anyway, sweet fairy queen? There's a fire, and wine."

Lisanne was suddenly undecided. She'd come this far out of necessity, but her courage was failing her at actually facing the rogue. He was large and broad-shouldered, wearing a shirt with an open collar, no neck cloth. With his reddish hair fallen over his forehead, he looked sleepy, unfinished. Mayhaps this was a bad idea after all.

While Lisanne was studying the duke, St. Sevrin was owlishly peering out the window at her. "No, you cannot be Titania, for surely you haven't enough years in your dish to be queen of the ether. But come in out of the chill, fairy child."

For a moment Lisanne's heart soared. He understood! He knew about the woods! But no, she realized, he was only teasing, flirting with her. He was a rake, after all.

St. Sevrin watched the expressions flitter across the beautiful face. That smile lit her whole being, as if the moon rivaled the sun when she was happy. Sloane thought he'd move mountains to bring it back. "Come, sweetings, do."

Lisanne thought the clunch would fall out of the window if he leaned any farther out. She could smell the spirits on his breath even from where she stood. But she had no choice. Muttering under her breath, *"Ave atque, Caesar, mortituri est te salutamus,"* she raised her arms to be hoisted through the window.

When he lifted her, Sloane was surprised to find that his guest was flesh and blood after all, although she weighed about as much as a moonbeam, and her hand trembled in his like a captured butterfly. But her eyes never wavered from his and that clear blue gaze seemed to sear his very soul, like the eyes of the children of war, the children of poverty. St. Sevrin prayed this angel-child would find what she came for. Lud knew he had little enough to offer.

He kicked the fallen bottle aside and made a fairly creditable bow, for a fellow half seas over. "St. Sevrin, at your service."

Lisanne bobbed an awkward curtsy, being out of practice since Miss Armbruster had left. She had to stifle a nervous giggle to think of worrying over drawing-room manners at a time like this. Then she took a deep breath and poured forth her prepared speech: "I am Lisanne Neville, and you can have my fortune if you'll marry me."

St. Sevrin decided he really had to give up drinking.

Chapter Seven

St. Sevrin sank down in a chair. It wasn't the polite thing to do, of course, sitting before a lady, but he felt it was more courteous than falling in a heap at her feet. Many years had passed since he'd been knocked so cock-a-hoop. "Could you repeat that?"

The girl cleared her throat. "I am Lisanne Neville." She jerked one angular shoulder toward the woods and beyond. "I am very wealthy, and I . . . I should like to marry you."

Now there, he thought, that made everything clear. Clear as Kelly's coffee. The outrageous chit just stood near the window, ready to flee, he thought, but giving him time to recover his wits and look his fill.

Miss Lisanne Neville was a tiny scrap of a thing, bird-bone thin. Those big blue eyes gave her an even more waiflike appearance as they made their own inspection. She didn't like what she saw, he could tell by the downward pull to her soft lips, but she held her ground, only the clenched hands and white knuckles betraying her fear. Sloane had seen seasoned foot soldiers show less courage. Whatever her mission, the girl had bottom.

She also had dirt on her hem, twigs in her skirts, and

smudges down the front of her poorly fitted gown. There were leaves in her streaked blond hair, which was every which way around her face and down her back. No wonder he took her for some elven being; she even smelled of forest and earth. At least Miss Neville didn't chatter on like most other females of his acquaintance, highborn or low.

Of course she didn't blather; Lisanne was struck dumb now that she was face-to-face with the duke. He was everything she'd been warned about, and worse. No one had mentioned he might be half dressed. Naturally no one thought she'd come to call after midnight, either. No one had warned her he was such a firm, muscular man, obvious under the form-fitting breeches and the white shirt that was open enough to reveal reddish hairs on his chest. Did all men have hair on their chest, or only the devilish ones? Lisanne made herself look away from his body. It was even more unnerving than his frown.

Returning her gaze to his face, she could see the firm chin and well-defined planes of the hero; she could also see the lines of dissipation, the sallow complexion, the bloodshot, puffy eyes of the libertine. The duke's auburn hair had no shine to it, and those eyes, hazel, she thought from this distance, seemed cold and weary, empty.

St. Sevrin, meanwhile, was trying to recall what he'd heard of the Neville offspring. The parents were dead of course, that was ages ago. Were there more children? He thought not. And there was something, some rumor or other that hadn't mattered at the time, about the daughter. He'd only listened because the Nevilles were old neighbors. Was it that she was sickly? The chit didn't look febrile despite her thinness. She had a golden outdoor tan, unless that was dirt on her face. And the talk couldn't have been that she was a simpleton, for she'd quoted Latin and Shakespeare back at him. Most likely someone had mentioned she was a wayward baggage, hot to hand. What else could she be, wandering around the countryside at night, visiting bachelor quarters? Most likely this was some schoolroom prank, or a dare from her giddy girlfriends, who were undoubtedly safe asleep in their warm beds while this little wren was flitting through the forest at night.

No matter, the gossip would come to him later. For now he had to get the infant home before her guardians tossed a gauntlet in his face, or whatever it was that rustics did when great hulking lechers besmirched their innocent womenfolk. For if there was anything St. Sevrin knew, it was that this little girl wore the face of innocence.

"I'm sorry, sweetings," he told her, deliberately drawing the words out, "you might have a yearning to be a duchess, but I'm not in the market for a bride. If I were, I most decidedly would not choose a hobbledehoy urchin."

"That's a hobbledehoy baroness, sirrah," she retorted, "and the least you could do is listen to my proposition." Her eyes ran around the room, noting the moth-eaten drapes, the water stains on the paneling. "I don't see where you have much to lose."

Some of the old baronies were like that, St. Sevrin knew, passing through the female lines. "Very well, Baroness, I acquit you of coveting my title. You still have to leave. It's past your bedtime."

Lisanne drew herself up to her five feet naught height, the naught giving her dignity. "I am eight and ten, Your Grace, not a child."

"Forgive me, Baroness, but you appear to be no more than fifteen."

"And you are said to be twenty and seven, yet you look nearly forty."

"Touché," he acknowledged. "Very well, you are not a child. Therefore, you know you have no business here. For one thing, the woods can be a dangerous place at night. I suppose you must have played there all your life, but there are unseen hazards in the darkness."

That earned him a disdainful look. Compared to her uncle's wrath and this gentleman's uncertain temper, Sevrin Woods was the last danger she had to worry about.

"Bats? Spiders? Poachers?" She didn't flinch. It was a peculiar female he had on his hands, but St. Sevrin was determined to make his point. "What about the witch who's supposed to live there, casting spells?"

Lisanne laughed. *She* was the enchantress everyone feared! Then she laughed again, in relief. The duke wasn't a total ogre, not if he cared about her well-being. She found a chair whose seat cover wasn't totally ripped and sat down.

Her laughter was like honey, sweet and soft. The duke let it flow around him, but he wasn't to be swayed. "Don't get comfortable, my intrepid lady, for there's still a matter of reputation."

"Yours or mine?"

"Both. Someone has sullied your tender ears with mine, I'm certain." He quirked an eyebrow in inquiry; Lisanne nodded. "Therefore the meanest intelligence could calculate the damage this visit could do to yours."

Lisanne brushed that aside. "I have no reputation to speak of, and no one whose high esteem I desire."

Thunderation, Sloane wished he'd listened harder to the gossip about this chit. "What, have you blotted your copybook so badly that you were denied vouchers at Almack's? If you are of age, you should have been presented at court this past year." The duke was sure he would have remembered that. Gossip about a debutante baroness would have penetrated even his alcoholic fog. "You should be in London now, dancing at balls in silk gowns, having mooncalves write sonnets to your eyebrows." They were very fetching eyebrows, he couldn't help noticing, a bit ragged, as though his fingers could smooth the golden hairs into line.

"Is that what those cabbage-heads do? I'm even more

glad I never went, then. My cousin Esmé comes out in the fall. She'll be thrilled, although I'm not sure . . ."

"Platter-faced, is she?"

"Spots," Lisanne confided. "Uncle Alfred and Aunt Cherise are hopeful she'll outgrow them over the summer."

St. Sevrin was positive the spotted Esmé wore silks and lace. "What about you? Shall you go to Town with them?"

"Oh, no, I don't want to, and Uncle does not want to lay out the expenses for a Season for me, so we are agreed for once."

"Ah, the wicked uncle. I knew there had to be a villain in this piece."

Lisanne gave her answer serious consideration. Actually the man in front of her was the villain, but she didn't think she ought to say that.

He seemed to read her thoughts. "No, no, sweetings. I cannot be the villain and the hero both. You did come to me for rescuing, didn't you?"

"I don't think Uncle Alfred is wicked, precisely. He is greedy, certainly, and miserly. Mostly he is discontented that the Nevilles have so much and the Findleys—that's Uncle Arthur's family—have so little."

"I believe certain Frenchmen felt the same way about their monarchs, and look what happened there. You are very forgiving, Baroness."

St. Sevrin wasn't. He already despised this unknown Alfred Findley for keeping his niece in rags and letting her go unguarded, hidden away in Devonshire. The man should be finding a splendid young husband for his ward, someone of equal rank and fortune to cherish her and protect her from evil beasts like the Duke of St. Sevrin.

"Go home, sweetheart. You've got your fairy tale all wrong. The dragon isn't allowed to rescue the damsel in distress." He closed his eyes and leaned his head back on the chair.

A moment later he felt a gossamer touch on his shoulder. "Sir? Your Grace?"

She was so close Sloane could smell rose water under the other, more earthy scents. He opened his eyes. "What, still here, Baroness? You are a stubborn little thing, aren't you?"

"When I have to be, Your Grace. Won't you hear me out?"

"Will you go home after?"

She nodded.

"Then bring me the bottle over there, child, and let's have your story."

Lisanne found the bottle on the floor near the window, with some brandy miraculously still in it, and handed it to the duke. She searched for a glass.

"But I'm not half civilized, Baroness, haven't you heard?" He tipped the bottle to his lips and swallowed. "I'd offer you some, but I'm sure one of us ought to stay sober."

Drunk, unmannerly, bitter . . . could she bear this in a man? She'd have to. Lisanne found the glass where it had fallen behind a chair still in holland covers. She took the bottle from his limp fingers and poured out a scant thimbleful. "I'd think you'd want a clear head to hear my proposition," she told him, handing over the glass instead of the bottle.

"If I had a clear head, *chérie*, you'd be home in your bed, or upstairs in mine. Now, say your piece, little lady, and get out."

Lisanne put the bottle out of his reach and pulled her chair a little closer. She closed her eyes a moment. "I am the only child of Lord and Lady Neville," she began. "When they died, I inherited the title and great wealth. I cannot give you exact amounts, for no one shows me the account books, but I believe my fortune to be over a hundred thousand pounds."

57

He whistled. "Now, that's a number to gain any man's attention."

"That's without the income from Neville Hall, which has been earning a handsome profit, and the returns on Papa's investments, which fluctuate. My solicitors in London could give you the precise details. They hold the funds while Uncle Alfred . . . holds me, until I marry or reach five and twenty. But I think—no, I know—that he has plans to extend his control by legal means after I reach my majority."

"What, does the dirty dish want you to marry his nephew or something, to keep the money in the family?"

"No, I think he intends that I never marry."

"What, never give his permission? Never let you go into Society?"

"That needn't concern you, Your Grace. What must is that I have all these funds I don't need and cannot touch, and you have none."

It would be useless to deny the obvious. St. Sevrin stared at the minute amount of wine in his glass. "Why me? A hundred thousand pounds could net you any number of handsome young beaux ready to sweep you away from Uncle Alfred and off to Gretna Green. What could I possibly have that you'd want? A crumbling monastery, a hellish reputation, a mountain of bills? Perhaps this old, battered body?"

If he thought to put her to the blush, he was wrong. "Sevrin Woods" was all Lisanne said.

"Excuse me?"

"Sevrin Woods. That's what you have that I want. I can put a fortune in your hands, if you'll give me Sevrin Woods."

Sloane thought he must be more foxed than he realized—or she was. "Sweetings, if I could sell Sevrin Woods or any part of this monstrosity I've inherited, I wouldn't need your fortune."

She brushed his objection aside impatiently. "I know

58

you cannot sell the property; I wasn't born yesterday. It's what's on it that I want, what's in the woods. I cannot simply buy the trees and such like the lumber mills can. I told you, I cannot touch my moneys. But Sevrin Woods could be written into the marriage settlements, that the woods are to be mine, absolutely inviolate in perpetuity."

"Trade a king's ransom for marriage to a curst rum touch like me—to get a forestful of trees? Lady, you're crazy!"

Lisanne jumped to her feet, fists clenched at her sides. "Never, ever, say that to me!"

He watched her through narrowed eyes. "And prickly as a hedgehog. Almost as grubby, too. Well, I wasn't born yesterday, either. What's in Sevrin Woods you want so badly, you're willing to marry me to get? Did you find gold under the surface? A diamond mine? The fountain of youth in one of the streams?"

"It's nothing like that." Lisanne stared at the mud on her shoes. "It's hard to explain. I spent my childhood playing among the trees. After my parents died my only friends were the, ah, sylvan creatures."

Although Sloane had spent his childhood at schools or being passed from relative to relative, he sympathized with her. "Poor puss."

"No, no, I was never sad in the forest. My happiest memories are there. That's why I cannot bear to see it all destroyed to pay your gaming debts. No, I shouldn't have said that. I know you inherited debts and mortgages you could never have repaid. I don't blame you, truly, but I can help."

"What did you say your name was?"

Chapter Eight

$\mathcal{H}$e was listening! More important, he was hearing her! Self-interest was a wondrous tool sometimes, Lisanne decided, and who could be more self-centered than a hedonistic, care-for-nothing rake? Instead of disdaining the duke for his profligate ways, she was relieved. Given enough time and his favorite peppermint drops, even Lester Roarke's most cantankerous bull could be gentled a bit.

"My name is Lisanne. Lisanne Margaret Finella Neville. My cousins call me Annie, but I hate it."

"As do I. It's common. Lisanne suits you, something that's a combination of many things, but with its own flow, its own grace."

That may have been the first compliment Lisanne ever received from a man. She didn't need flattery from this cup-shot stranger, only his cooperation, but she was pleased all the same. "And you, Your Grace? Do you prefer something to your title? Or does that suit your consequence?"

"Consequence be damned. My father made sure there was no distinction in those ducal strawberry leaves. I've only continued the slide. I was born Sloane Jarrett Shelton Shearingham, with more titles and dignities than I can recite now. My fellow officers used to call me Sherry. I was Lieutenant Shearingham at the time, you see, so it was natural, given the reddish color of my hair and my fondness for the grape."

She looked at the bottle. No, she would not call him Sherry. "St. Sevrin fits you better. Or Sloane."

"Slow to pay what's owed? Securing a loan? No, don't answer. Call me whatever you will. After all, we should be on a more familiar footing. It's not every day a chap has an offer of marriage. Or an offer for his home woods, since that's what this so flattering proposition amounts to. No, no, I'm not offended," he said when she would reply, holding up his hand with the glass. A drop or two spilled on the threadbare carpet. "I admire your honesty."

"In that case I'd better tell you that I do have a few other conditions."

"Ah, now, why am I not surprised?"

"But these are negotiable, of course."

"Unlike the deed to the woods, which is to be bound in a blood oath and witnessed by an archangel."

"The rest are nothing so terrible." Lisanne fished in her skirt pockets, pulling out her usual hodgepodge of stuff, until she found a folded paper.

To St. Sevrin's amusement, she shoved the rest of the junk willy-nilly back in her pockets till she looked like a tattered Elizabethan doll with panniers. This ragamuffin thought she could be a duchess? As she smoothed the page on her lap, Sloane noted, "I can see you've put some thought into this, at least."

"Oh, I thought and thought. I would not have come to you if there was another way."

"Thank you for that, my lady."

Lisanne colored up again. "I'm sorry. I'm not in the habit of dissembling."

"Never learn, sweetings. Go on, let me hear the rest of your terms."

She consulted the paper, as if trying to decide which stipulation he'd find least insulting. "Firstly, I should wish part of the money to go to restore the Priory. This must have been a wondrous place. It shouldn't be allowed to crumble into dust."

"I am not comfortable in such conditions, you may be assured. This rubbish heap makes Portugal look like a well-run hostelry. The London house needs refurbishing, too."

"And the farms?"

"A given. It only makes sense to invest some of the ready back into the land so it can turn a profit. What's next?"

She had to moisten her lips with her tongue. "I would want a portion of the moneys, perhaps the income from Neville Hall, to be kept separate for my use."

"I thought you said you didn't need the blunt, *chérie*. Never tell me you're going to turn into one of those fashionable belles who spend their husbands' incomes on feathers and furbelows? Hiding your fashion sense under a bushel, are you? Or do you hanker for jewels, perhaps a diamond tiara to go with the leaves in your hair?"

Lisanne reached up to remove the offending articles, disarranging what remained of the braid. She pulled the ribbon away and shook out the rest of her long blond hair, over her shoulders and past her breasts. St. Sevrin watched her unconscious sensuality and shook his head. Zounds, the chit didn't even know what she could do to a man. She could unman him with her words, too.

"I want a sum settled on me, perhaps the amount my dowry would have been, so that you cannot gamble it away if you manage to lose all the rest."

At his indrawn breath, Lisanne glanced toward the window, gauging the distance if she had to escape. "You said I should be honest."

So his little hedgehog had teeth, too. "Fencing with naked swords, are we, Baroness?"

He had reverted back to formal titles. So be it. "I wouldn't want my children going hungry, Your Grace, or reduced to living in the gamekeeper's cottage when you get yourself killed in some brothel brawl. My children's future must not depend on which horse wins at Epsom."

"Oh, so there are to be children of this union? S'truth, I thought it was to be a financial transaction, accrued interest the only outcome."

There was no blush this time, just the matter-of-fact: "You need an heir. And yes, I would like children . . . someday. After we know each other better."

And after she had a bath. "I would derive great satisfaction in eliminating my current heir, my cousin Humbert, from the succession." St. Sevrin also thought he might find a bit of satisfaction in introducing this hurly-burly baroness to the joys of lovemaking.

"Then why haven't you married?" she asked in that disconcertingly straightforward manner of hers.

Because he couldn't ask a decent female to share his miserable life; because if he could have fed another mouth, he'd have bought a racehorse; because he hadn't yet met a woman who didn't bore him to death after twenty minutes, ten if he was in a hurry.

Until tonight. Tonight this female was full of surprises. Sloane didn't think she could ever bore him, with her eccentric mix of worldly wisdom and naïveté. Lady Lisanne was the one who let her thoughts rule her tongue, however, not him. Sloane was used to keeping his cards close to his chest, so his answer was, "What, marry and settle on one woman?"

Lisanne nodded. "I've thought of that also, and I promise not to interfere with your life. I know you have other interests, and I don't mean to hang on your sleeve, you know. I don't care if I never go to London, and you don't have to dance attendance on me here."

"You have an odd notion of where the heir is coming from, then, my dear, if we live separate lives."

Lisanne refused to be embarrassed. "I believe it's done all the time in arranged marriages. I wouldn't care, as long as you do not embarrass me. I realize you haven't had reason to be discreet in the past. I understand, truly."

"You do?" Then she understood more than Sloane could himself. He didn't want to continue this particular line of conversation. "Is that it, then? Have you finished your shopping list? Let me reiterate, Baroness, to make sure I have it correct. You want the woods, or what's in them."

"Sworn and inviolate. Forever."

"Right, forever. Marriage to me would get you Sevrin Woods and get you out from under Uncle Alfred's thumb, with a substantial amount settled on you and your children. For a rainy day, of course." At her nod he continued: "In return, I get my bills paid, my property restored, a fortune to fritter away, and my freedom, as long as I don't embarrass you. I also increase my holdings with Neville Hall and your father's investments."

"There's a town house in London, too. It's part of the entail so cannot be sold, but you could lease it out."

"Rental income," he said, ticking another bonus off on his fingers. "And, of course, a wife and heirs, sometime in the future. I think I have covered everything."

Sloane reached over for the bottle, about to pour a healthy amount of the brandy into his glass.

"There is one more thing." Lisanne stared at the paper in her hand. "You must promise . . . never to lock me up."

The glass's stem snapped off in the duke's left hand. "That bastard. Is that what he threatened you with if you went to the magistrate, that he'd send you to Bedlam? Is that how he was going to keep your fortune when you came of age? Snakes like that should be boiled in oil."

Lisanne was rummaging in her pockets again. She found what she wanted, a clean handkerchief, and poured brandy onto the linen square. She reached for the duke's hand.

"What? Oh." St. Sevrin hadn't felt the cut or seen the blood. "Hold now, that's expensive brandy!"

"And it will do you more good outside than inside." When Lisanne was finished cleaning the wound, making sure no glass remained, she went back to her pocket for the small book. She opened its pages and carefully removed a spiderweb.

"What the deuce . . . ?"

"It helps stop the bleeding, Your Grace, and holds the cut edges together so they don't need to be sewn. And the spider doesn't need it anymore. She makes a new one each night."

The spider doesn't need it? Sewn? No, he would not be bored with Lady Lisanne Neville. While she was busy tying yet another handkerchief around his hand, he apologized for his clumsiness. "That was just my bad arm, weakened from a war wound that never healed right."

"I might be able to help. I know a lot of remedies, oils, potions, that sort of thing." She started to lift his shirt.

He clamped his good right hand over hers. "Here now, none of that until we're wed."

Lisanne's whole face lit up. "Then you agree to marry me? You'll really do it?"

St. Sevrin leaned his head back and let his eyes drift closed, but he kept his hand over hers, on his warm shoulder. "Devil a bit, poppet, I don't know. I suppose I need time to think on it. It's an offer that could tempt a saint, which I never pretended to be, but I still have some honor. I cannot take advantage of a tender little bud like you."

"How could it be taking advantage when it's what I want?"

"When you're too young and innocent to know what's best for you, that's how. I'll call on your uncle tomorrow, to sound him out on plans for your future. Perhaps he has some likely candidate for your hand waiting in the wings."

"No, you mustn't do that! He'll never tell you the truth anyway. And he'll forbid you to call."

"My title ought to be enough to have him consider my suit, should I decide to make the offer for his ward's hand."

She moaned. "What's a title for me compared to control of all my money, for him? No, he'd find a way to ruin everything. We have to present him with a fait accompli. It's better for you to go speak to my London trustee, to make sure he'll release the estate to you." She took her hand back to search through the pockets again. "I wrote Mr. Mackensie a letter, telling him my wishes."

"Sure of your charms, were you?"

"Sure of my worth, rather, and sure of your need. Your Grace, Sloane, marriages are made for much worse reasons all the time. I know I'm not any Society Toast. I'll never make a political hostess. And I'm not a beauty, tall and willowy or all rounded like the current mode. Aunt Cherise despairs of me in a polite drawing room. But I would try my hardest to manage your household and make your children happy."

"And me? Would you try to make me happy?"

"I . . . I wouldn't know how to begin." It had never occurred to Lisanne that he might want something from her beyond the monetary, beyond that other marital duty. "Yes, I'd try, if you wished."

"And you? I suppose you'd be happy here, with children and a great forest to romp in. You wouldn't even need me, would you? No, don't answer. Leave a man some pride." He sighed. "Very well, I promise to consider this mad bargain. If it doesn't all turn into a whiskey dream when I wake up, I'll travel back to London and talk to your man. He'll likely throw me out on my ear. I would. But now it's time for you to go. Let me get my coat and a lantern."

"Oh, you needn't accompany me."

"What, you only need a husband, not an escort through haunted forests in the middle of the night?"

"The forests aren't haunted. You know there's nothing in them to fear."

"Still, I cannot let you go alone."

"But I'm not alone." The cavernous pockets yielded a carved flute this time. Lisanne played three high lilting notes, then repeated them.

In moments a great lumbering black beast galloped out of the forest, across the field of onetime-lawn, and through the open window without breaking stride. The shaggy monster took up a stance in front of Lisanne, blocking all but her upper body, and slavering in Sloane's direction.

"This is Becka."

St. Sevrin knew better than to step forward or to raise his voice. "What *is* Becka? I've seen handsomer creatures at the bottom of a bottle of Blue Ruin."

"Becka is beautiful! Her mother was Homer Phelps's prize mastiff bitch."

"What was her father, a troll from under a bridge?"

Lisanne shrugged. "Homer thought so, too. He tried to drown the puppies. Becka was the only one I could save."

St. Sevrin could foresee a lifetime of rescued kittens and orphaned lambs. Was he to be one of her acts of charity? "You're too soft, Lady Lisanne."

"No, I am strong, Your Grace, like Becka. Strong enough to make Homer Phelps swim into the pond to get her out. Strong enough to be your duchess."

"We'll see."

Lisanne flitted out the window before he could go to assist, the oversize dog right behind her. St. Sevrin watched the baroness scampering across the moonlit lawn toward the woods, just like some fairy sprite.

Maybe it was all a dream.

Chapter Nine

*E*ighteen years old. Lud, St. Sevrin didn't even remember being eighteen. He must have been so young, somewhere in the murky past. And it was true, many chits the baroness's age were already married and breeding. Some of them were even married to men older than he was. It wasn't as if he were losing his hair or his teeth, either, Sloane told himself, standing by the window as he watched his visitor disappear into the woods. He could still cross swords with the best of the fencers at Antoine's, and go a few rounds with Gentleman Jackson himself despite his weak left punch. No, ten years wasn't such a big difference, until you measured it in experience.

Every scrap of honor he had left told Sloane to stay away from Lisanne Neville. Boys don't pull wings off butterflies; men don't destroy innocence.

But she already knew about him: the drinking, the gaming, the whoring, things no decent female acknowledged. The baroness acknowledged, accepted, forgave, and gave him future permission to repeat his sins. She wasn't a lovesick peagoose who'd wake up three months into the marriage to discover she was wed to a cad.

Maybe she really wouldn't mind living alone here in seclusion when Sloane resumed his dissolute life in London as he was bound to. And maybe pigs would fly.

She had come to him. That had to count for something, such as how desperate she was. Sloane could no more make a chit like Lisanne a decent husband than he could make his horse do somersaults. But if her alternative was no husband at all, no family of her own but that mawworm Findley, then maybe the Duke of St. Sevrin wasn't so bad a choice. Lisanne had offered Sloane his freedom in the union, but maybe it was her own she was seeking. Money of her own, an absentee husband—a lot of chits did far worse in marriage. Lisanne Neville looked to be doing far worse now.

Unfortunately St. Sevrin wasn't the one in the business of rescuing fallen sparrows. Lud, what was he thinking of, to entertain the notion of wedding the appealing little waif? Worse, what was he thinking of to let her go home alone through the woods? She didn't even have a light. St. Sevrin pushed himself away from the window and went to the kitchen, where his greatcoat hung on a peg.

Kelly was sitting at the scarred table, having a cup of well-fortified tea. Another of those precious bottles of brandy sat half empty next to him.

"You went into the village today," St. Sevrin casually remarked. "Did you happen to hear anything about a Miss Neville, the baron's daughter?"

Kelly whistled. "What, we been here a whole day now and you're tumbling into trouble already?" The ex-soldier shook his grizzled head. "I don't see how you do it, Yer Grace. I swear I don't."

The duke frowned. "What do you mean, trouble?"

"The Neville gal. She's trouble. You've hardly been out of your own stable, and you're up to your neck in manure already."

"Come on, old man, what have you heard?"

"The chit's all they find to talk about around here. Except you, a'course. But after trying to get me to open my budget about Yer Grace, which I ain't about to, a'course, it's Lady Annie this and Lady Neville that. Or worse."

St. Sevrin left his coat on the hook and took a seat across from his manservant, who got up and found another chipped cup. The baroness would be long gone into the woods, Sloane realized, and he'd never find her in the dark. He'd just have to trust in that dog to see her home safely.

"But what are they saying about her, Kelly?" he asked.

"Fey."

"Faye? No, her name is Lisanne."

"Fey. Touched. Fairy-dusted. Pixilated."

"That's absurd. There's no such thing, just ignorant folks trying to explain away someone else's peculiarities."

"A wee lass what can charm birds down from the trees sounds a tad peculiar to me, too." Kelly scratched his head. "But there's others who say she's a natural. You know, simpleminded."

"They're far off the mark there. The lady quoted me Latin, French, and Shakespeare."

Kelly slapped his hands down on the table, jostling the cups and bottle. "I knew it. You've gone and met the female somehow, not hours after that guardian of hers spread word around the village that he'd have your hide if you so much as looked at the chit. Warned all the locals to lock their daughters up, too."

"What, did he think I was in the habit of ravishing milkmaids and dressmakers' assistants? Forget about Findley for now. What else do they say about the baroness?"

"One man claimed he'd never heard her speak a word in ten years."

"Nonsense. She most likely had nothing to say to the dolt." She'd had plenty to say to St. Sevrin tonight. "Anything else?"

"Well, they was all agreed she had the healing hands." Kelly stared at the handkerchief wrapped and neatly tied around the duke's hand. "But you wouldn't be knowing nothing about that neither, would you?"

"What a lot of claptrap. I forgot how narrow-minded and superstitious people were in these small villages and outlying shires. Did anyone happen to mention anything about the Neville inheritance? How it was divided, that kind of thing."

"Weren't divided at all. Every last farthing comes to this female, what the uncle doesn't manage to skim off. He's too smart to let the land go to waste, unlike some others I could name, but that handsome profit the bailiff collects ain't all making it to the London bank. They might split hairs about the girl, but no one hereabouts has a decent word to say about the uncle. A regular dirty dish, I figure. Miserly and mean, he turned off all the Neville staff without a groat when he took over. Brought in London servants. What with the Priory gone to the dogs, there's a heap of folks nearby on the dole."

"A few more hints like that, old man, and you could be joining them."

Kelly ignored his employer, as usual. "They say the old baron was a downy cove what tied up most of his fortune with a London solicitor so Findley couldn't get at it. So now the scurvy bastard makes money by charging a fee to anyone doing business at the Hall. You know, the carter, the coal man, the chandler. Some London butlers pull that rig. First I heard of the gentry doing it."

St. Sevrin was staring at his cup. "I don't suppose the solicitor is aware of any of this. I've a good mind to go tell him."

"Now, why would you want to go and stick your nose in someone else's business? It'll just get bitten off. And ain't we got enough in our dish right now?"

"Yes, but there's a lady who needs rescuing, and she

72

just might be the salvation of us all." Sloane took a swallow. "Tell me, old man, do you think I'm beyond hope?"

"The devil hisself is not beyond hope. They call it religion. Why don't you try going to church instead of to that accountant bloke?"

"I wasn't thinking of divine intervention. Let's start off with small miracles."

"Oh, dear; oh, dear. This is all my fault." Mr. Mackensie had been shocked when the Duke of St. Sevrin sent in his card that morning, asking for an interview with the Neville solicitor. From what Mackensie heard, the duke never took the time nor made an effort on anyone's behalf but his own.

"I remembered the baron and his lady fondly from my own childhood," Sloane lied when he read the suspicion on the elderly gentleman's face. "I thought it my duty to help their daughter. As a concerned neighbor, don't you know."

"Much obliged, Your Grace, to be sure. And you say things aren't what they ought to be?"

Mr. Mackensie was even more shocked after he'd listened to St. Sevrin's claims against Sir Arthur, but not precisely surprised, Sloane thought.

"I should have gone in person," the solicitor bemoaned, "when I first heard those rumors. But . . ."

St. Sevrin understood. Mr. Mackensie was a white-haired, bespectacled old man, with fingers bent and swollen with arthritis. Two canes were propped against his desk in the well-appointed office. The roomful of clerks in the outer office would run all of the gentleman's errands here in Town, but he could never have traveled to Devon. "I'm sure you did not want to give credence to idle rumor."

Mr. Mackensie nodded, thankful for the rescue. "I did send one of my assistants with some papers to be signed some years back. I could have put them in the post, of course, but I asked the lad to look around. He found everything in order."

"Did he actually see Lady Lisanne? Speak to her?"

"Unfortunately no, she had a putrid sore throat at the time. The baronet was very concerned. He wrote me as soon as she was recovered."

"I'm sure he included a tidy bundle of doctor's fees, too. I doubt the chit ever saw a physician. She's the one the villagers call on for their aches and pains."

"But my clerk saw nothing untoward."

"Possibly he was gulled, but more likely greedy. Sir Alfred would have given him a handsome douceur to insure a good report."

"I take it you have no high regard for human nature, Your Grace."

St. Sevrin brushed that aside. It was a fact. "Did that clerk stay in your employ? Is he here now? Can we speak to him?"

"Unhappily I had to dismiss him from my employ several years ago for irregularities in his accounts." Mr. Mackensie was looking even more old and pained. He kept rubbing at his swollen fingers. "I should have sent another when I started to hear those disturbing rumors. One of my other clients told me word was going around the clubs that the child was sickly. Her mother was, do you recall?"

St. Sevrin could honestly say no. He had no memory of Lady Neville whatsoever, and still hadn't remembered the gossip he had more recently heard. "I daresay that Lady Lisanne is in better health than either of us, sir."

Mr. Mackensie smiled, reassured. "Then there was talk that the heiress was high-strung, of a nervous disposition. I didn't know what to think. An old bachelor like me, what did I understand about children, female children besides? I thought her aunt and uncle would know what was best for her."

"I fear, sir, that they were worrying about what was best for themselves."

Mr. Mackensie removed his spectacles and painstakingly wiped them with his handkerchief. Not until he was done and the glasses were back on his nose did he continue. "I was relieved when Sir Alfred sent notice that he was bringing my client to Town for the coming fall Little Season. It's more than time. I don't know why he's putting it off so long; most debutantes make their curtsies in the spring. I suggested my staff could have Neville House opened, aired, and ready by mid-April."

"Most likely his own daughter is still too young."

"Yes, well, I thought I could see Lady Lisanne for myself, then talk to the poor dear."

"I seriously doubt you'd have been given the chance. Lady Lisanne believes she would not be permitted to come to Town if she had intentions of doing so. Findley will give some excuse or other: a lasting fever, a broken ankle. Frankly, sir, she is not ready to make a come-out. From what I saw, the baroness has no wardrobe, no care for her appearance, no drawing-room accomplishments, no sense of decorum." Hell, if he told this old gent how she climbed through bachelor windows in the middle of the night, the solicitor was liable to have apoplexy right there, and St. Sevrin needed him safe and sound.

"But the estate has been paying for expensive governesses for years," Mr. Mackensie protested.

"I'd wager the estate has been paying for a great many things Lady Lisanne never received. Oh, there may have been an instructress—for the younger girl. No governess worth her salt would turn out a hoyden like the baroness; she'd never find another position with such a recommendation. Lady Lisanne's education does not seem lacking, just her social skills. The villagers say she hardly speaks, she runs barefoot in the woods . . ."

"Oh, my; oh, my. I'll have to send someone. Perhaps two so they cannot be suborned if what you surmise is correct. But with the Findleys named my lady's legal guardians, it would mean a scandalous court case to have them declared unfit. I cannot think that will help Lady Lisanne's chances of making an eligible match. And there is no one else, no other family on either side except very distant cousins. I know of no one who could arrange the proper introductions and smooth her path."

"I thought perhaps a match might have been arranged in infancy or some such, since Sir Alfred does not seem concerned with putting his ward in the way of eligible gentlemen. Maybe he's contracted with a wellborn family in Devon."

"Oh, no, I would have been notified at once. The settlements, don't you know. And there was nothing like that in Lord Neville's will, you may be assured. You say she is eighteen and has never been to a local assembly?"

"She is past eighteen, plaits her hair in schoolgirl braids, and wears her cousin's castoffs."

Mr. Mackensie pawed through a thick folder of papers. "But these are dressmakers' bills from this past quarter."

"I'm sure they are. Sir Arthur's wife and daughter are very à la mode, according to the local vicar. I spoke with him because I wanted to verify my facts before coming to you, without stirring up a hornet's nest."

"Oh, dear, what is to be done now?"

St. Sevrin handed over Lisanne's letter.

The poor old solicitor almost fell off his seat. If things were bad before, this was disastrous. "Oh, my stars. She wants to marry—you?"

St. Sevrin inspected his boots. "As they say, there's no accounting for tastes."

"This is a love match?" Mackensie asked hopefully.

"Don't be ridiculous, man. I hardly know the chit. The union's to her advantage, though. She's positive no one else will be allowed near her until she's twenty-five. She'll be firmly on the shelf by then, and so set in freakish ways that no one will have her, no matter how large the fortune."

"But, Your Grace . . ."

"I know, Mr. Mackensie. I wouldn't wish a female in my care to throw herself away on a loose screw like myself, either. But Lady Lisanne wishes it. She needs it. And I'm not fool enough to turn her down. I know you have no reason to trust me and years of indiscretions not to, but I do mean to improve. Furthermore, you shall see that her settlements are so securely tied that Lisanne will never be at the mercy of any man again, myself or any other. Neville Hall is to remain hers and her issue's, along with its income. Whatever would have been her dowry joins her portion. You might have to stay on until she is of age to satisfy the law, but the money is hers, to do with as she wishes."

"Ahem. That's very generous, Your Grace."

"I need to pay my bills and mortgages. I need to reclaim my estates from bankruptcy. I do not need to look in my mirror every morning and see a fortune hunter looking back. As soon as my own property turns a profit, I will pay her back. I swear to you Lisanne will want for nothing."

Except a decent man as husband. Mr. Mackensie could foresee the little baroness abandoned within a month of the wedding, in favor of the card tables. Leopards didn't change their spots. "And you'll bring her to court for presentation, as her parents would have wished?" he tried.

"If she is willing, yes, I can do it. There are certain advantages to playing cards with Prinny, don't you know. The lady is much happier decocting herbal remedies and going for walks with her dog, though. I cannot imagine what the polite world will make of a lady with snails and spiderwebs in her pocket, but I can try. It would not suit me to have my duchess outcast from Society." Actually it wouldn't bother him a whit—Society be damned—but

St. Sevrin was of a mind to rub Sir Alfred's nose in the mud, and Cousin Humbert's, too.

Mr. Mackensie sighed. "I can't see how I can refuse if it is what my lady wants."

"That's how I looked at it."

Chapter Ten

*A*lone. Alone. Alone.

St. Sevrin had gone back to London. Lisanne's uncle had gone back to ignoring her. And she had gone back to the forest, where silence reverberated in her mind.

Lisanne visited all the secret places, called all the names, played all the songs on her flute. No one came, no one answered. She was alone.

In her mind she'd known how it would be. You can't play cards with the devil and not come away smelling of fire and brimstone. St. Sevrin had gone to London, so there was hope that she'd won; but, either way, she'd lost. She'd lost her innocence by selling herself, even if it was for the best of causes.

Besides, she was too old. Fairy tales were for children, with their wide-eyed sense of wonder. Children knew how to play; adults forgot.

In Lisanne's mind she understood. She even knew she'd been fortunate longer than most. In her heart, though, she felt abandoned. "It isn't fair," she cried the eternal lament into the void. "I did it for you. Please don't leave me alone like this! I cannot help growing older. Please. Without you I have nothing."

Under the ages-old trees, where violets tried to find a patch of sunlight, Lisanne cried for her lost parents, her lost childhood. She faced a terrifying future with a dangerous stranger, or an equally uncertain future without him, under her uncle's domination. The only creature in the world who cared about her was her dog, whose motley fur was soon damp with the first tears Lisanne had cried since her mother's death.

Like a newborn crying at being thrust from her safe womb into the world for the first time, Lisanne lay on the forest floor and sobbed her heartbreak.

She didn't know how long she wept there, and she never heard his footsteps. Becka didn't even growl when strong arms reached for Lisanne and lifted her into his lap, cuddling her against his chest while he leaned back against a tree trunk. St. Sevrin let her cry her fill, even though her tears were soaking through his shirt in front, and the tree's rough bark was digging into his skin in back. And Becka was drooling on his Hessian boots.

"Everyone has left me" was all he could understand between her wrenching sobs.

"Ah, and I feared you were crying because I came back."

"But, but my friends are all gone." She tried to move from his embrace to find a handkerchief, but he already had one to hand, knowing how long it would take her to sort through the clutter in her pockets.

He gently wiped her eyes. "I'll be your friend, sweetings. I haven't much practice at it, but I'll try."

She took the cloth from him and blew her nose, not a delicate gesture. Since she was already covered in dirt and debris from the forest floor—as was St. Sevrin now—one more inelegance didn't count, to Sloane's thinking.

Coming upon her crying in the woods, all splotchy-faced and disheveled, St. Sevrin felt something twist in his guts. Women's tears hadn't moved him in ages, manipulative and on cue as they usually were, yet these sobs had brought him to his knees literally and figuratively. He didn't know the problem, only that he had to protect her, even if from himself. Whatever was wrong, he'd make right.

This new feeling of protectiveness wasn't passion, which the duke was used to, or even casual attraction. It was more like brotherly affection, paternal almost, which was not a comfortable role for him. Sloane did not want to think of Lisanne as a child, as too young for his attentions. If comforting was what she needed, however, comforting was what she'd get.

As she sat there in his lap with his arms around her, though, Sloane could feel her rounded bottom against his thighs, her softness against his chest. She was not a child, he told himself. It was her small stature that was deceiving, and her thinness. Lady Lisanne was not his sister, daughter, or ward. She was the woman he was prepared to marry if she'd still have him, if she wasn't crying at the mare's nest she'd dug up with her offer.

"What, is the idea of being a duchess so terrible, then?" he asked. "Or just my duchess?"

She sniffed and squirmed off his lap to a position across from him, sitting cross-legged in the leaf mold, her skirts hiked up past her ankles. "You decided, then."

"Only if you're still sure it's what you want. You can back out now, Baroness, and I'll understand."

The magic was lost to her either way, but the forest would be safe. She didn't even hesitate, especially when the duke had shown how gentle he could be holding her. If there was an ounce of tenderness in this war hero turned rake, that was one ounce more than Uncle Alfred possessed. "I am sure."

"Then, here." He reached into his coat pocket for a small jewel box and opened it to show her a gold ring with a pearl surrounded by tiny diamonds. "It's the lightest ring in the St. Sevrin collection. The emeralds would have weighed you down, *ma petite.*"

"It's lovely." Lisanne started to admire the ring on her finger until she realized the duke was trying not to laugh at her dirty hands and ragged fingernails. She hid both hands and ring in her skirts. "But do you mean you have a fortune in gems somewhere? Why ever didn't you sell them to pay your bills?"

"The entail, of course. Cousin Humbert would be after me with a court order before the ink was dry on the jeweler's check. I did take the lot 'round to Rundell and Bridges for cleaning while I was at the vault, to make sure my esteemed father hadn't switched them for paste. You can have them reset later. And Mackensie says he's holding a box full of your mother's jewelry for your request, too, so you'll outshine all the other sprites in your forest."

Lisanne didn't want to talk about the forest. "Then he gave his permission?"

"Reluctantly, but yes. Your estate was even larger than you thought, so a goodly portion of it is being tied up for you and your progeny, besides Neville Hall and its income. I told him to add a codicil to keep your father's title from being absorbed into the dukedom, naming our second son to the barony."

"Or daughter."

"Or daughter," he agreed. "See? I'm really an easy fellow to get along with." Especially when handed a fortune to rival Golden Ball's.

"And Sevrin Woods?" she had to ask.

"Mackensie's writing a book, it seems. I'd be surprised if a crow will be allowed to nest in one of the trees without your permission when he's done."

"That's it, then." She was relieved, of course, but anxious. "When? That is, how soon . . . ?"

"Until the execution? Poor poppet, between the devil and the deep blue sea, are you?"

82

"Oh, no, you mustn't think I'm having second thoughts."

"Third and fourth ones, too, if you've any common sense." He patted his inside pocket. "The venerable Mr. Mackensie helped me get a special license. We can be wed as soon as you wish."

"Soon, then. You'll be wanting to settle your accounts and start the renovations."

"No fancy June wedding?" He couldn't imagine this ragtag urchin at a grand social event at St. George's, but it was her money, her wedding. He had to ask.

"No, if we marry now, there's still time for spring planting if you get the tenant farmers back."

He nodded. "Practical little puss. I'll go speak to Uncle Alfred this very afternoon."

"No, you mustn't! He won't allow it."

"He cannot stop it. And I'm not about to steal you away from him like a thief in the night. I don't want the sheriff coming after me for kidnapping an heiress, and I don't want anyone thinking this was some hole-in-corner affair."

"But he'll ruin everything. You don't know him."

"No, Baroness, he doesn't know me. If he causes any problems, we'll make other plans. Don't look for trouble." The marriage itself was going to be hard enough, heaven knew. "Now come, sweetings, a smile. I hear you can charm the birds out of the trees. Is it true?"

Lisanne did manage a wan smile. She pulled a heel of bread out of her pocket and played a few notes on her flute. "Be very quiet." Soon enough, little black and white birds came and took crumbs out of her hand.

When the crumbs were all gone, St. Sevrin kissed her hand, dirt and all. "I bet no other duchess can do that."

He stood to leave, brushing at the damp spot where he'd been sitting. Now he'd have to go back to the Priory and change clothes before calling on Sir Alfred. Kelly was going to have a fit.

As he turned to go, Lisanne asked, "How did you find me? No one else ever comes through the forest. I could have been anywhere."

"It wasn't hard. There was a path right from the edge of the Priory's old lawns. I can't imagine how I missed it the morning after your visit."

Lisanne could. It hadn't been there then. So she wasn't quite alone after all.

The duke sent his card in. Then, to make sure Sir Alfred didn't deny his presence, he followed the niffy-naffy butler into an airy parlor done in the Chinese style. An older woman was pouring tea for Findley, a chinless youth, and a plump miss who was obviously and unfortunately the spotted Esmé, all rigged out in the height of fashion. The ladies' gowns were made in London by a French modiste, if Sloane didn't miss his guess.

Findley took the card from the butler's silver salver and cursed when he read the name. "St. Sevrin, damn his effrontery in calling at a decent house. Pomfrey, tell the makebait I'm not—" Sir Alfred stood abruptly when he saw who stood behind the butler in the doorway. "Why, Your Grace, what an unexpected pleasure."

St. Sevrin made his bows, murmuring some fustian about calling on neighbors, while Sir Alfred begrudged the introductions without offering tea. Out of spite, Sloane raised Esmé's hand to his lips and lingered over her baby-fat fingers. Not until he thought Lady Cherise was about to have palpitations and Sir Alfred to have conniptions, did he release the pudgy hand. At least the chit's face was now so red you couldn't see the spots. Sloane asked for a moment of the baronet's time, on a private matter. Sir Alfred was only too happy to get him away from his starry-eyed peagoose of a daughter.

There was no sign of Lisanne until they moved to a small room, apparently the estate office. St. Sevrin could spot the baroness out of the corner of his eye, standing behind a large potted fern in the hall. She'd changed her gown to another unhappy selection, an ill-fitted beige lutestring that looked like a grain sack with a bow around it, an unevenly tied, frayed bow at that. Her uncle didn't acknowledge her presence, didn't bother making an introduction, as if she were a servant. Of course the servants all wore immaculate livery, not rags.

Sloane noted how everything in the house was of the first stare, right down to the smuggled cognac Sir Alfred offered. He declined in favor of keeping a clear head, but he did accept a seat opposite the baronet at the handsome cherry-wood desk.

"I hear you are interested in selling off your timber." Sir Alfred was making conversation while letting his own glass of cognac settle his nerves. "Sorry I can't be of service, but the man in Honiton is supposed to be reputable. He'll give you a fair price."

St. Sevrin adjusted his cuffs. "Oh, I am no longer interested in selling off the home woods. I won't need to, after I marry your niece."

Sir Alfred jumped up, overturning the inkwell on the desk. "What did you say? Never! I wouldn't give permission for a basket scrambler like you to get within five feet of her. I know my duty to my dead sister's child better than that." He stomped over to the door and called for a servant. "Clean this mess. And show this man out."

The footman who entered looked at the spreading black puddle, then he looked at the black expression on the duke's face. "I'll be fetching some rags, milord."

He didn't come back, which St. Sevrin thought was a shame; it really was a lovely old desk. "I have Mackensie's permission, you know. I am here only for the formality of the thing."

"He's not her guardian!" Sir Alfred was growing red in the face. "He cannot make that decision."

Lisanne came in then. She did not look at the duke, but addressed her uncle. "Mr. Mackensie didn't make the decision, sir. I did."

"What? You? How the deuce did you ever see him? I'll have your hide for disobeying me, you wretched brat. I told you to stay away."

"I wouldn't advise such intemperance, Findley. I do protect what is mine, you know." No emotion showed on the duke's face now, but his voice was quiet, sinister.

Findley didn't take the warning. "She's not yours, blast you, and never will be! What, are you going to claim you've fallen top over trees with this . . . this ragamuffin? The dustman wouldn't have her!"

Sloane took his eyes from Findley's beaked nose, which he was going to flatten if the man didn't shut up soon. He glanced at Lisanne, who had gone pale enough that a row of freckles stood out on her cheeks and her eyes were wide with distress. He saw all those other children who haunted his nightmares, their hungry, hopeless eyes.

"Nevertheless, I aim to have her."

"Over my dead body!"

"It's coming to that, you clodpole," the duke muttered under his breath, but Sir Alfred was too enraged to hear. He turned to Lisanne with his ranting: "And you, Annie, do you want to tie yourself to a rake and a wastrel, a degenerate womanizer? Why, the man's nothing but a fortune hunter. You'd be penniless in a month. He'll have his whores at your breakfast table, wager your house or your services on the turn of a card."

St. Sevrin stood and leaned threateningly over the desk, one hand on either side of the ink blot, prepared to slam this maggot's face into the mess.

It was Lisanne, though, who quietly interjected: "He

may be all of those things, and worse, Uncle, but I doubt he has ever struck a woman."

Findley's face turned purple now, and St. Sevrin had all he could do not to strangle the man as the import of her words sank in. "Enough, sirrah. Lady Lisanne and I have come to an agreement that suits both our needs. We do not require your blessing. At this point I do not even care for your presence at the wedding. I have fulfilled my honor-bound duty in advising you." He stepped back to leave.

Sir Alfred called him back. "I'll fulfill mine, Duke, by telling you what a Smithfield bargain you'll be getting. What do you think, that Annie is some pretty little rustic tomboy you can dress up and teach to make polite conversation? Well, it can't be done. God knows I've tried. Annie's no hoyden, no high-spirited filly. She's a lunatic, that's what!"

Now he remembered the rumors. Sloane stared at Lisanne while her uncle continued his harangue. Damn, he knew this deal was too good to be true. He murmured to himself, *"Timeo Danaos et dona ferentes."*

Lisanne snapped back, "Then never look a gift horse in the mouth."

"She's insane," Sir Alfred raged on. "She talks to fairies. She lives in a dreamworld in that forest of yours. Addled Annie, everyone calls her. The only reason I never saw fit to lock her away is that she seemed harmless enough. Now look what my kindheartedness has done."

"You didn't lock me up, Uncle, because then you'd have no excuse to stay at Neville Hall at my expense. If asylum fees were paid from my estate, there'd be no need for a well-fed, well-kept guardian and his family. And I might have died in such a place. Most bedlamites do, don't they? Then you'd never see a groat of my income."

"You see, Duke? See what madness she speaks? No

child in her right mind would so accuse her loving guardian. With such suspicions, she'll see a plot to assassinate her next." Sir Alfred was practically frothing. Beads of spittle had joined the ink on the desktop.

St. Sevrin turned to Lisanne. "Are you insane?"

"Can you afford to be so particular?" she replied, pointed chin raised, blue eyes flashing.

"Dash it, girl, I'm on your side!"

Findley pounded the desk, sending droplets of ink and saliva flying. "You may as well ask a liar if he's telling the truth. That's what makes a crazy person crazy, isn't it? A lunatic doesn't know reality from cloud-cuckoo land."

"They say the king knows when he is having one of his spells. It upsets him, but he realizes when he is all about in his head. I think the baroness knows very well the state of her mind. What say you, my lady?"

"I am not daft. Sir Alfred chooses to make me out to be for his own purposes."

Sloane stared into her eyes. There was no guile in their blue depths, no blank look he'd seen on soldiers with head injuries, only intelligence, bravery, and a plea for help. He nodded. "The marriage will take place tomorrow morning. I'll make arrangements with the vicar. See that my bride has a clean gown to wear at least, Findley, or you'll be wearing your teeth on your tonsils."

"Are you threatening me?"

"Of course not. I never waste my time threatening pigs like you. That was a promise."

"I'm not afraid of you, Duke," Sir Alfred sputtered.

St. Sevrin shrugged. "Then you're a fool besides a blackguard." He stepped closer to Lisanne and clasped her hand, where she was shredding the already frayed ribbon on her gown. He made sure Sir Alfred saw the ring before he brought her fingers up to his lips. "Mine."

No one in the room made the mistake of thinking he meant the ring.

"A demain, chérie."

No one knew what to make of it. No one had anything to say about the fire.

(... blurred lines ...)

Chapter Eleven

"*O*h, the shame of it! Oh, the disgrace of being connected to that family!" moaned Aunt Cherise.

"Oh, shut up," snarled Uncle Alfred back.

The rest of the family had rushed into the estate room as soon as the duke left, leaving their tea in the parlor. Aunt Cherise wanted to know what all the yelling was about. What could a bounder like St. Sevrin want with Sir Alfred?

"He what?" she shrieked, clutching her vinaigrette. "My nerves cannot take such a calamity, Sir Alfred, I tell you. I'm sure to be laid in my bed for a week."

"Stubble it, woman. He means to have the plaguey chit, your nerves or not, blast him to perdition! Wants me to buy her a trousseau, no less!"

The plaguey chit was standing near the fireplace, as far from the Findleys as she could get. If Nigel and Esmé hadn't been crowded in the doorway, she would have fled lest Sir Alfred decide to ignore the duke's warning and take his ire out on her, as usual.

This time it was Aunt Cherise who turned on Lisanne before she could make her escape. "You ungrateful child! How could you do this to us? Why, that man is not acknowledged among the best houses. With that connection we'll never be received by the highest sticklers. Dear Esmeralda won't receive invitations to the best parties, where she can meet the most eligible *partis*."

"What about Almack's, Ma? I'll still get my vouchers there, won't I?" Esmé demanded.

"Oh, my precious, I fear not."

"What?" screamed that devastated miss, who'd secretly harbored the notion that the dashing rake had come to ask Papa permission to pay his addresses to her, Esmé. "Why, you jade, Annie! You've ruined everything! I hate you! I hate you! If I can't go to Almack's, my come-out will be a failure. I may as well stay in Devon!"

"Where?" Sir Alfred snidely asked. "You cannot have thought, miss, nor you, madame," he said with a nod toward his wife. "Neville Hall will become the duke's property. And it's not merely a matter of receiving the proper invitations to those dreary subscription balls when we go to London; we cannot go to London! In case you forgot, the site of that grand debutante ball you've been planning for months, Neville House in Cavendish Square, will belong to the dastard also!"

Aunt Cherise fainted into Nigel's arms, never yet swooning when no one was nearby to catch her. Nigel quickly lowered his mama's bulk to a leather-covered chair. Esmé was drumming her feet into the carpet, screaming that her life was over, that she hated all of them.

"Neville House is to be mine. Mr. Mackensie is drawing up the papers." Lisanne ignored her uncle's narrowed eyes, his fury at how much she had done behind his back, and addressed Esmé. "You may still have your ball there. His Grace has a home of his own in London. He cannot live in two houses at once."

Aunt Cherise sat up, and Esmé sniffed, "Well, that's the least you could do."

"And the most, I'm afraid. His Grace will naturally

control the bulk of the estate. You'll have to bear the expenses yourself, Uncle. Unless, of course, you wish to ask my lord St. Sevrin to sponsor your daughter's come-out."

Aunt Cherise fainted again. Sir Alfred pushed past his children and out the door, slamming it behind him. No one mentioned Lisanne's trousseau.

Lisanne took dinner on a tray in her room, what little she could eat atop the knot of uncertainty in her stomach. She thought of asking the serving girl to help her find a gown, but the maid was already rushed off her feet since Aunt Cherise and Esmé had also requested trays, tisanes, and soothing teas. Findley and Nigel were left alone in the dining room to bedevil the other servants with their ill temper.

Searching through her closet brought Lisanne no closer to an acceptable gown in which to be married. For her own sake, she couldn't see what the to-do was about a dress. The wedding was a formality only, a ritual binding of the arranged contract. Any of the serviceable gowns in her closet should have done, spots, stains, gathered seams and all. But His Grace had requested a clean, decent gown. Appearances obviously meant more to him. The veneer of a proper bride must suit his self-consequence, although Lisanne knew she was no such thing. St. Sevrin must be worrying over his decision as mightily as she was hers, Lisanne thought, so she owed him the attempt to satisfy his wishes.

She would not think about what other desires of his might need satisfying. She would not think about tomorrow at all. He had stood up for her—for his own reasons, she must never forget—and he wanted a conventional bride. So a dress was her mission for the evening, not fretting herself to flinders over decisions already made.

Scratching on Esmé's door produced nothing but more

vitriol. "Go away, you loony. I hate you! You've ruined my life."

Her aunt's French dresser opened the door to Lisanne's knock, took one look at who called, and shut the door in her face. "Madame is prostrate with *une crise de nerfs*. Good night, mademoiselle.

So Lisanne took herself upstairs past the servants' quarters, to the attics. It took some time for her to find what she wanted in the dim light of two small wall lamps and the candle she carried. Even after she found the right trunks, she had to struggle to uncover them, to move heavier items off their lids. For once she wasn't concerned with collecting cobwebs, although her hair and hands did a good job of it. At last she gave up trying to drag the weighty trunks toward better light and just started opening them. First she wiped her hands on her already filthy skirts.

Gowns were fuller in her mother's time, she quickly realized, pulling out one opulent gown after another, trying to ignore the smell of camphor. They were meant to be worn over the voluminous crinolines that filled a nearby trunk. Contrary to Aunt Cherise's estimate, Lisanne could ply a pretty needle indeed—she had to, to mend broken wings and injured paws. But remodeling one of these gowns was entirely beyond her. Why, it would take all night just to hem the wide skirts.

She kept opening more trunks, almost in despair, when she came upon her mother's undergarments and night rail. Silk and lawn, they were, the finest muslin with lace and embroidery. One white silk nightgown had a rounded neckline, a high waist, and small puffed sleeves, similar to the muslins Esmé wore year-round. It was a narrow slip of a gown, meant to be worn under a satin robe with matching embroidery. It was the embroidery that caught Lisanne's eye. Flowers of all hues and tints twined around the entire bodice and trailed down the skirt, with here and there a butterfly sewn into the design. Perfect.

Of course the gown was almost transparent, so Lisanne unpacked the trunk onto a blanket she placed on the floor until she found a silk slip, a batiste shift, and an entire layer of neatly folded stockings. She left the whalebone corsets in the bottom of the trunk. Not even for His Grace would she lace herself into one of those contraptions.

There was a pier glass in the attic, its silvered mirror turned cloudy. Still, it was better than going downstairs to try on her finds, then returning to the attics if she wasn't satisfied. Lisanne quickly undressed—there was no heat here in the attics—and drew on the gown. Her mother had been thin, so the fit was better than Esmé's rejects, although the hem would need to be taken up.

An old sewing box leaned against a dressmaker's dummy near the mirror, so Lisanne held the skirt off the floor and went to search for pins to mark the hem before removing what was to be her wedding gown. There were a few pins, not even rusted.

It was when she bent down to fold the fabric under that Lisanne heard voices. At first she thought she must be hearing the servants in their nearby rooms, but the voices sounded like Uncle Alfred's and Aunt Cherise's. Looking around to get her bearings, Lisanne realized she must be directly over the master suite, which her aunt and uncle would *not* have after her marriage. They might stay until they removed to London in the fall, but that was the end of her charity, and her patience.

She was gathering up a handful of pins and the other items she had selected from her mother's trunks, thinking to take them back to her room since she had no desire whatsoever to be privy to her relatives' bedroom conversations traveling up the chimney flue. As she bent to retrieve the dress she'd been wearing, though, she heard Uncle Alfred's voice clearly state: "I tell you, the wedding will not occur."

Lisanne sat on top of one of the trunks.

"What do you mean?" Aunt Cherise asked. "St. Sevrin

94

has a special license and permission from that awful man in London. He doesn't need her guardian's approval, so how are you going to stop it?"

Lisanne could hear her uncle chuckle. "Oh, Nigel has his orders. He'll take care of things."

"Nigel?" shrieked Aunt Cherise loudly enough to be heard down in the kitchens. "He's not going to challenge that disgusting man to a duel, is he? They say St. Sevrin never misses his mark. And he's a master swordsman. My baby will be killed!"

"Don't be absurd. Nigel will merely make sure that the chit is, shall we say, less desirable."

"Less desirable? I don't understand. You said that reprobate wants her for her money, not her appearance. Annie's already an unkempt, unmanageable sort of female. However could Nigel make her any less appealing?"

Lisanne wanted to know, too, but she had an idea. Her suspicions were confirmed when Uncle Alfred's voice rose through the flooring: "If you cannot understand, madame, then I suggest you put your head to it. Not even Satyr St. Sevrin will take used goods for his duchess. He might spend his life whore-mongering, but he won't marry one of them."

There was a gasp. Lisanne didn't know if it came from her own mouth or Aunt Cherise's.

Sir Alfred was going on: "Nigel will make sure of it tonight."

"I don't want to hear anymore!" Lady Findley cried. Lisanne could picture Aunt Cherise pulling her sleeping cap down over her ears.

"It's a masterful plan," Sir Alfred boasted, ignoring his wife's mewling sounds of distress. "I don't know why I didn't think of it years ago, except there was no need. Who would have thought that any man, no matter how badly dipped, would marry that farouche female? No, she'll just have to marry Nigel. That way all her lovely blunt stays in the family where it belongs. The curst solicitor will have to give his permission. He'll understand Annie'll be ruined, else."

"But . . . but my baby is a good boy. He wouldn't want to . . . to . . ."

"Oh, wouldn't he just. Our niece is turning into a dashed attractive female, if one doesn't mind a little muck and mire. Some men might even find that attractive in a primitive, earthy way. Besides, your baby Nigel is at the age when he'd lift the skirts of the fat lady at the fair, if he thought he could fit between her thighs."

"Sir Arthur, my tender sensibilities!"

"Blister your sensibilities. This isn't the time for the vapors. Nigel knows what he's supposed to do. Annie is richer than he, more highly titled than he, and God knows is smarter than he. The only thing she's not is stronger than he. Nigel understands it's the only way."

"Fetch my laudanum. No, the big bottle. I intend to sleep until tomorrow afternoon."

The pins were all over the floor. Numbly, Lisanne gathered them into her hand and then tried to put them into her pocket, out of habit. The nightgown she wore didn't have a pocket, so the pins landed on the floor again.

Dear heavens, what was she supposed to do now? Lisanne knew she couldn't overpower Nigel, and it was too late to put a sleeping draught in *his* evening brew.

Servants were still moving around, thank goodness, making a great deal of noise. Nigel would never go beyond the line when a scream could bring a roomful of curious spectators—unless that was what Uncle Alfred wanted, enough people to witness her disgrace.

She couldn't stay up here because someone was sure to come looking. She couldn't go to her room, for Uncle held the key to her door from when he used to lock her in. The furniture was too heavy to make into a barricade, and what was she supposed to do, hold off her cousin with the fireplace poker? For how long?

The pins were bundled into a beaded reticule from one of the trunks, the embroidered nightgown and undergarments carefully folded into the matching robe. In her dusty old gown and scuffed half boots, with cobwebs in her hair and the scent of camphor on her skin, Lisanne crept down the servants' stairway. She tiptoed past the family's bedroom level and then the public rooms, descending one level farther toward the kitchens without seeing anyone. The kitchens were blessedly empty, too. Lisanne unlatched the back door and let herself out into the night, whistling for Becka.

There was only one place she could go, one place she could be safe, and it wasn't Sevrin Woods.

Chapter Twelve

"We really have to stop meeting like this, sweetings." St. Sevrin was in that small back parlor again, the one with the working fireplace. He had been making inventories and estimates, lists of loans and mortgages, debts and past-due bills. He had no way of figuring how much it would cost to restore the estate to solvency or where to start. He was making great headway, however, with the new bottle of brandy on his desk.

Then he'd heard a dog barking and a tapping at the window. His fiancée, it seemed, did not care much for doors. Or propriety.

"Confound it, Baroness," he chided as he helped her over the windowsill, "what the devil are you doing prowling about the countryside in the middle of the night?"

Instead of answering, Lisanne turned to make sure the dog was inside, the window closed and latched. She was as messy as ever, but also seemed stiff and cold, which was no wonder, with the nights still chilly so early in the spring. Sloane drew her over to the fire, then pried her fingers away from the basket she carried. A cloth fell away to reveal a mound of raspberry tarts and a shank of ham.

"Well, at least you brought the wedding breakfast. Kelly will be thrilled. His culinary efforts don't extend to pastries, and we're growing tired of eggs and poultry. I daresay the chickens will be glad for the reprieve also."

"They're for Becka."

"What, all?" Sloane eyed the raspberry tarts with disappointment, but he eyed his bride-to-be with concern. She'd hardly said a word or moved an inch. He decided she needed a bit of internal warming, so he brought over his glass of brandy. "Here, sip this. You may as well be hung for a sheep as a lamb, alone in a bachelor's rooms, awash in Demon Rum. Dash it, don't you care anything about your reputation, my lady? My rep is bad enough for both of us."

"I care," she said in a toneless voice, staring at the fire. Sloane stared at the tarts. Becka stared at him, showing teeth that would have made a wolf envious. The duke forced his mind away from his stomach and onto his betrothed. She hadn't touched the brandy. She hadn't moved. "What if someone had seen you?" he prodded.

"I care," she repeated. "That's why I came. They . . . Uncle told Nigel to . . ."

"Findley and Nigel were going to do what?" His hands were on her arms. He didn't notice how tightly until she winced. "Sorry. But you were saying?"

"I was in the attics. I could hear his voice, telling my aunt. Nigel was going to . . . going to make certain I was ruined."

"Are you sure that's what he said? Maybe you misunderstood his meaning."

"You mean maybe my imagination ran away with me, and I invented the whole thing? Or maybe I was hearing voices? Maybe you don't believe me because you think I don't know the difference between truth and fantasy."

"No, no, I didn't mean anything of the kind. I was just

surprised. Your own relatives, by Jupiter." He was stroking her shoulders now. "I shouldn't have doubted you, sweetheart. I'm sorry."

She finally seemed to relax under his soothing caress. "You do believe me, that I wouldn't be safe there?"

"I believe you. It's the scurvy kind of trick that slimy bastard would try. I should have figured he'd pull something like this. You tried to tell me, didn't you? Thank goodness you had the sense to come to me."

"What shall we do?"

"Do? We shall get married, that's what." He strode to the hallway and shouted, "Kelly, on the double."

Kelly rushed into the room, then stopped short when he saw the disheveled female and the very large dog. He'd heard about the female, naturally, since he'd been the one trying to get this house in order for her while His Grace was chasing all over London after special licenses and such. No one had mentioned the dog. He bowed and uttered, "My lady," all the while eyeing the huge slobbering canine. Kelly didn't like dogs. The bigger they were, the more he didn't like them.

"My dear," said St. Sevrin, making the introductions, "this is the estimable Kelly. I couldn't manage without him. And Kelly, may I present your future mistress and duchess, Baroness Lisanne Neville. And her dog, Becka, who might be convinced to trade her raspberry tarts for some of your chicken stew."

Kelly's eyes lit up when he saw the tarts, all golden and dripping fruit. He took one step toward the basket, though, and Becka growled. The windows rattled with the force of it.

"Or perhaps not. We'll work on it later. For now I need you to take the curricle and go fetch us the vicar."

"But, Major, that is, Yer Grace, the vicar's due here in the morning."

Lisanne added her objection. "You can't just go awaken the poor man in the middle of the night."

St. Sevrin motioned Kelly to get going. "Tell him it's a matter of life and death." When the batman left, Sloane turned to Lisanne. "I wouldn't mind putting a bullet through your uncle, but I would mind having to flee the country at this point. The vicar is the only one who can eliminate the necessity."

"I don't see how. Uncle Alfred never listened to the vicar before."

"It's not a question of listening. Findley will be coming after you, I have no doubt of that. Until we are married, he is your legal guardian, so I have no rights but the power of my pistol to keep you from him. Therefore it's either shoot him or let him take you back with him, for whatever evil plan he has in mind."

"I wouldn't go."

He shrugged. "Then it's definitely pistols. Of course, if we were already married by the time he got here, he could just go shoot himself. Now *that* would be a fine wedding gift."

"You still want to marry me, even though there's bound to be an awful row?"

Even if he wasn't drowning in an ocean of bills, Sloane wouldn't send her back to that spawning ground of slugs. He was finding he had more of a sense of responsibility for Lisanne by the day. It wasn't an altogether uncomfortable discovery. "It's the only way, sweetings. How much time do you think we have? Kelly should be back within the hour with the vicar."

"The household was still awake when I left, so I doubt Nigel would come looking for me for yet a while."

"From what I saw of him, he'll spend half the night drinking his courage up. I've seen enough raw recruits to recognize a coward at first glance."

Lisanne couldn't deny Nigel's lack of bravery, and saw less reason to defend his honor. "They'll have to search through the house first. Maybe they'll just think I'm in the woods."

"No, Findley won't chance it. He has too much at stake, too little time. He knows the wedding is on for tomorrow."

"Well, they'll never come through the woods. Nigel is terrified of the place, even if Uncle could find the right path. If they ride around to the gate of the Hall, then down the road to the gate of the Priory and up the drive, the trip will add almost an hour in the dark, after they saddle the horses."

"That's cutting it close, but you do have a little time to rest. Kelly always has hot water on the boil. Perhaps you'd like to have some tea, or to wash up?"

Shyly, Lisanne pointed toward the basket. "I found a gown. It was my mother's."

And it was now under a ham. "Let's shake it out, shall we?" St. Sevrin took a step toward the basket. Becka growled, but Lisanne jumped to clutch the basket to her. "You mustn't see it. Not before the wedding. That would be bad luck."

Bad luck? Why not, this farce of a marriage had everything else going for it. Sloane shrugged. "You can change upstairs in my room—it's the only one uncovered yet—but the fire hasn't been started. The kitchen would be warmer, and there's a copper tub by the stove that we've been using for bathing. I can fill it for you."

"The kitchen will be lovely." She called the dog to follow them.

As he led his odd band down the corridor, St. Sevrin apologized. "I'm sorry this won't be any picture-perfect wedding. I was going to have Kelly scour the countryside for some flowers for you. Squire used to have a fine conservatory."

"There are flowers on my gown."

He had to laugh at her practicality. "Well, that's all right, then. I'm sure it's lovely, and you'll be a beautiful bride. Your mother would be proud."

* * *

102

The duke must think she was going to wear her mother's wedding dress, not her nightgown, Lisanne thought as she nearly scrubbed her skin raw in the tub.

The bath was placed behind a screen for warmth, not modesty, and Lisanne stayed there as she dried herself and dressed, hoping that the heat from the water would steam out some of the gown's wrinkles. She sorely doubted that her mother would be proud. More likely Mama would be turning over in her grave to see her only daughter getting married in a creased nightgown that smelled of camphor and smoked ham, with its skirt pinned up. There was no time to sew the hem, and with every movement she made, the pins jabbed into Lisanne's legs and snagged her stockings. Besides, Lisanne refused to wear the heavy, muddy boots she'd run through the forest in, not with this gossamer flower-garden gown. So she was going to go barefoot at her wedding. No, she didn't think Mama would be proud.

Lisanne took baby steps toward the back door, where ivy was growing over the walls, and pulled down enough to make a wreath of sorts for her hair. As she was sitting at the table, trying to weave the vines with fingers that insisted on trembling, Kelly scratched on the kitchen entry.

"Vicar said we needed another witness, ma'am, so I brung his housekeeper's daughter Mary. His Grace said as how you might need help."

"Yes, please. Come in, Mary."

Mary was a sturdy country girl a few years older than Lisanne with work-roughened hands and a smile that showed overlapping front teeth. She had a little snub of a nose. "Oh, don't you look a treat, miss. My lady, I mean. Won't me mum be that sorry she missed seeing a real duchess get hitched."

Mary pulled a comb out of her pocket and got to work on Lisanne's hair. She didn't pull much more than she would plucking a chicken, but she chattered the while, so

Lisanne didn't have to think about what was waiting for her outside this room.

"Feeling poorly, she was," Mary explained. Lisanne knew very well that the vicar's housekeeper felt poorly about the Nevilles' attics-to-let orphan who ran around like a heathen savage. Mary's mother crossed to the other side of the street when she saw Lisanne coming, the hypocrite. There was no father to Mary that anyone had ever heard of, which was why Mary was still unwed and likely to remain so. Her mother was fierce in her piety now, though. Lisanne could just imagine what the housekeeper had said about being woken to attend Addled Annie's wedding—to a gazetted rake.

"I didn't bring no hairpins, Miss Annie. That is, my lady. That nice Mr. Kelly says as how we're to call you Lady Neville today, and Your Grace tomorrow."

"Lisanne is fine, Mary, and don't worry about the pins. At least you've taken out the snarls and debris. I'll just plait my hair as usual."

"Oh, that would be a sore shame, miss." Mary fluffed out the long blond locks till they fell halfway down Lisanne's back, with the slightest ripple left over from the braid. "And isn't a bride supposed to wed with her hair down? I heard that somewhere."

"In medieval times, I believe. But it will have to do. I've lost the ribbon, and could only tie the braid with this old piece of string from my pocket."

So they placed the ivy circlet atop Lisanne's head and declared her ready, which was a good thing, for His Grace was wearing a hole in the threadbare carpet in the little parlor and the vicar was developing mal de mer just watching.

While Lisanne bathed, St. Sevrin had gone upstairs and changed into formal dress. When he returned to the parlor, he was relieved to see that his bride's dog was still gone. Too bad the tarts were, too. He then primed and loaded his pistols and made sure his sword was ready to hand. He felt the same hum of excitement he used to feel on the eve of a battle. Too bad he was getting married instead.

Chapter Thirteen

"My God, you're beautiful." St. Sevrin didn't see the bare toes or the pins. That is, he saw them, but they didn't matter. He would have been surprised if his duchess—as he was already thinking of this Pocket Venus at Kelly's side—had appeared in normal garb. No wonder the rustics thought her fey. If ever there was a female who could pass for a fairy princess, it was Lisanne Neville in a gown of flowers with her sun-lightened gold hair trailing down her back.

Kelly escorted Lisanne farther into the room, Mary following behind. Becka had elected to remain in the kitchen with the ham. St. Sevrin approached Lisanne and took her small, trembling hand in his to lead her closer to where the vicar stood by the mantel.

"I count myself the most fortunate of men," he told her, softly pressing his lips to her palm. "But are you still sure you want to go through with this? Zeus, you could take London by storm and have any man you chose, even if you didn't have a shilling. I'd find a way to keep you out of Findley's clutches, I swear. You don't have to settle for a rackety old warhorse like me."

Lisanne looked up at him. In his black swallow-tailed

coat and white satin knee breeches, Sloane St. Sevrin had to be the most elegant gentleman she'd ever seen. His auburn hair was still damp from a recent combing, just now beginning to fall forward onto his forehead. He was willing to defend her, and every inch of his well-muscled frame bespoke the ability to do just that. More important, his brown eyes looked kind, and he held her hand gently. He needed her money and perhaps her understanding.

"I'm sure."

The duke was sure. Lisanne was sure. The vicar was not sure. All that time watching St. Sevrin pace had not convinced him that this was a suitable match. He was tired and irritable and couldn't see what all the fuss was about. "If you're both so determined to marry, I don't see why you cannot have the banns read." That would take three weeks, during which time cooler heads might prevail. "And you could hold the ceremony in the church, with a proper wedding." And he could go back to bed.

"Oh, this is much more romantic," cooed Mary, but no one listened.

"It's entirely legal, sir, so what's the difference if we wed tonight or tomorrow?" Lisanne asked.

"But without your guardian's approval, child, I cannot be comfortable."

Kelly muttered, "What, is that bounder such a big contributor to the church poor box?"

The vicar prepared to get even more annoyed that his honor was being impugned. "My judgment is not based on financial considerations, sirrah."

"Of course it is," St. Sevrin answered for Kelly, "else you would have written to Lady Lisanne's London solicitor ages ago about her treatment at Findley's hands."

When the vicar started to bluster about rendering unto Caesar what was Caesar's, and leaving him to God's work, the duke held up his hand. "I am sure the baroness—the duchess—and I shall be most generous to the community. For a start, we intend to rehire as many of the dismissed Neville Hall staff who are still in the neighborhood and might be convinced to work here at the Priory. If any of the old Priory retainers are still alive, they might apply, too."

"Now, that would be good for the village," the vicar had to admit.

Mary wanted to know if His Grace meant they wouldn't hire any new people. "All those maids and footmen is old folks by now. You need some younger hands to get this job done." She waved her arms around the decrepit surroundings.

"You can be my personal maid," Lisanne told her. "I shouldn't like strangers around."

"Coo, and won't those uppity servants choke on that! A'course, I never been a maid, my lady."

"That's fine. I've never had one."

It was St. Sevrin who called them back to order by clearing his throat. "The wedding? Nothing goes forward without the ceremony and the reverend's signature on the license."

The vicar still hesitated. Money was one thing, but the man's reputation . . .

The duke was out of patience. "My lady is spending the night here under my roof. Would you prefer she do so under the protection of my name, or under the cloud of other, even less reputable names? Make no mistake, I do intend to make this woman my wife, with or without benefit of clergy."

The vicar started reading, and faster when St. Sevrin started tapping his foot on the floor.

At last he was almost done. Out of breath, he was gasping, ". . . Let no man put asunder," when they heard a furious rapping on the front door.

"Go on," Lisanne urged. "Finish."

St. Sevrin nodded, so the vicar repeated, "What God

has joined together, let no man put asunder. I now pro-
nounce—"

Footsteps were pounding down the hall.

Lisanne looked at the duke in disbelief. "Didn't you
lock the door?"

"What, and deny Sir Alfred his grand entrance?"

"—You man and wife. You may kiss the bride."

"Like hell he can," roared the baronet from the doorway. He and Nigel came charging into the room along
with the local sheriff, whose pistol was drawn.

Without thought, St. Sevrin stepped in front of
Lisanne, protecting her. She peered around him to see a
smile on his face. "Why, you're enjoying this!" she ac-
cused in a harsh whisper.

"Haven't had as much fun since Coruña," he admitted,
pushing her back behind him, out of the line of fire in
case he had to draw his own weapon. He was pleased he
had Findley's measure: Like most bullies, the man was
too cowardly to take him on by himself, so he'd brought
an armed reinforcement. Of course, Findley hadn't
counted on finding the matrimonial deed done, so was
now having apoplexy.

"Unhand my niece, you scoundrel!" he was shouting.
"This ceremony is a travesty. The marriage is illegal!"

The vicar was holding his pen above the papers, signing the license and the marriage certificate. "Oh, no, I
made sure everything was in order. It's a proper marriage,
Sir Alfred, all right and tight, so we can all go home and
get a good night's sleep. There's no law I know of that
says a bride and groom have to kiss at the end of the ceremony to make it legal."

"Oh, but I'm willing," St. Sevrin drawled for Findley's
benefit.

"Don't you dare! Sheriff, shoot him if he tries! This
marriage is illegal, I say! If you won't rip up those papers
now, Vicar, I'll just have to go to the trouble of an annul-

ment. Breach of promise. Foresworn vows. The jade was already promised to my son."

"Never!" Lisanne shouted, stepping out from St. Sevrin's shadow. She did allow him to keep her hand in his. "I wouldn't marry that toad if he were the last man on earth."

"Well, it ain't as though I'm in any great hurry to marry a great gaby like you, neither, Annie," Nigel was heard to respond before his father's elbow landed in his midsection, halting his disclaimer.

The vicar was shaking his balding head. "Oh, I don't approve of first cousins marrying. Too many children born with too little wit, don't you know."

"Like my niece, you mean," Sir Alfred said, but everyone was looking at Nigel, wondering at the proximity of his parents' relation. "I say she was promised to my son and that promise invalidates this farcical ceremony."

"It's a farce, all right," St. Sevrin muttered. "If Lady Lisanne was affianced to your son, Findley, why didn't her London trustee know anything about it? Here's his letter of permission. His name is on the license, too."

"They were too young," Sir Alfred blustered. "There was no reason to involve the solicitors yet. It was an understanding between my deceased brother-in-law and myself."

"An understanding that the baron didn't happen to mention in his will? Gammon. I saw his will, and he planned for every eventuality of his daughter's future. None mentioned your son. In fact, if you'll recall, he didn't even name you as full guardian. It won't wash, Findley. Give it up as a bad hand. The marriage is done. Fact. History."

"No! I'll have it annulled, I swear! I can do it, too. You won't like having your name spread through the mud."

St. Sevrin just laughed. It was not a pretty sound. "My name? You'd have to invent a new shade of black before you could darken my reputation any."

"Well, you won't like what I'll be forced to do to hers." Findley pointed at Lisanne and sneered. "Look at her, all decked out like a bird of paradise."

Not understanding, Lisanne thought it a rather nice compliment until she saw the darker frown on St. Sevrin's face. Mary came closer and whispered an explanation in her ear that made Lisanne gasp. "A trollop? Me?"

Sir Alfred hadn't paused. "I can have it annulled because the doxy's not in her right mind. Lunatics cannot enter legal contracts; everyone knows that. That London trustee had no business giving his permission. Only her guardian can."

"I am no doxy, Uncle, although you tried to make me one. And I am no lunatic."

He curled his lip. "I can have five doctors prove you are, and a houseful of servants, an army of witnesses, to swear to your freakish behavior."

The sheriff felt it was his duty to speak up. First he wiped his dripping nose on his sleeve. "I seen it myself, her going off in those woods, staring into space."

The vicar had to admit there had been a deal of talk that Miss Neville was short a sheet. Even his own housekeeper, this very evening, had called her by that old nickname, Addled Annie. "There may be some grounds here for deliberation, gentlemen."

"No," St. Sevrin thundered. "The lady has had an irregular upbringing, which can be laid at your doorstep, Findley. That's all. Ignorant country folk have always seen hobgoblins behind every turnip patch. They don't understand anyone different, and fear what they don't understand."

"Here now, who are you calling ignorant?" the sheriff demanded.

"Anyone stupid enough to mistake a lonely child for a moonling, that's who."

Sir Alfred returned to the fray. "The sheriff is right, St.

Sevrin, Annie is crackbrained. Everyone knows it but you. If you persist in this idiocy, we'll take it to a court of law and they'll overturn the marriage. Meantime the sheriff's duty is to see that you release the girl to her loving family."

"So loving that you'd have your son rape her?"

The vicar choked. Even the sheriff was taken aback. "Here, here, what's this, then?"

"You're as totty-headed as she is, Duke, to even suggest Nigel is capable of such a heinous act. No, I have my duty and the sheriff has his, to bring Annie away with us. I'm not leaving her here where you can force yourself upon her so that the marriage has to stand as consummated."

"Now, why does that have a familiar ring to it?" the duke wondered, crossing his arms.

Sir Alfred ignored St. Sevrin's facetious remark. "Take her, Sheriff."

"But what if he's already had her, Pa? She's been here for hours, and who knows when they met. And you said he's the devil with the females."

St. Sevrin didn't even bother taking aim. He just swung around and landed Nigel a facer. The clunch went down, blood spurting from his nose. "It's bad enough," the duke told Findley, "that you denied your niece the ladylike upbringing her birth deserved. It's worse that you didn't teach your son to be a gentleman."

Mary went over to the fallen youth and bent down to see if Nigel was still alive. When she saw his chest rise and fall, she kicked him in the ribs. "And that's for trying to get a feel of all the girls in town, you swine."

The sheriff sniffed. "I gots to take her." He took a step toward Lisanne, but now Becka was at her right side, the duke at her left, his own pistol drawn. The minion of the law wasn't sure which was the more formidable opponent. A distinctive click behind him said that Kelly had drawn the hammer on his gun, too. "I gots my duty."

"What you've got is a head cold, Sheriff. That's about all you can manage at one time." St. Sevrin was deadly serious now. "And no, you are not going to take Lady Lisanne—my wife—anywhere. We'll settle this tonight."

That sounded too much like a duel to Findley, and he was certain a rogue of St. Sevrin's caliber wouldn't challenge a runny-nosed bumpkin of a sheriff. He'd be the one looking down the barrel of that deadly pistol next. "It's not for you to settle anything, Duke. I demand a London tribunal to hear the case."

"Where you can hire a hundred so-called experts to tell any story you feed them? I've seen proceedings like that. The side with the most money and the most convincing quacks wins. No, Findley, you're trying a bluff because I wouldn't want *my wife* to have to face such an ordeal. Nor would anyone who truly cared for her welfare."

"I'll do it, I swear, to keep her out of your evil clutches. You rip up those papers or I'll challenge the marriage in every court in the land."

St. Sevrin turned to Lisanne. "Is Squire Pemberton still magistrate for the shire?" When she nodded yes, he asked, "And is he still regarded as an honest man? A fair man?"

"I think so," the vicar agreed. Mary bobbed her head when the duke looked at her questioningly.

"Then go get him, Sheriff. That's a job you ought to be able to accomplish. Kelly, you go with the officer to make sure he doesn't fill Pemberton's head with fustian before he even gets here. None of us is budging until this is settled."

The vicar groaned. So did Nigel. St. Sevrin ignored them both. He led Lisanne away from her fuming uncle to a chair at the other end of the room, and sent Mary to the kitchen for some tea.

Lisanne clutched his arm. "But what if he . . . ?"

Sloane patted her hand. "Don't worry, sweetings, you're not the one crazy enough to get between me and what I want. Your uncle is."

Chapter Fourteen

*S*quire Pemberton had his own system of justice: murderers were hanged, thieves were transported. That kept the criminal element out of his shire one way or the other. Any other miscreant coming before him, vandal, pickpocket, or public nuisance, was put to work. The poorhouse was kept in firewood, the church was repainted yearly, the roads were in good repair—and all at no expense to the worthy taxpayers. Everything neat, efficient, and equitable, that's how Pemberton liked to administer the law. He was good at it, he was fair at it, and he was fast at it.

This current mess of potage, however, fit into none of his guidelines. Getting up in the middle of the night to adjudicate an ugly situation didn't fit into any of his notions of justice, either. Pemberton was old, he was tired, and he'd earned every right to be cranky. Not even the glass of excellent brandy the duke offered was going to reconcile the squire to a night's disturbed slumber. Not even the sight of that jackanapes Nigel Findley with a wet cloth over his nose and claret down his shirtfront could make up for a cold, uncomfortable ride. The only high point that Pemberton could see was his old friend Neville's daughter finally turned out like a lady for once.

"All grown up, eh, missy?" he said, pinching her cheek on his way to the seat Kelly held out for him. "And pretty as a picture, besides."

"Here, here." Sir Alfred jumped up. "You can't go taking the chit's side without hearing all the evidence."

Pemberton settled his bulk in the chair and looked over his spectacles at the baronet. "Her side, is it? I thought we were here to decide what was best for the gel's future. I deuced well will take her side, with her welfare at the heart of any consideration. I'll just assume that's what *every* concerned party here wants, shall I?"

"Of course. I am only trying to make the best provision for my dear sister's only child." Findley could do nothing but take his seat again. At least he had one. He hadn't been offered any brandy, tea, or hospitality, not that he expected it in this den of infamy. He'd even had to tend to Nigel's nosebleed on his own, to his disgust.

Pemberton was going on: "And you can stop looking thunderclouds at me, St. Sevrin. I've known you since you were in short coats, and you were a resty lad then. Would have thought the army'd smooth out the rough edges. Guess not. But sit down anyway. There will be no more, ah, accidents like young Findley here suffered, or I'll charge you with contempt of court. That means three days' labor. The schoolhouse needs new steps. Don't suppose you'd be much good at it anyway, so don't aggravate me with any show of temper."

St. Sevrin sat down on the threadbare sofa next to Lisanne, sending a cloud of dust into the tea she was pouring for the vicar. She also offered the reverend gentleman on her other side a plate of raspberry tarts. Becka must be full of ham, St. Sevrin decided, for the big dog didn't even raise her head off Lisanne's feet when he helped himself to one of the pastries. Good, let the shaggy mongrel stay there so no one could see that his bride was barefoot.

The sofa smelled of mildew, but St. Sevrin also recognized the scent of musty old clothes coming from Lisanne and a whiff of the soap he used. She also had an inchworm climbing out of the ivy tiara she wore. Damn! That wasn't going to win any points with the magistrate. While Pemberton was greeting the vicar, St. Sevrin reached up and removed the offending wildlife, then had to look around for a place to put it. The sugar bowl seemed the likeliest until Pemberton changed his mind and wanted tea instead of the brandy. Gads, Squire would think they all had breezes in their cocklofts.

Lisanne had frown lines on her forehead he wished he could wipe away, so he tried a smile for her. Lud, what a damnable thing to put a sensitive female through. She looked like a wood nymph that could be blown away on a gentle breeze.

For himself, St. Sevrin wasn't worried. He was a gambler, after all. Of course this was the biggest gamble of his life—or Lisanne's. Usually when he wagered, Sloane knew the odds and could calculate his chances. He seldom put his precious blunt on the line for games of random chance or luck, only science and logic.

Tonight, though, Pemberton was the wild card, the joker in the deck. Sloane had no way of figuring which way the old man would lean. Of course he still had his hole cards, but the duke didn't want to use them unless necessary.

He lightly squeezed Lisanne's hand, between them, for what reassurance he could give. She squeezed his back. The girl had pluck, thank goodness. They'd get through this.

Squire was ordering the sheriff to put down his pistol in the name of civilization, if not out of fear the lobcock would sneeze and shoot the ceiling down on their heads. Kelly, too, had to lay his weapon aside before the magistrate would begin. St. Sevrin didn't mind; his was tucked into his waistcoat, ready to hand. He wasn't that much of a gambler.

First Pemberton listened to the vicar without letting Findley interrupt. He looked over all the papers: the special license, the marriage lines, the letter from the estate administrator. This last not only gave permission, but stated that the marriage settlements were extremely favorable to Mackensie's client.

"So you thought everything was in order?" Pemberton asked the vicar.

"I did question the need for such haste, although now I see why His Grace wished to get the wedding performed in a timely fashion."

"And to your thinking the marriage is legitimate?"

"In the eyes of the Church, certainly, with the archbishop's signature on the special license and two attendants to witness the vows. I truly thought I could go seek my bed."

"And do you still feel the marriage is lawful and binding?"

"Oh, there's no question of that. They're well and truly married. The question is whether they should stay so. Sir Alfred believes I have only to tear up the papers to have the marriage disappear, which is patently untrue. On the other hand, the gentleman did present some feasible grounds for having the proceedings annulled. He claimed that the bride's hand had been promised elsewhere, to his son Nigel, in fact, and that she was of such diminished mental capacity that her vows should not be binding."

Sir Alfred was smirking. "Not just feasible grounds for dissolution, but legal certainties. Do you want to hear me now?"

"I'd like to hear my wife snoring now, but I suppose I have to hear you out if the vicar is done. Vicar? Reverend?" The clergyman had nodded off, thinking his part in the proceedings was at an end. "Lucky devil."

So Pemberton listened to Sir Alfred spout about his beloved, befuddled niece, how she needed the care of her family, not some avaricious villain who chanced upon a pigeon for plucking, etc., etc. There was so much *cetera* that Pemberton was ready for a nap himself. He shut Findley up and listened to the sheriff swear how he thought he was protecting a loony, by trying to get her back home.

When St. Sevrin would have spoken, thinking it must be his turn, Pemberton bade him hold his horses. "I'll get to you next, Your Grace." He picked up his teacup, stared at the contents a moment, then set it aside. "I'll have that brandy after all."

Kelly started forward, as did Mary. Both should have left long ago, but since no one had ordered them out, they stayed. Even Sloane attempted to get to the bottle first, but Lisanne hopped up before he could rise. Unfortunately one of the pins in her hem stuck in the frayed fabric of the sofa's skirt. *"Merde,"* she cursed, and pulled at her entangled gown, revealing her bare toes. Nigel snickered through the cloth over his face, and St. Sevrin groaned. The vicar snored.

Pemberton wiped his spectacles, replaced them on the bridge of his nose, and took another look. "Thank you, my dear" was all he said when she put the glass in his hand. He waited until her back was turned on her way toward the sofa, to check the snifter for other life-forms. Then he addressed the baronet: "Sir Alfred, I am having a problem with your claims. If, as you say, your niece is of unsound mind, why should you wish to pursue her marriage to your son? You cannot want your grandchildren to be Bedlam-bred. No, you cannot have it both ways. If she is not competent to marry St. Sevrin, she is not fit to marry your son."

"So they won't marry."

Nigel was heard to mumble "Thank goodness" before

his father drowned him out with, "We'll just make sure Annie is kept safe at home."

"Her money, you mean," St. Sevrin put in, which drew the magistrate's attention his way.

"Findley's motives are suspect, Your Grace, but yours are transparent. Everyone knows you're badly dipped."

The duke just nodded, tight-lipped.

"And you have a devilish reputation as a womanizer. Who is to say you didn't seduce an innocent young girl away from her family?"

"I am," the duke replied. "I married Lady Neville in good faith."

"Yes, but you are a practiced rake who could find it all too easy to take advantage of a poor harebrained heiress."

St. Sevrin was on his feet. "I did not, and my *wife* is not a simpleton to be led astray by a facile tongue. My *wife* is an intelligent woman who knows her own mind."

"Intelligent enough to curse in French, although I'm sure her parents never intended her to learn such. Sit down, Your Grace, the lady's intelligence has never been in question. You're forgetting I've known her since she was born. I've even seen some of the translations she's done to continue her father's work. Very well received in learned journals, I assure you. What are you reading now, my dear?"

Lisanne searched for pockets to find her book. "I'm sorry, it's in my other gown. I am rereading Plato's *Phaedo*, sir. As extensive as Papa's library is, it hasn't been kept current and most of the volumes on agriculture do not bear a second reading."

"I'm sure, I'm sure. And in what language did you say you were reading Socrates, my dear?"

"Why, the Greek, of course. Oh, but I am also reading Herr Mittlebaum's book of natural medicines. His publisher has promised to make the necessary corrections."

Squire Pemberton turned to Nigel. "What was the last book you read, young man?"

"Book?" Nigel tried to think of one. "Well, a fellow doesn't want to fill his head with all that rumgumption."

"And your daughter?" the magistrate asked Sir Findley. "What books has she been reading?"

"How the devil should I know? And what's that got to—"

Lisanne knew. "Oh, Esmé is a prodigious reader, Squire. She reads Maria Edgeworth and Mrs. Radcliffe, all the Minerva Press novels she can find."

"Which put more nonsensical notions in a miss's head than any seven silver-tongued devils," Squire declared. "I know, my wife reads 'em and sighs when I can't make pretty speeches or ride *ventre à terre* to her rescue. Rescue her from what, I say, her lisping French coiffeur? Bah. Forty years, and she wants pretty speeches." He harrumphed again at the thought. "Anyway, I suppose we are all now in accord that Lady Neville's intelligence is not in question?"

Sir Alfred had to nod his agreement. "But—"

"And as to whether she can sew or paint or play a pretty tune, that has nothing to say to her competence to enter the married state. All that caterwauling and banging on the ivories always gives me the headache anyway. The only good thing about getting old is you don't hear it so well."

"But—" Sir Alfred was determined to be heard.

Squire Pemberton was growing deafer by the moment, it seemed. "Now, there is an important question to this annulment business that no one's mentioned yet. The likeliest cause for dissolving a marriage is when the bride cannot or will not perform her marital duties. Is that a problem, my dear?"

Without so much as blinking, Lisanne answered that it was no problem whatsoever. "His Grace requires a son for the dukedom and another for the barony."

"I see you've your work cut out for you, lad," the

squire chuckled, bringing the first blush to St. Sevrin's cheeks in more years than he could remember.

Pemberton sighed. "So we're left with the issue of mental competency. There's no doubt that there's an odd kick to missy's gallop." He pointedly stared at her bare feet. "The villagers talk, the country folk whisper. I ignore most of it, but I've heard tales even before yours, Sir Alfred, and the sheriff's tonight. Now, I don't claim to be any physician, but I am the one you asked to decide this argle-bargle."

"Ask her about the fairies," Nigel prompted, and his father took it up. "Yes, ask her if she speaks to the Little People in the woods, Squire, so we can all go home."

Lisanne looked at the duke, trying to judge his reaction. Sloane merely raised one eyebrow. "It's your call, sweetings."

She studied her hands a moment, when the only sounds were the vicar's snores and the sheriff's snivels. "Yes," she finally answered. "I did think I spoke to the Wood Folk, when I was a child."

"And now?"

Sadly she shook her head no. "Now I am grown up."

"She's lying!" her uncle insisted, shouting so loudly he woke up the vicar. "Make her say whether she believes in fairies or not."

"Fairs?" the vicar asked. "Are we discussing the village fairs?"

"Go back to sleep, Reverend," Squire Pemberton directed, waiting for Lisanne's answer.

Instead she asked him a question: "Is your wife insane? She's said time and again that she refuses to step foot on Priory land because it's haunted. But has she ever seen a ghost? Spoken to one? Has anyone who claims to believe in ghosts seen one? And you, sir," she inquired of the yawning vicar, "do you believe in angels?"

"Why, of course I do, child."

"Yet you've never seen one or spoken to one, have you?"

The vicar laughed. "You have to be a saint to speak to an angel, or in heaven among them."

"Yes, but you believe anyway. And without meaning any blasphemy, there is the belief in God Himself. How many people do you know who have ever seen Him, or spoken to Him—and gotten a reply?"

"But we see His works, child. That is enough. It is for the prophets and the martyrs to converse with the Almighty."

Squire nodded. "I get your point, missy. 'There are more things in heaven and earth, Horatio, than are dreamt of in your philosophy.' "

"And belief is an act of faith, not an act of lunacy."

"Is this place really haunted, Pa?" Nigel wanted to know, looking over his shoulder.

Findley hadn't quite followed the discussion, either. "Didn't she just admit she believes in pixies?"

"I believe anything is possible."

"Well then, missy," Squire asked, "do you think it's possible to make a go of this marriage?"

123

Chapter Fifteen

"You mean you're going to let her marry this wastrel?" Findley squawked, as if the hand of doom were closing around his throat.

St. Sevrin's patience was seconds away from doing just that, but it was the magistrate who answered: "I'm not going to *let* her do anything. She's already done it."

"But, but he's a ne'er-do-well, just marrying her for the money. He'll gamble it all away in a sennight and leave her destitute."

"I doubt even St. Sevrin could go through Neville's fortune in a sennight." Pemberton glanced at the papers again. "According to this, Her Grace will have a handsome jointure of her own that the duke can't touch."

Findley threw his hands in the air. "Fine, then she'll waste it herself. Most likely give it all to beggars and orphans, the way she does with whatever money I give her. Can't even trust her with an allowance, like my Esmé."

"Tut, tut," the vicar put in. "There's nothing wrong with charity, Sir Alfred."

Pemberton agreed. "She might even manage to do some good with her fortune, Findley, amazing as it might seem to you."

"Then let her give *your* blunt away!" Findley yelled, tripping over his own greed.

Squire coughed. That was all.

"Well, she don't know what she's getting into, then. Her aunt and I kept her insulated from the evils"—a sidelong sneer in the duke's direction—"of men such as St. Sevrin. Wild to a fault, profligate with money they never earn, careless of their own lives or others', and as immoral as a band of baboons."

"Actually, baboons have close-knit families," Lisanne began, to be shushed by St. Sevrin with a laugh.

"I've heard better defenses from a pickpocket caught red-handed."

Squire wasn't laughing. "I regret that Sir Alfred does have a point, my dear. I've never seen you at the assemblies or tea parties in the neighborhood. You've had no London come-out, no exposure whatsoever to young men that I know of." He ignored Nigel completely. "Are you certain you know what you are doing, marrying a man with His Grace's lamentable reputation?"

Lisanne looked at her new husband, the lines on his face, the puffiness near his eyes, the brandy glass never far from his hand. She also saw the strong jaw and straight nose. More important, she saw the damp spot near his knee where he'd let Becka rest her drooling chin while he scratched her ears.

"Major Lord Shearingham was a hero," she said. "General Wellesley trusted him with his plans and his platoons. I can trust the Duke of St. Sevrin no less."

Kelly, from the back of the room, called out, "Here, here."

Sloane lifted her hand to his lips and spoke for her ears only: "Thank you, Duchess. I shall do my damnedest to live up to your confidence."

Squire wasn't quite satisfied that Lisanne knew what she was in for, taking on a here-and-thereain. "Some women get the deuced romantical notion that a reformed

125

rake makes the best husband. Most likely from that drivel they read. I say the tiger doesn't change its stripes until it's a fur rug. You aren't thinking of trying to reform St. Sevrin, are you, my dear?"

She smiled and softly answered: "I thought we had determined that I am not crazy, sir."

The magistrate and the vicar laughed. Even St. Sevrin's mouth turned up.

"You'll do, lass," Squire Pemberton pronounced. "You'll do fine. Congratulations, Your Grace, you've won a fine wife for yourself. See that you deserve her." He started to lift his bulk out of the chair. The vicar was already heading for the door.

"No!" Sir Alfred screamed. "No, I am not satisfied. Justice has not been served! This travesty of a wedding has to be annulled. I'll go to the lord high magistrate in London. I'll go to the archbishop himself!"

"Why not the prince?" St. Sevrin taunted. "Our Regent would do anything to get out of his own marriage. Perhaps he'd look more kindly on your petition." He stood slowly and flexed his fingers before forming them into fists. "Damn weak left," he muttered, then warned the baronet, "Of course, if you approach Prinny or the courts or the Church, if you so much as breathe the word annulment ever again, I'll tear you limb from limb."

Findley stepped closer to the sheriff. "You . . . you can't do that! This is England, you devil, not some army outpost or battlefield." He turned to Pemberton. "Tell him he can't do that!"

"Oh, but I can," St. Sevrin breathed while Squire looked on, "and I would derive great pleasure out of it, too, after what you've done to my lady; but I don't need to." He paced closer to the baronet, who seemed to shrink with every step the duke took. "No, I do not need to, because you aren't going to make any more trouble. I let you play the game out your way, Findley, so you would be satisfied, so there would be no question of the legality of this marriage. I let you embarrass my wife with this inquest, and I let you abuse the hospitality of my house. But you still aren't content, are you?"

"I'll never rest, I tell you, until I have Annie back where she belongs! I'm not afraid of your threats." Everyone could see his spindly knees knocking together.

"Very well, then, it's time I laid the rest of my cards on the table. First, my wife's name is Lisanne, not Annie. That's 'Her Grace' to you. Second, if you don't shut up, don't get out of my sight with your spineless sprig of a son, I'll be the one to go to court. I'll have you charged with embezzlement so fast your head will spin. You'll have to answer to the magistrates and Mr. Mackensie for every shilling you've spent on your wife and children, not on your niece. I'll bring in the local merchants to discuss your so-called contracts, and the Neville tenants to discuss improvements that were never done to their farms."

"A bunch of country yokels? You can't prove anything!"

"Mr. Mackensie never throws anything away. Every inflated bill you sent, every bogus expenditure, they are all there, just waiting for you to make a peep about the state of my marriage or my wife's mind."

"No one will believe you. Everyone knows you're a drunk and a debaucher."

St. Sevrin studied his fingernails. "You really are getting on my nerves, Findley. Do you actually believe anyone in London will take the word of a jumped-up bartholemew babe over a duke's? Over that of a wealthy duchess and her eminently respected solicitor? Think for once, Findley. You would have to make reparation of all that money. Do you have that much squirreled away? I doubt it. You'd be ruined. You could even land in gaol or the penal colonies."

Squire nodded. "Thieves get transported. That's the way of it."

"Wouldn't do much for Esmé's Season, neither, Pa," Nigel volunteered.

"The nodcock is right for once. Your entire family will be ostracized, Findley. Think, man. One word from you about my wife means one word from me to Prinny. You won't be accepted anywhere except Botany Bay. I am willing to let it rest, Findley—I won't even sue for reparations—if you are willing to let us alone."

"Let's go, Pa," Nigel urged. "Before he sets the dog on us. He's done everything else."

Defeated, deflated, Sir Alfred turned to leave.

"I'll have your word, Findley," St. Sevrin called after him. "Your word as a gentleman, for what it's worth, in front of witnesses, that you accept this marriage."

The bitter flavor of failure was too strong in Findley's mouth for him to answer. He jerked his head in acquiescence and left. Kelly slammed the door behind him and his little entourage.

Champagne would have been a nice touch, had there been any. Instead Squire lifted his glass of brandy and toasted the newlyweds. The vicar raised his cup of tea to their health, and Kelly gave Mary a sip from his flask to put their seal on the marriage.

"Good health, long life, strong sons ... Did I forget anything, Reverend?"

The vicar had to think a moment, so sleepy was his brain. It was gone after two in the morning, and his tea was cold. "Uh, happiness and understanding, joy in each other, that's what I always wish for the young people I wed." Right now he wished them all to the devil, the good Lord forgive him.

Kelly had one more toast to make: "And no more plaguey relatives."

Then they were gone. Squire Pemberton had his own rig, but Kelly had to drive the others back to the vicarage. Mary would gather her belongings, tell her mum the good news, and return in the morning to take up her new employment. Kelly allowed as how he may as well sleep with the horses in the little stable behind the manse, for otherwise he'd no more get home than he'd have to turn around to fetch Mary back.

Mostly they were all giving the Duke and Duchess of St. Sevrin privacy, which was the last thing their graces wanted, unless it was another visit from Uncle Alfred.

Sloane helped Lisanne carry the tea things and the glasses back to the kitchen, neither knowing what to say or what to do. Becka padded after them and the remaining pastries.

"I could brew a fresh pot of tea, if you'd like," she offered, and "Are you warm enough? You could wrap yourself twice around in my greatcoat on the peg there," he suggested. They both declined. The dog started gnawing on the ham bone.

When the sound started grating on his nerves, Sloane cleared his throat. "I don't think we'll have any more problems with your relations."

"No, I don't suppose so. You gave Uncle Alfred no choice. Thank you for what you did. And for what you didn't do."

"What I didn't do?"

"You didn't shoot him or strangle him or knock him down. I shouldn't have liked to see that, even if he deserved it. Reasoning is always better than brute force. Nigel doesn't count because he has no reason."

"I daresay we've seen the last of them either way. Findley has a small holding in Richmond, doesn't he?"

Lisanne licked her dry lips. "Yes, outside of London. I, ah, did tell Esmé that she could still make her come-out from Neville House. It's right in Town and has a huge ballroom."

"And a much more prestigious address to boot. But don't you think we should have discussed it first?"

Her chin came up. "You said Neville House was to be mine, to do with as I would."

"Yes, and I also thought you would be more comfortable there while St. Sevrin House undergoes repairs."

"Don't you think we should have discussed *that* first?" Sloane ran his hand through his already disarranged hair. "I see we both have a great deal to learn about being married. The vicar did wish us understanding."

"And I thought you understood I had no wish to go to London, to either house. I told you I didn't intend to live in your pocket, and I am more comfortable in the country."

"Yes, you did tell me all that, but I thought that going to Town as a married lady, as a duchess, would be different. You wouldn't be on the marriage mart or dependent on the goodwill of those high-in-the-instep hypocrites who rule Almack's." And he wouldn't have to worry about leaving her here alone.

"No, it makes no difference. I prefer to stay in the country. I have my work with the botanical medicines, and the tenants will need some direction until you find a competent bailiff. The steward from Neville Hall is a good man and can begin improvements, but there is too much work on the two estates for one man."

"And you would help?" No other female of his acquaintance would turn down a London Season for the farmyard. No other female of his acquaintance would be a ha'penny's bit of good there, either. In her pretty gown and neatly combed hair, she'd let him forget for a moment how very different his bride was from women of her class. Hell, she was different from women of *any* class. He didn't want to think about that right now.

"I can help," she was saying, without artifice or boasting. "I know the land." Not "I have studied the land," or "I have read agricultural journals," but "I know the land." Lisanne was trying to tell him, trying to make him understand, as the vicar said they should. "In the woods—"

"No." He didn't want to hear about that right now, either. "It's late, Duchess, and your eyelids are drooping. Go to bed. We'll talk another time. I'm afraid my room is the only one made up for now. I'll show you the way."

Her eyelids weren't drooping at all now. Lisanne's blue eyes were wide-open as they flew to his. She didn't even have to put the question into words. "No, I am not going to join you tonight, Duchess. We're both too tired and upset. I'll take Kelly's pallet here by the stove. It's no hardship after the army."

Instead of arguing as he thought she might, Lisanne merely gathered up her old dress and her boots and followed him down the hall. As he lit her way up the stairs and down the echoing corridor, Sloane felt he had to reassure his barefoot bride that she was safe. "The Priory ghosts only appear when there's a death or disaster in the family, or so the story goes. There's nothing to be frightened of."

"Oh, I'm not afraid of ghosts, Your Grace. Besides, Becka will be with me."

Fine, St. Sevrin thought on his way back down the stairs, he got to sleep on a thin mattress on the floor while a great hulking dog shared his bed upstairs. And he'd never even got to kiss the bride.

Chapter Sixteen

*N*othing to be frightened of? Lisanne was alone in this great ramshackle mansion with a complete and total stranger who now had her life in his keeping. She very well knew that all the signed settlements and legal documents in the world wouldn't change the fact that a woman was her husband's property. The duke could force her to go to London. He could force her to share his bed.

He said he wouldn't come to her tonight. But that's what he was saying now. In a few hours, after a few more bottles of spirits, what then? She'd seen Nigel in his cups too often to trust a man's promises. Even her uncle's meanness was magnified tenfold by a night at the bottle. And this man, her husband, was already a creature of violence and strength, used to getting his own way, reveling in the challenge. What could be more challenging than a woman—no, a wife—who refused her favors?

And what of tomorrow or next week if he couldn't find some village girl to satisfy his needs? How long would Sloane be willing to wait? Lisanne wasn't ready. Nothing to be frightened of? Perhaps St. Sevrin had taken too many hits to the head at Gentleman Jackson's Boxing Parlor.

Lisanne looked around the bedroom for hints of the man's character, even knowing he'd only been here a matter of days. The room had his mark already, or his man Kelly's. The massive canopied bed was neatly made, albeit with a bedstead that appeared moth-eaten. The comb, brush, and mirror on the dresser were aligned with military precision. The book on the nightstand was a history of the Mahratta Wars. Lisanne was not surprised, nor at the wine bottle and glass next to it. He'd been a good soldier. Lately he'd been drinking a good deal of his life away. Perhaps he was in pain from that wound he'd mentioned. She'd have to ask about it when she knew him better.

The pitcher and basin were chipped, the towel slightly damp, the mirror tarnished, but those told nothing of the man. There was no other sign that anyone had stayed here. Lisanne unfolded her old dress and emptied the pockets. Books, bottles, stones, an iris root, various bits of bark and greenery wrapped in scraps of cloth came forth, with paper and pencil, sewing kit, a handful of pins and half of a roll gone hard. She fed the last to Becka and scattered the rest on the night table, the dresser, the washstand. Now the dark-paneled room had life, her life.

Despite its original purpose, Lisanne didn't want to sleep in her lovely wedding gown, nor in the dusty, creased muslin she'd worn all day and would likely wear on the morrow. Even less did she want to sleep in her shift and slip, in case St. Sevrin came into the room for his book or his bottle—or his bride.

Feeling like a trespasser but having no choice, Lisanne opened the clothespress. The neatly hung coats and breeches were not many, but even her untutored eye could tell they were of the finest quality. Among them Lisanne found a white lawn nightshirt. She put it on instead of her mama's gown, which she tenderly hung between the rows of waistcoats.

Lisanne was comforted by the nightshirt's softness, the lingering scent of her husband's lemon and spice cologne, and the fact that it trailed down past her feet.

She put another log on the fire and sank down in front of it, her arms around Becka. As she was wrapped in his nightshirt, she knew she could be wrapped in the security of knowing Sloane would look out for her interests. He terrified her, but he could make her feel protected. He wouldn't let anything happen to her.

In a way, that was even more frightening. Lisanne had just given up her name and her fortune. She was liable to lose her self to him next.

She could get used to having someone to lean on. She could learn to depend on his strength and his honor. And then she'd have nothing when he left.

He'd take care of her, she had no doubt, maybe even come to care *for* her, but he'd go his own way. Lisanne knew she couldn't hold a man like St. Sevrin. She'd never thought she could, so wouldn't let herself hope for the impossible. She wouldn't let herself grow fonder of his daring, his infrequent half smile, or that lock of auburn hair that fell into his eyes.

Nothing to be frightened of? Giving her heart into the keeping of a man like St. Sevrin was scarier than facing a hundred moaning medieval monks.

Lisanne couldn't fall asleep, not in his bed with his scent on his pillow. She was being suffocated. Her books and notes couldn't interest her tonight, nor his volume on the India campaign. She was too anxious to sleep, too anxious to concentrate on anything else. What had she done? And what could she do now?

She could put the robe that matched her mother's nightgown on over his nightshirt. She could carry her boots in one hand, a candle in the other, and leave.

She and Becka did not head for Neville House—

Lisanne would never give her uncle the satisfaction of seeing that she was worried over her choice. Instead she set out for where she would find peace, where she could be the Lisanne Neville she knew, nobody's wife, nobody's fool.

Sloane didn't believe in ghosts. He didn't need them to disturb his rest; he had specters of his own. Not ready for sleep, he took the brandy bottle back to the parlor. He wasn't castaway, not even slightly above par, not nearly foxed enough to dull his mind to what he'd done.

The Duke of St. Sevrin had taken a child-bride, for her money. The devil could worry about what the world might say; Sloane was outraged enough himself. Lisanne Neville was too innocent to touch, too unworldly to understand his corruption. She hadn't known what a vile deed he was committing by binding her clear light to his murky shadows. He knew. He'd done it anyway.

In a way he was worse than that bastard uncle of hers who let Lisanne stay a child for his own gain. Sloane was forcing her to be a woman for *his* own gain. Findley had kept her from meeting the decent young men she could choose from; Sloane was keeping her from marrying the man she deserved. A beautiful, intelligent, and wealthy female making a marriage of convenience without ever knowing an infatuation, calf-love, or grand passion was bad enough. The bargain Lisanne was getting was horrid.

Sloane had taken the baroness from the elegant comfort of her home to this crumbling heap of his. Not even Findley, with his lax guidance and grasping, conniving ways, kept her in such deplorable conditions: a dented copper bathtub in the kitchen, a tea set with no two cups matching and half of those chipped, and worse meals than her dog usually ate. Zeus, Sloane hoped Becka liked chicken. The dog and the duchess were in the one passable bedroom the vast pile boasted, passable if you kept your eyes closed to the warped paneling and your nose closed to the mildewed hangings. The wind whistled through the cracks in the windowpanes and under the rotted sash, and something nibbled noisily behind the wainscoting. He couldn't even offer her a decent night's rest. This place wasn't going to be liveable for ages, if he could find anyone willing to work where ghosts supposedly roamed the halls.

The souls of the dead monks were said to stir at the death of a Shearingham or a disaster befalling the household. Most likely the old shades were celebrating the misfortune of their nemesis, for it had been a Shearingham who razed their monastery and claimed the surrounding fertile lands. Presumably the steady decline in the St. Sevrin fortunes gave the ghosts many an opportunity to rejoice in the halls and attics of the rebuilt manor, and gave the local Devonshire population many a cold shiver. Sloane remembered his father tossing in a losing hand and calling it another merry monk. He wondered now if Lisanne would hear the wind howling through the cracks and crannies, and think the monks were abroad, proving this day another disaster.

No, she'd said she didn't believe in ghosts. She believed in—St. Sevrin would not think about that now. He poured himself another glass of brandy and contemplated the number of panes of glass the Priory would be needing. He finally had the money to fix the windows and seal all the drafts, to put on a new roof to stop the leaks. He would have the blunt as soon as he got to London and completed the arrangements with Mr. Mackensie.

The expense was going to be enormous, Sloane knew, and the effort even greater. There were priorities to be set, adjustments to be made. The land had to come first, but he was a soldier and a gambler, not a farmer. How the hell was he to make the right decisions? St. Sevrin did not intend to go through the Neville treasury without making sure he'd get a return on his investment, enough to repay Lisanne. It might take forever, but he'd die trying to give back her riches rather than go to his grave a fortune hunter. What the deuce was he giving her right now?

Those blasted woods, that's what. St. Sevrin carried his glass over to the window where he'd first seen Lisanne appear like a mist from the woods. Her woods now, where she could study nature's secret remedies to her heart's content. It was an odd interest for a young woman, extraordinary actually, but a rationale his mind could accept.

He stared out, almost knowing what he would see if he waited long enough. Yes, there she was, looking like a ghost indeed in flowing white robes with her pale hair streaming behind, crossing the lawn. She was going to the woods in the middle of the night rather than sleep in his house, in his bed. A dark shadow at her side meant that Becka was with her, keeping Lisanne safer than he could. Hell, Sloane had missed the path back from Neville House this afternoon and wandered for an hour before he found himself back at his starting point, having to ride all the way around by way of the road.

No, Sloane wouldn't go chasing after his wife or make a cake of himself by getting lost in his own home woods. If she'd wanted company, she knew where he was.

But the duke didn't know where she was, not really. No scientific investigations took place at night in a dark forest. Was Lisanne in the woods or in a world of her own creating, as her uncle had implied? What was she, this wife, this duchess, this fairy child?

She'd wanted the woods, and he'd given them to her. Had he done the right thing, right for her? Lud, he didn't know. Lisanne didn't want parties and gowns, jewels or foreign travel, nothing he could buy for her with her own money. If there was anything she did crave, she could purchase it herself now that he'd granted her control of her own funds. There was, however, one other thing he could give to make her happy: his absence. St. Sevrin had seen the fear in his wife's eyes, fear of him. No female should fear the man sworn to protect her. He could save Lisanne that, at least.

He was afraid, too, afraid of what could happen to her away from the woods, out in his world. Sloane thought he now understood how a father must feel giving his beloved daughter away in marriage. But no girl could stay a child forever, and this lady was his wife, not his daughter. She was almost nineteen, St. Sevrin reminded himself, old enough to bear children.

Children. Two sons at least. His Grace rather thought he'd like a little golden-haired daughter also. But what if his children were born . . . odd? No, he might as well say the word to himself, here in the solitude of his empty house, where only the dead monks could laugh at another Shearingham's comeuppance. What if his heirs, his successors, his bid for immortality, were crazy, like their mother?

No, this duchess wasn't ready for children. Let her grow up, he thought, get used to being mistress of a household of her own. Let her find her way out of the woods.

St. Sevrin had all those papers to sign, business to transact, and bankers to meet in London anyway. He had to put a wedding notice in the newspapers. After he settled his own accounts, then he had to see about finding agricultural advisers and architects, workmen and wise investments. Mackensie would help—and Mackensie was in Town.

Kelly would stay on here, starting to organize things and looking after the duchess. St. Sevrin went over to the desk and pulled out a sheet of paper to begin a list of instructions. He felt better immediately, getting something done. This was more like it, rather than sitting around fretting. He wouldn't be gone all that long anyway, the duke rationalized to himself; and they both, he and Lisanne, needed time to come to terms with this marriage. It was going to be one hell of a honeymoon. The devil take it, it had been one hell of a wedding.

There was no sense going to bed, Sloane decided, especially not on Kelly's hard pallet. This wouldn't be the first time he'd stayed up all night, not by half. And he could fetch his things from the bedroom now while Lisanne was out, without having her panic at his presence in her chamber.

It was better this way, he told himself. He'd be gone before she returned to the house, unless the fairies decided to keep her this time.

Chapter Seventeen

ℰither his London business was more complicated than he thought, or St. Sevrin was more cowardly. Either way, he did not return in the sennight or so he promised Kelly, who got left in Devon.

"What, now that you're a duke, you figure an old batman ain't hoity-toity enough for your new consequence? I'll be handing in my resignation, then. Save you the bother of dismissing me."

"Stubble it, Kelly. I always was a duke, since selling out, anyway. Now I can finally afford to pay you what you're worth, if I get to Town and get the finances squared away." His Grace was still in the small parlor making lists when Kelly returned in the morning with Mary. The duke was packed and ready to go. "But I need to leave you in charge here now." He indicated the pages of directions and instructions, the foremost of which was to look after the duchess.

Whatever Kelly hadn't heard at the wedding and the magistrate's hearing, he'd gotten an earful of from Mary on the way back this morning. Kelly didn't truck with gossip, but his new mistress was a puzzle and a problem, that was for sure. And that dog of hers was a hound from hell. "I ain't no nanny," he complained.

"No, you're the only man I would trust with my life, or my wife."

"Why don't you take her with you, then, if you're so worried about the missus?"

"Because she doesn't wish to go, and she is not ready to be presented to the ton. You might have noticed my lady is not exactly rigged out in the height of fashion."

"Don't seem much of a duchess to me." Kelly remembered the bare feet.

"She was a baroness long before I was a duke. And she's bright. She'll figure it out. You just need to help her along with hiring servants and such to get a start on cleaning this place and the grounds. I wager there will be lines applying for positions as soon as the vicar eats breakfast. Your job is to make sure no one shows Her Grace any disrespect and that those slimy relatives of hers don't come around. I'll be returned before you know it, with your back pay and a bonus, old man, so quit your grousing. Furthermore, I'll lay you odds that you and Becka will be firm friends by then."

Kelly hoped His Grace didn't put any of his new cash on the bet, but he didn't say anything, just took up the pages of instructions again.

"Oh, and Kelly, that girl Mary who is to work here . . ."

"Yer Grace?"

"She's young and innocent. Hands off."

"Could say the same for yer lady, Yer Grace."

"And I married her, by George. I won't have you carrying on under my wife's roof."

"What, married one night and turning Reformer, are you? You never frowned at a little slap and tickle before."

"I wasn't head of a respectable household before, either. Mary's a comely lass, but it just won't do. Vicar's connections and all."

"Next you'll be telling me you won't be enjoying a

141

quick tumble or two whilst you're in London and I'm stuck here like one of the blasted monks."

"I'm telling you I mean to be more discreet." The duke tossed some coins in Kelly's direction. "Here's just about the last of my pocket money till I get to the bankers. Find yourself a wench who works on her back, not one who works in my house."

St. Sevrin had no trouble with the bankers or Mr. Mackensie. He was quick to send a draft for Kelly to open a household account in Devon to pay the new servants and keep Lisanne in comfort. Next the mortgages got paid, so he wasn't laying out interest on top of interest on his father's loans. Then he settled long-outstanding bills with various delighted tradesmen who'd written him off as a bad debt ages ago. It was an unusual and pleasant experience to be warmly welcomed by the merchants he visited to start the refurbishment of St. Sevrin House. Yes, being beforehand with the world had its definite advantages. Better vintages of wine, for one.

Sloane might awaken these mornings with his usual hangover, but he didn't suffer from the load of worry and guilt that had been weighing heavily on his shoulders— except when he thought of his duchess, that is. So he sent more money to Kelly, new books from Hatchard's he thought Lisanne might enjoy, trinkets, fabrics, and the most expensive French modiste he could convince to leave her own establishment and travel to Devon to outfit a duchess. Then he didn't feel so like her money-grubbing uncle when he thought of Lisanne. And he was pleased with the refurbished suite he was having decorated for her at the town house. The duchess's apartment was going to resemble a garden bower, no matter how many consultants he had to hire and fire.

That's what St. Sevrin told everyone to explain why his bride wasn't in Town with him, that he was preparing the house for her. The wedding notice had been in the papers the day after he arrived in London and questions were rife. She'd be coming once the Season was in full swing, the duke told his cousin Humbert, taking great satisfaction from the prig's deflated ambitions.

Aunt Hattie, his mother's half sister and the only blood relation he cared for, was not as easy to put off. Harriet, Lady Comstock, was a walking repository of genealogy and gossip. She wasn't happy with the match.

"The breeding's sound, even if Neville did marry beneath him, and the fortune is certainly welcome," Hattie acknowledged, "but the mother was delicate. No getting around it, she was sickly, and there are some deuced odd rumors going around about the chit. You'd do best to puff her off soon, let the tabbies see she's not got two heads or anything."

When Sloane explained how St. Sevrin House wasn't ready to receive its mistress, Lady Comstock snorted. "Then put her up at the Clarendon, boy. It doesn't look right, keeping her hidden away in Devon. What, is she platter-faced? You wouldn't be the first connoisseur to lower his sights to the pocketbook."

"Not at all. In fact, she's quite stunningly beautiful in a unique way." St. Sevrin found himself at a loss to explain what made Lisanne so different from other pretty chits. "She's a tiny bit of fluff, looks like she could fly away. And she's young. There's plenty of time to introduce her around."

"She's what? Eighteen, almost nineteen? I was married three years by my nineteenth birthday."

"Lisanne is a young eighteen," St. Sevrin admitted uncomfortably. "She has no Town bronze, no sophistication. No mother, don't you know."

"Hoydenish, eh?"

"Not precisely." He didn't elucidate, feeling disloyal to be discussing Lisanne this way.

Aunt Hattie had no such scruples. "Then what? Shy? Stupid? No, I cannot imagine you shackled to a mutton-head, no matter the purse. So what's wrong with the gel that you don't want to show her off? You need her on your arm if you hope to be received in polite Society again, you know."

The devil take polite Society. "She's neither tongue-tied nor bacon-brained. She just wouldn't know how to go on."

"That flibbertigibbet Findley woman couldn't teach a dog how to bark. And you're no better, you cawker, leaving the gel in the country. How do you expect the chit to take her place in the world if you don't show her?" She batted at him with her lorgnette. "Bah! I'll just have to go take her in hand myself. 'Twould be better done in the country, away from the wagging tongues. Time enough for the harpies to get their claws into your diamond after we've polished her up a bit."

Since this was precisely the result the duke had hoped for with this morning call, he left his aunt's house satisfied, promising to join her in Devon as soon as his business was concluded.

Some of his business was taking a bit longer than expected. With members of the Quality just now trickling back to Town for the Season, St. Sevrin was hard-pressed to find all the gentlemen who held his personal vouchers. When he did, he had to suffer their congratulations, ribald comments, and sly references to his well-filled pockets. It was only polite to accept their toasts and their invitations for a hand of whist or a round of piquet. Now that he didn't need the money, the duke's luck was in, but his patience was quickly wearing out. Members of White's could be stared down with a frosty St. Sevrin sneer; the denizens of the lesser haunts of the gambling set soon learned that the Duchess of St. Sevrin was not a topic for conversation, not if they wanted to finish the night with all their teeth.

* * *

The duke had left a sheaf of directions for his man Kelly, and a one-page note for his wife: *Enjoy yourself, Duchess.* How was she supposed to do that, when she was so busy?

He was right: maids and footmen and gardeners and stable hands started parading onto Priory grounds the same morning St. Sevrin had left. Some were Neville Hall retainers dismissed when the Findleys brought in their own staff. Lisanne recalled many of them and made them welcome. Others declared themselves to be previous employees of the Priory, let go without their back pay. A third group had no claim on the available positions except that they were poor and needed the work. Lisanne hired them all.

When Kelly protested, she insisted that there was certainly enough work for all of them. "But some is too old to do a day's labor, Yer Grace."

"Then they shall do half a day's labor. Or, if the older maids cannot help with the scrubbing, perhaps they can sew. And footmen who cannot repair shingles can polish the banisters. I am sure you can find jobs for everybody."

Kelly was sure they didn't need seven grooms, not when His Grace owned three horses, and one of them was in London with him. For that matter, the ex-soldier saw no need for a kennel master when the only canine on the premises slept in the master bedroom. But his instructions were clear: he was to make sure the duchess was happy. If she was happy filling the stables with a crippled goat and an ancient, abandoned peddler's pony, the kennels with baby birds fallen out of nests and sick rabbits, and the Priory itself with servants older than the dirt they were cleaning, he wasn't about to argue. It was her money.

And the money started coming in from London. Kelly opened a household account for Lisanne at the bank in Honiton, and a separate, personal one for the duchess's generous allowance plus her income from the Neville holdings.

With which the duchess hired more derelict dependents to trip over each other. She had them working on the servants' quarters first so they'd have somewhere decent to sleep, and the kitchens so they could have nourishing meals. The people from her parents' household remembered a sweet, sunny child. They were proud their lady was thinking just as she ought. The Priory workers had never known an employer to care a whit about the hired help. There was a lot of head-shaking. Those rumors must be true, that the new duchess was dicked in the nob. Her disappearing for hours into that patch of trees didn't sit easy, either, not once someone resurrected those old stories about haunted woods.

Then Neville Hall's previous housekeeper arrived from her daughter's overcrowded cottage and took over the chatelaine duties, to Kelly's temporary relief. She had the crews working in shifts, getting the walls, rugs, and furniture spotless until repairs and replacements could be ordered. Kelly had the gardeners and grounds people in military formations, stripping overgrown ivy off the stone walls, scything the lawns, reclaiming what was left of formal plantings.

Now Lisanne could turn her efforts to the Priory farmland, with Kelly trailing behind arguing that His Grace had left definite instructions concerning the hiring of a bailiff.

"Oh, the man arrived this morning while you were at the bank. He wanted to evict what tenant farmers still remain and turn the entire property into sheep pasturage. I dismissed him."

"You dismissed the duke's man?"

"He thought the home woods would offer good hunting."

"So you sacked him the same day he got here?" No one had ever disobeyed Kelly's master, not when he was

146

a fresh lieutenant, not when he was a major, and absolutely not when he was a duke. "Oh, lud, His Grace'll have my head for sure."

"Nonsense. He'll see how much progress we've made." With the help of Neville Hall's steward, Lisanne found families willing to move into the abandoned farmsteads, and men to help make repairs so they'd be comfortable. She had Kelly order new seed drills from Taunton and plowshares from Manchester. She was knee-deep in mangel-wurzels and manure, when she wasn't writing away for the latest strain of wheat or inspecting farms for breeding stocks of sheep, cattle, and pigs. And there was a new crop of orphaned lambs and cows with swollen udders for her to tend.

Kelly had to admit Her Grace had an eye for livestock, but he didn't think farming was any more suitable an occupation for the duke's lady than captaining the mop brigade. Of course, it was better than the hours she spent trudging around in the woods with her dog and coming back to brew Zeus only knew what. With all the oldsters in the house, the duchess was constantly concocting remedies for chilblains and shingles, sore gums and inflamed joints. She even interrogated Kelly about the duke's troublesome war wounds and packed a bottle of salve for him to send on to London. No, it wasn't fitting at all, but what Kelly was supposed to do about it he couldn't begin to guess. From what he heard, no one had ever changed Lady Lisanne's mind about anything, though Findley had almost died trying.

The old retainers and the new tenants were all grateful to the duchess, and were all afraid of her. The Priory ghosts were as nothing to Lady St. Sevrin. The people didn't dare talk when Kelly might hear, but he knew. The hushed voices and the sideways looks told the tale. There was no disrespect, but there was a distance.

The only one Kelly could trust with his worries was Mary, who was as devoted to the duchess as the dog was.

Mary was waging her own campaign to get Lisanne to behave more in keeping with her—and Mary's—high estate. She started by burning the dresses sent over from Neville Hall.

"Spotted and stained every one, I tell you, Mr. Kelly. Why, I wouldn't wear such a thing to clean the vicar's cellars. It's no wonder these ninnies whisper about our lady when we ain't looking. So I fixed them. Set some of the old maids, them as can still see good enough, to altering some gowns we found in one of the closets. His Grace's mother's, maybe."

Kelly sighed over the tea the two were enjoying in the butler's pantry. Since Kelly was doing that job, he felt entitled to that privacy. There was a bit of the bottle in his tea, none in Mary's. Kelly sighed again over lost opportunities. "No matter, Her Grace'll just get them new gowns soiled. I never seen such a one for mucking about."

Mary took offense at the slur to her mistress. "Lots of high-born ladies garden. Don't they have them fancy rose societies?"

"When ladies of Quality grow their own flowers, they have three gardeners to do the dirty work. And they wear gloves to keep their hands smooth and hats to keep the sun off their faces and smocks to protect their gowns."

So Mary set the old maids to making smocks out of old bed ticking and sheets. And she made sure her lady was wearing gloves when she left the house. The duchess usually came back with the gloves in her pocket, along with sundry other items Mary was reluctant to handle, but at least the altered gowns stayed fairly neat. No afternoon caller, tenant farmer, or tradesman was going to mistake the duchess for one of her own scullery maids.

"I'll work on hats next week."

Kelly poured some of his brandy into Mary's teacup. "You'll need this."

Then parcels and packages started arriving daily from His Grace in London. He was detained on business, he wrote, but meantime he sent bonnets and shawls and slippers that had Mary in alt, and books—Miss Austen's novels, Scott's romantic tales, Wordsworth's poetry— that had Lisanne staying up half the night in the library after she was finished with the day's accounts.

Next to arrive was a French dressmaker with enough yard goods to guarantee the aged seamstresses sinecures for life. Lisanne couldn't have cared less about her new wardrobe. She refused to be fitted, in fact, or make decisions about colors, styles, or trims, but the modiste had her orders and her deposit. The Duchess of St. Sevrin was going to be dressed like a lady, even if she persisted in rambling around the countryside like a Gypsy.

And then the duke sent his aunt. Lisanne wanted a new mule for the plows. Lady Comstock came close.

Chapter Eighteen

"And what time do we take dinner, my dear?" Aunt Hattie, as she told Lisanne to call her, was standing in the Priory hall amid bags and boxes and an army of servants.

"Dinner?" Lisanne blinked. She was used to asking for a tray at whatever hour she came in from the fields or the woods, or wandering to the kitchen and helping herself and Becka to whatever she found. The habit would have wreaked havoc in any respectable kitchen, with the staff never knowing when or what the mistress would be wanting, but the duchess hardly ate enough to keep a bird alive. In fact, had Cook known it, most of her breads and rolls and cakes did just that—go to keep the birds alive. If a particular cut of beef or a slab of mutton went missing from the servants' own meal, no one was going to argue with the big dog over it. There was enough to go around, thank heaven and marriages of convenience.

Such slipshod scheduling was not at all *convenable* for a duke's household. Or a duke's aunt. "Yes, my dear, dinner. I prefer Town hours, of course, but I would understand if you'd like to dine earlier, shall we say seven? That way we have a lovely evening to become better acquainted and catch up on our needlework. Perhaps play a hand of cards or read aloud. Then there's music. So soothing to the digestion, I find. You do play, don't you, my dear? That's when we don't have company, of course. I haven't seen Mrs. Squire Pemberton in ages, I swear."

Lisanne was inching toward the door. She and Becka could live in the woods, or in that derelict cottage no one wanted. Then two of the footmen carried in a large portrait in a heavy gilt frame. The painted gentleman was in wig and satin breeches, and held a bust of Homer. The footmen set the picture down, awaiting instructions.

"Ah, Lionel, there you are."

"I'm sorry, Lady Comstock, ah, Aunt Hattie, but that's James, and this is Harry."

"No, not the footmen, dear, the portrait." Lady Comstock whipped a scrap of lace out of her black crepe sleeve and dabbed at her eyes. "I keep dear Lord Comstock's portrait with me so that I don't feel so alone. Dear Lionel was lofted above ten years ago."

He'd gone in a hot air balloon? Lisanne didn't have time to ask the question, for Lady Comstock was making the introductions. "Lionel, dear, this is our new niece, St. Sevrin's duchess."

Gracious, Lisanne thought, the lady was as balmy as . . . as she herself was supposed to be. No wonder Sloane had sent the poor unfortunate widow to Devon for a repairing lease. Lady Comstock was the duke's aunt, and this was the duke's house. His wife could do no less than show proper courtesy. The poor thing likely had no one to talk to except a picture of her deceased husband. Besides, perhaps she was as below hatches as the rest of the duke's connections and had nowhere else to go. "Did you say you preferred to dine at seven, my—Aunt Hattie? I'll just go notify Cook. There is much for me to be doing about the estate, but I shall be pleased to keep you company in the evenings."

Lady Comstock went upstairs behind the housekeeper, satisfied for now. The girl was as beautiful as St. Sevrin had claimed. Those big blue eyes alone could have made her fortune if she didn't already possess one, but Hattie couldn't decide if they were full of innocence or wisdom. The chit was decidedly not the standard milk-and-water miss. And that hair was impossible, of course, and the browned skin. The pastel gown was all wrong, too, over-fussy for such a little dab of a thing. No, the gel wasn't ready for London, aside from the fact that she had the social graces of a newborn chick.

Luckily Hattie had planned on spending a month or so with the girl, getting her in shape before her jackanapes of a nephew arrived to take over. Meantime Lady Comstock could have a lovely time with St. Sevrin's carte blanche at Ackerman's Repository, helping the duchess order new furnishings for the Priory. There was nothing Hattie liked so much as spending other people's money, unless it was ordering other people's lives.

She had the footmen put Lionel's portrait over the mantel in a clean but shabby bedchamber, right where she could see him every day, and rejoice that the dastard was dead and she was alive to enjoy his wealth. "And no," she told him, not for the first time, "that bust of Homer doesn't make you look one groat smarter, you old nincompoop."

The campaign began. Lisanne knew she was being manipulated, but didn't have the heart to disappoint the duke's unfortunate relict. If Lady Comstock was content to play with fabric swatches and furniture patterns all day while the duchess accomplished something worthwhile, Lisanne couldn't mind approving the choices or giving an opinion when she had one. "I like light colors better than dark," she offered. "And florals rather than stripes."

She knew Aunt Hattie was also busy with the French dressmaker, for the gowns Mary now laid out for her in the evenings were of brighter, prettier colors and simpler styles. Mary was learning from Lady Comstock's fancy dresser, too, for she begged to try new hairdos on her mistress. "Just for the practice, like." Some of them even stayed up through dinner.

And bonnets. With Lady Comstock trimming the chip straw herself after dinner—a favorite hobby of hers, she declared—Lisanne could not refuse to wear them. The silk flowers sewn to the brims were rather pretty, and they did keep the sun out of her eyes now that the weather was getting nicer and nicer. Best of all, the hats were the perfect size for transporting the nests of field mice disturbed by the plows.

Even company dinners were not so terrible. Squire Pemberton was always ready to debate the classics, while his wife enjoyed Aunt Hattie's Town gossip. Mrs. Squire Pemberton finally even stopped looking over her shoulder for the Priory ghosts. Lisanne didn't mention Lord Comstock upstairs in his wife's bedchamber, and her guests never mentioned Sevrin Woods. The vicar was eager to discuss Lisanne's plans for a new school, now that she had the poorhouse almost empty, and he didn't mind taking up a hand of whist, either. Everyone learned to ignore what Lisanne ate, or didn't, after the time Aunt Hattie asked why she wasn't eating the superb beef Bourguignonne Cook had prepared for the guests. Lisanne's reply, that it was Spotted George on the platter, cost everyone their appetites. No one asked again.

There weren't many return invitations, which aggravated the normally active Lady Comstock to no end. Not even Devon could be this dull. Hattie was giving up the London Season, for heaven's sake; she didn't mean to give up all social entertainments. And how was the chit going to learn how to go on if she never got out? It was Mary who heard through her mum at the vicarage, who heard everything, that there were no big parties, period. None of the better families were throwing lawn picnics or country balls, because no one wanted to have the duke's relatives under the same roof as the duchess's relatives, not after hearing how St. Sevrin had threatened Sir Alfred.

So Lady Comstock decided to get rid of the Findleys. They were sponging on Lisanne's generosity, after all. She called on Cherise Findley while the duchess was overseeing a ditch-draining or something equally as disgusting—but in a hat.

Lady Comstock's mission didn't take the twenty minutes assigned for a morning call. Lady Findley wasn't half done complaining about her ills when Aunt Hattie suggested a sojourn to Brighton. Sea bathing was relaxing for the nerves, she advised, and might even clear up Esmé's complexion. Personally she would have taken the bonbons away from that plump little peagoose, but that was none of Lady Comstock's concern. Getting these mushrooms out of Devon was.

The prince might be in Brighton soon, she emphasized, and all the truly fashionable members of the ton would summer there. Just the place to begin introducing a young deb. Lady Comstock even offered to write some letters of introduction, smoothing the chit's way. Or the Findleys could stay on here at Neville Hall, Hattie allowed, inspecting her manicure. Of course they expected the duke back anyday now. . . .

The Findleys were gone by the end of the week, their servants with them since Sir Alfred wasn't about to pay the staff for a summer vacation. Aunt Hattie sent a box of bonbons to enliven their journey. Then she sent to Neville Hall all the superannuated servants Lisanne insisted on keeping on her payroll. The place needed a caretaking staff, she explained, and Lisanne was satisfied the people were given healthy, productive lives. Lady Comstock was satisfied that the Priory was at last beginning to look like a gentleman's residence, not a retirement home for domestic help.

Things were going so swimmingly, in fact, that Kelly decided to travel up to London and see what was keeping His Grace. With that battle-ax aunt of the duke's in charge, Kelly hadn't had a bout of dyspepsia in weeks. He also hadn't had a night on the Town. The senior footman was promoted to butler.

Kelly left and he didn't come back, either, to Lady Comstock's consternation. Lisanne didn't seem to notice as spring changed to summer, and there were plants to tend and crops to watch, but Aunt Hattie fretted over her nephew's long stay in Town, away from his bride. Letters availed Hattie nothing, for the dratted boy sent money, not answers. And Lisanne never mentioned his name.

Hattie was beginning to get a bad feeling about this marriage. She loved the girl as a daughter by now . . . no, as a niece. No daughter of hers would be caught dead at a sheepshearing. Lisanne stood by with a salve, in case the sheep got nicked. His Grace wasn't to know, but it was the same salve she'd sent for his wound. Then again, she wasn't to know that he'd used it on his new stallion's scraped leg. Communication between the two, now that Kelly was gone, was nil, which pleased Lady Comstock even less. Lisanne could be the redemption of her wild nephew, and Sloane could keep the girl from getting lost in her books and botanicals—if they ever spoke to each other.

Lisanne was as ready for London as she'd ever be, Aunt Hattie felt. Whether London was ready for such an original remained to be seen, but with her contacts and connections Hattie would see the little duchess creditably established. The job would be easier with the Season winding down and everyone leaving Town for country house parties and seaside resorts. St. Sevrin's bride would be a nine days' wonder this year, and be just another eccentric aristocrat by next fall's Little Season. The problem was, of course, that Lisanne refused to leave Devon.

By now Lisanne knew Lady Comstock was no grieving widow. She also knew that Hattie kept Lord Comstock's portrait nearby just to aggravate the man if he was listening, as much as Lionel's nip-farthing ways had aggravated Hattie during their marriage. The duke's aunt kept to her widow's weeds because they were a perfect foil to her silver hair and the Comstock diamonds, not because she was in perpetual mourning. Her blacks were elegant, expensive, and fashionable silks and lace. No dreary black bombazine for this widow.

Lisanne quickly realized that St. Sevrin's aunt wasn't in Devon on any repairing lease, either. She was ruralizing because it suited her managing ways to refurbish a huge manor house and rearrange Lisanne's life. By the vast correspondence Lady Comstock sent and received, she was no humble relict of some minor lord; Mathilda Comstock was a force to be reckoned with among the *belle monde*, knowing everyone and everything that went on among the Upper Ten Thousand.

Lisanne had been well and truly diddled, but she didn't mind. In fact, she respected the older woman's family loyalty. Lady Comstock was only doing her best to make Lisanne an acceptable member of the duke's world. It was an impossible task, of course, but most likely Aunt Hattie had a long list of instructions from the duke, too.

Because of her fondness for the lady, Lisanne did not take offense when Aunt Hattie complained yet again that St. Sevrin hadn't returned from London, and that Lisanne refused to accompany her to go find him.

"If you have some place else to go, ma'am, please

don't feel you have to stay on my account. I know you're missing the opera and theater and all the balls. I have my work here."

"You have no proper companion here if I leave. And your place is at your husband's side."

"Why, no, ma'am. The duke and I agreed that we wouldn't hang on each other's sleeves."

"Well, I do not approve of these modern marriages when the husband and wife go their separate ways as soon as the heir is born."

"Neither do I. We need two heirs."

"Don't be pert, girl. And if you and my nephew are so agreed that you require two sons, the wretch should be here seeing about the successions, unless you're already breeding." She ended this last on a hopeful note, which Lisanne had to disappoint.

"Then, by all that's holy, what is keeping that clunch in London?"

"Why, I suppose all the entertainments you've been so eager to tell me about, to lure me there. St. Sevrin loves London, ma'am. It's his way of life. He wouldn't be happy in the country. I do not look for him anytime soon."

"Fustian. He hates London and all the shallow posturing that goes on. He's chided me often enough for being a vain, silly creature who only cares for gowns and gossip. He couldn't wait to buy his colors and be gone off soldiering."

"That was in his younger days. He seems to have adapted recently."

"What, by cutting a swathe through the *demi monde*? What else was he to do, with no future, no occupation? That's why he drinks and gambles to excess, just for something to do."

"Well, there's plenty for him to do here. Do you think St. Sevrin is any good at baling hay? Painting the barn? Darning the tapestries?" Lisanne held up her corner of the hanging currently under repair, trying to keep the hurt from her voice. If he disliked London so much, but stayed there anyway, it could only mean he disliked his wife in Devon even more. "No, he won't come."

Chapter Nineteen

St. Sevrin was ready to go home. He'd paid his debts and worked out his investments so they were already returning a profit. He wouldn't have to dip so deeply into the Neville capital for the rest of the major improvements needed at the Priory.

And after a month or two—almost three, he admitted to himself—of Aunt Hattie's company, even his ugly phiz should look good to his bride. If he knew his aunt, Lisanne had the benefits of the best finishing school in the country without ever leaving Devon. The old Tartar's wily ways, sharp tongue, and encyclopedic knowledge of the upper class would have the young duchess up to snuff by now. He wouldn't be returning to that odd, appealing little waif.

In a way St. Sevrin was sorry. Such a child of nature shouldn't be forced into a prunes-and-prisms world. He shrugged and sipped his wine. No one said life was fair.

Aunt Hattie hadn't said the girl was mad. Different, an original, refreshing, yes. Mad, no. Of course the breeze blowing through Hattie's upper story was so strong she mightn't recognize windmills in anyone else's attics.

Trying to disturb Uncle Lionel's eternal rest by toting his portrait around was barmy enough.

No matter, if there was a hint of lunacy, Hattie's frequent letters wouldn't be urging Sloane to return to the Priory to start setting up his nursery. She cared too much about the *haut monde*'s opinion to try to foist moonlings into their midst.

So Sloane was ready to go do his duty for God, King, and country. The marriage would be consummated.

Then Kelly came to Town. On vacation, he said, not supplanting the man St. Sevrin had valeting him, nor the butler who almost slammed the door in the grizzled veteran's face. He needed a holiday, Kelly declared, after chasing after the duchess for all those weeks. " 'Twere like trying to catch a butterfly on horseback, without a net or a saddle." He was ready to rejoin the regiment, Kelly told his employer reproachfully, unless His Grace was relieving him of guard duty.

"What, that little thing running you ragged? Maybe you better think of retiring altogether, Kelly. Lady Comstock writes she's got the chit in hand, so you couldn't have much to do."

Kelly helped himself to a glass of wine. "That's as may be, but Lady Comstock only sees Her Grace for a few hours at night. I'm trailing after her all day, when I can keep up. This farm, that field, a sickly calf here, a mildewed row there. It's more'n a body can bear, never sitting still less'n she's at the accounts or in the library."

"But she has no business doing anything but her embroidery and flower gardening. That's why I hired a new bailiff."

"I wrote you, Her Grace didn't like the man."

"So she didn't like him. I—" St. Sevrin tossed back the contents of his glass. "My God, she fired him, didn't she? Who the hell is running the place and making the improvements I requested? Did spring crops even get planted?" There went his hopes of keeping the Priory self-sufficient and solvent. Another chunk of investment money would have to be withdrawn to meet expenses.

"Now, I told you everything is aces, Yer Grace. I wouldn't of left, otherwise. Her Grace has everything in hand. Them cottages are all repaired, with good families moving in to work the farms, that stream's been rerouted so the bottom land don't flood, new breeding herds are getting fat, and the school is half finished." Kelly scratched his head. "Did I write you about the school? Not much for letters, don't you know."

"I'd never have guessed," the duke answered dryly. "But Lady Lisanne can't be running the estate. Those old tenant farmers won't accept a woman in charge, especially not one who's—"

"They don't like it, but they listen. When she picks up a handful of dirt and tells them how much manure to put in the field, how much lime and how much ashes, they listen. And if she says they should plant wheat here and corn there and turnips in the lower acre, they do it. They know your man wanted to throw them all off the land and turn it over to sheepherding."

"What, get rid of the farms? They've been there since the monks had the Priory. And what about the dairy cows? The Priory used to make a profit on the milk."

"That's what Her Grace said, before giving the new bailiff his walking papers."

"And you say she's doing all right?"

"Better'n all right, I'd guess. Everyone's saying it'll be the best harvest in memory if the weather holds."

St. Sevrin poured out another glass of wine for himself and one for Kelly. Here he'd been spending hours poring over the agricultural journals, trying to learn a lifetime of responsible landlording in a month. He'd been corresponding with Coke about new methods and visiting the patent office for new tools. He was cluttering up his mind with boring claptrap, stuff his lady wife knew by instinct, or whatever.

The Priory didn't need his sad lack of expertise. It had the baroness. The baroness's money. The baroness's skills. He may as well stay in London.

The Priory mightn't need St. Sevrin's help, but he found someone who did. A roistering night at Horse Guards with old Army comrades ended with a sobering message from the Peninsula. The sketchy information reported a devastating battle near Formieva, with many British deaths and casualties. Hardest hit was St. Sevrin's old regiment, which had valiantly held the line under Lieutenant Trevor Roe after the commanding officers had fallen. Lieutenant Roe was not expected to survive the loss of his leg.

If he was being treated in the field hospital, he didn't stand a chance. Sloane had enough experience to know the surgeons killed more soldiers than they saved. And any who did manage to recover from the savage amputations and bullet extractions were prey to blood poisoning from the filthy conditions and fevers from the infections. Then they had to face the weather-wracked hospital ships, when the generals chose to dispatch them, and the epidemic influenzas and dysentery. Major Lord Shearingham had gone through it all.

Trevor Roe wasn't going to. They'd been friends since school days and had signed up together. Trev had been the one to pull Sloane out from under his horse after he'd gone down from the saber slash that opened his chest and side. Trev had dragged him off the field, dodging bullets and flying hooves, stuffing his own uniform jacket into the wound to stop the bleeding.

No, St. Sevrin wasn't going to let his friend die in some stinking, fly-infested field hospital. He went to the docks to hire a yacht while Kelly purchased bandages, medicines, sheets, and blankets. None of the suitable craft were for lease, so the duke bought one, crew and all. This he could do. He went home to gather his own bags—and that jar of Lisanne's salve he'd been using on his stallion's cut leg. It worked for the horse.

It worked for Lieutenant Roe, and the three other wounded officers St. Sevrin managed to cram aboard his new vessel. Being warm and dry and tended around the clock with cooling drinks and nourishing broths had to speed their recovery also. Just being away from the contagion-ridden wards saved them from exposure to all manner of pestilences.

Lieutenant Roe's family was renting a place near Brighton for the summer, so St. Sevrin had his crew sail straight there. The Viscount Roehampton was so grateful to Sloane for bringing his son home that he insisted St. Sevrin stay on. He even invited the other wounded lads to recuperate in Brighton's healthful atmosphere, too, while Trevor finished his convalescence under his mother's loving care. Unfortunately the Viscountess Roehampton cried every time she looked at her son's crutches. Nor was she quite comfortable having five grown bachelors roistering under her roof, with the worst-reputed of them, St. Sevrin, being hale and hearty and a social pariah.

The other officers quickly removed to their own families or to the barracks in London. St. Sevrin was itching to leave, but Lord Roehampton, at his wife's urging, decided to put a flea in Prinny's ear about the duke's noble generosity. And his abysmal reputation.

As a result, St. Sevrin was to be awarded a medal for service to the Crown at one of the prince's extravagant, interminable dinners at his Oriental pavilion. Sloane couldn't insult the monarchy by leaving beforetimes, and he couldn't insult Trevor's father by expressing his wish that the Regent had seen fit to spend the nation's wealth on its loyal troops rather than on its overfed aristocrats. Bloody hell, he thought, a medal.

A medal wasn't enough for the prince. He wanted St. Sevrin to take his rightful place in decent Society. It was time the duke gave up his wicked ways, demanded one of the most debauched rulers in British history. The drinking, gambling, whoring—all of which the Regent practiced daily—had to stop, at least until St. Sevrin was respectable enough for the queen's drawing room. To attain such respectability, Prinny declared, St. Sevrin needed a wife. And not just any man's wife, he tittered in his latest mistress's married ear, but the Duchess of St. Sevrin herself. Prinny expected to meet the duke's bride at the fall Season. Country girl or not, she was a baron's daughter and could thus redeem the duke's reputation.

"If she doesn't pull a toad out of her pocket," Sloane muttered between clenched jaws as he bowed himself out of the royal presence.

"Well, what have you got against bringing her to London, anyway?" Trevor wanted to know when St. Sevrin arrived home in an ugly mood that hadn't been improved by enough bottles of ale to float an armada of grievances. Kelly's grin wasn't helping much, either, as he brushed off His Grace's formal attire.

"She doesn't want to come, that's why."

"So what? Hell, she's your wife. She has to."

Kelly laughed.

"You haven't met Lisanne."

"No, but I'd like to. Want to thank her for that stuff she sent with you. It helped a lot. Doctor here said it was one of the cleanest wounds he'd seen, fastest healing, too. Now all I have is pain in the leg I don't have. It's phantom pain, he says. Only imaginary."

"Then you'll really like my wife."

This time Kelly cleared his throat.

"Oh, hell, it doesn't matter. Prinny was three sheets to the wind himself. He won't remember."

But St. Sevrin's cousin Humbert remembered. He'd also been in Brighton, hanging on the prince's coattails. By chance or by design, he'd managed to meet Esmé and

Nigel Findley, who usually traveled in very different social circles. Lisanne's relatives were delighted to meet one of the prince's cronies; Humbert was delighted to hear about his new cousin by marriage. He was even more pleased to pass on what his groom heard from Esmé's maid.

The fall Season started with rumors flying about how Prinny was insisting St. Sevrin produce his bride, and how the duke was refusing because she was freakish. The prince wasn't happy, and the duke wasn't happy.

"Bloody hell. I should have run that bastard through ages ago."

"Which bastard?"

"Findley. Nigel. Humbert. Prinny. All of them."

Trevor looked over his shoulder to make sure no one in this alehouse heard his friend call the Prince of Wales a bastard or threaten his life. Then again, the tavern was such a low dive that half of its patrons were illegitimate. The other half would have killed their own mothers for the price of a bottle of Blue Ruin, much less the frivolous prince.

Sloane and Trevor were in London because Lieutenant Roe had been miserable in the bosom of his family. Their pity was smothering him, and his father's offer of an allowance was demeaning. He was a grown man, not a boy. He wasn't even the heir, just a second-rate second son. Trevor was depressed about his lost leg, his shattered career, and his bleak future. Even Whitehall, his last hope, had turned him down for a desk job. There were already too many crippled officers on the payroll.

That's why the two ex-soldiers were in an alehouse: so Trevor could drink himself into oblivion.

They were in *this* rat hole of a pub because St. Sevrin couldn't let his friend drink alone and the duke was playing least in sight. He and Trevor were staying at St. Sevrin House, which was looking more elegant every day under Kelly's supervision. The two friends were looking more seedy and degenerate every night. At least in this part of town St. Sevrin wouldn't be forced to defend his lady's name with his fists.

Thunderation, her name was mentioned in the betting books. St. Sevrin had never cared what anyone said about him, but Lisanne was his wife, by Jupiter! There were too many wagging tongues for Sloane to challenge, so he just let fly at the first man he saw smirking or simpering about the duke's fairy-tale match. His temper had seen him thrown out of White's and Watier's and Brooks's. The prince's disfavor, encouraged by Humbert, would keep him out. On the plus side, his left punch was getting stronger.

On the negative side, Trevor had started issuing challenges right and left in defense of the duchess. "Can't fence, but I can still shoot straight." He couldn't even see straight, but that hadn't stopped Lieutenant Roe. "M'best friend's wife, don't you know," he slurred. "M'hostess. M'benefactress, 'cause it was her blunt that brought me home so cozily."

So St. Sevrin landed Trevor a hard right to the jaw and carried him unconscious out of the Cocoa Tree to a hackney carriage, and to this gin mill the jarvey recommended.

Sloane pounded his bottle on the sticky, stained table. "It's a damnable situation."

"Right, when a man can't leave his wife in the country when he wants."

"No, not that situation. This one." St. Sevrin waved his hand around the dingy, smoke-filled room. "Here I am, a rich man finally, and I can't even drink in a decent club where the customers bathe occasionally."

"Uh, Sherry, I don't think it was a good idea to mention you were well-heeled. Not in a place like this."

Luckily Trevor was handy with his crutches, and St. Sevrin had his pistol.

Confound it, this couldn't go on. Sloane could turn

tail and drag himself and Trevor off to Devon, but he wouldn't give Humbert and the Findleys the satisfaction. He hadn't backed down from a challenge yet. Furthermore, if he left he'd never be able to return, not while Prinny was Regent . . . or King. There was nothing for it but to send for the infuriating chit and hope for the best: hope she came, and hope she was wearing shoes.

Besides, they were all out of that salve.

Chapter Twenty

*T*he duchess didn't answer St. Sevrin's summons to
present herself in London. His aunt did, in person.

Lady Comstock marched right past the new butler,
right past the new valet, and into her nephew's new bedchamber, where he was nursing a hangover, which was
nothing new.

"You look like you've been run over by a hay wagon,"
she began, pulling back the drapes to flood the room with
morning light.

"Several, thank you, Aunt Hattie," Sloane corrected,
wincing at the glare but dutifully reaching for his dressing gown. There would be no going back to sleep this
morning. He opened the door and bellowed for coffee.
And tea for the lady, he shouted as an afterthought. He
came back and sat in the chair across from his aunt.
"Where's my wife?"

"Oh, so you remember you have a wife, do you?"

Sloane got up, went back to the door, and shouted for a
bottle of brandy. He didn't reply until after the servants
had left. "Now, Aunt Hattie, you know very well that I recall my wife. Didn't I send her that fan from Brighton?
And what about the fancy lace headpiece from Portugal?

I wrote and told you I was going to the Peninsula to fetch Trev, I know I did."

Hattie raised her lorgnette at how much brandy was in his cup, how little coffee. "You think that's enough? A trinket? A footnote to your letters? How did you get to be such a fool?"

"I believe I was born that way, Aunt. You know, male. So where is my bride, at your house? She's in a pet over my lack of attention, is that it? Very well, I'll go beg her pardon."

"You don't know the girl at all, do you?" His aunt shook her head. "More's the pity." She made him wait while she buttered a scone, the sight of which did nothing for St. Sevrin's roiling stomach. "No, she's not at my house. She's not even at your house in Devon. She's gone home to Neville Hall to live in her own house, alone except for a parcel of old servants. She left one of the tenants' sons as overseer at the Priory and disappeared with her dog and her maid. She won't receive visitors or answer letters."

"Why the devil did she do a thing like that?"

"Not because the place held happy memories, from what I've gathered. No, somehow the child has got it in her head that you won't come home while she is at the Priory. Since you haven't yet—"

"Dash it, I've been busy. Bankers, solicitors, then helping Trevor get around."

"—Lisanne is convinced that she is keeping you here in London with her presence in Devon. If you don't have to deal with her in Devon, she's decided, then you'll leave this sinkhole of depravity. She feels responsible for your absence and even more responsible for your further slide into degradation." Lady Comstock fixed the duke with a gimlet stare, taking note of the bloodshot eyes and the bruises.

"That's absurd." It wasn't, of course. It was damn near the truth, that Sloane was running from his bride and

169

running amok defending her name, but that was none of Aunt Hattie's business. Or Lisanne's. "I'd like to know how in tarnation she heard anything about my 'further slide.' You wouldn't know anything about that, would you?" She knew everything else, with her network of letter-writing spies.

"What, do you think I would tell that sweet child that her husband is throwing drunken tantrums in the men's clubs because some chowderhead teases him over his wife's idiosyncracies?"

"Tantrums? Teases? Idiosyncracies? Madame, you certainly have a way with words. So what did you tell her?"

"I didn't have to tell her anything, you clunch. Your name is in every scandal sheet and gossip column. She can read, you jackass. And what tidbits Lisanne might have missed that harebrained cousin of hers makes sure to write. The little Findley twit thinks she's doing the duchess a favor, in exchange for having her Season at Neville House. So, yes, your wife knows all about your brawls and your binges. She is as well informed of Prinny's edicts as she is of the betting books at White's. And she knows every rumor making the rounds."

"Then why the deuce doesn't she come to London and disprove them all? That's why I sent for her, you know."

"Because she believes you wouldn't have done so unless your hand was forced. Lisanne thinks you don't want her here, that you're afraid she'll shame you worse. I think *she's* afraid of that, too."

"And will she? Will she make me an even bigger fool than I am now?"

"How could you ask that? You have to know she's intelligent and caring. You said yourself she was beautiful. Good heavens, boy, if you truly dislike her, by all that's holy, why did you marry her in the first place?"

Because of her eyes. Because she needed him to keep her safe. Because she wanted something so badly she was willing to bargain with the devil to get it. Sloane wiped his mouth with the napkin. "For the money, of course. That's what everyone is saying, isn't it?"

"Gammon. Everyone knows you were dished, but you could have found some cit's daughter to trade for your title ages ago if that's what you wanted."

"Ah, but I didn't . . . until things got so bad I had no choice. By then, of course, my reputation was so black no merchant banker would let me through the door. Lisanne Neville was the only heiress crazy enough to marry me."

Lady Comstock stood up and slapped him.

St. Sevrin wasn't in the mood for a long, boring carriage ride with its tolls and grooms and changes to inferior cattle. So he rode the roan stallion into Devon. The horse was the meanest brute St. Sevrin had ever owned, but had the strength to go forever on little rest. Sloane called him Diablo, Devil. The roan's previous owner hadn't called him anything intelligible, not with his jaw broken from a flying hoof. Not surprisingly, the duke had gotten a good price. He hoped to use the beast for breeding someday, if Diablo didn't kill him first.

The stallion took a bite out of the arm of an ostler in Reading, and kicked in his stall in Wincanton. There were two more places St. Sevrin wouldn't be welcomed to visit again, two more drafts on his bank.

At least Diablo wasn't boring, not by half. The manhater tried to unseat St. Sevrin every time the duke's thoughts wandered and his hands relaxed on the reins, which was often, with everything on St. Sevrin's mind. Most times Sloane stayed aboard, sometimes he didn't, but he always managed to hang onto the reins and not get trampled. By the time they reached Devon, the duke was bent and bruised. He was not defeated, however, which he considered good practice for the coming battle with his wife.

Lisanne *was* coming with him to London. He'd had

enough of this nonsense. So she had doubts. Everyone did. It made no never mind. They were married, by George, and by her own wishes.

St. Sevrin reached the Priory in late afternoon, in time to be awed at the difference in the old place. The drive was smooth and rut-free, and the grounds finally resembled lawns, not fields of grass and weeds. An army of gardeners was pruning hedges and trimming flower beds that were bouquets of vibrant colors.

A groom ran out to take his horse, then whistled up three more stable hands after St. Sevrin's warning and Diablo's flattened ears. They'd do. The duke turned his attention to the Priory itself. Every windowpane on the four-story building was in place and gleaming in the late-day sun. No ivy grew over the scrubbed brick facing, and fresh slates appeared on the roof. The ancient pile had never looked this good, not in Sloane's lifetime, not in his father's or grandfather's, either, he'd wager.

The front door opened before he could reach it, and a dignified, deferential butler bowed him inside. A nearby footman stepped forward to take his saddlebags. Another went to notify Cook, a third to order his bath.

My word, the duke wondered, was this the same place? The wood paneling shone, almost reflecting the patterns of the brilliant rugs on the floor. There were exquisite antique furnishings wherever he looked, even paintings on the walls. Good taste had failed in this one instance, for someone had managed to unearth or buy back the Shearingham ancestors' portraits. It was a waste of blunt, Sloane considered, for there was not an admirable one in the bunch, but it was a nice thought. The vases of flowers everywhere added a delightful touch of home—just not his home. Sloane could smell the late summer blooms, chrysanthemums, asters, and others he didn't recognize, instead of the mildew and mustiness of his last visit.

Upstairs, his bedchamber had been similarly transformed, complete with flowers on the nightstand. In minutes, more courteous help was bringing a hot bath and taking his clothes away to be pressed. Then the butler and a footman carried in an excellent meal, considering the kitchens had no warning of his arrival, and an excellent vintage of wine.

The servants weren't familiar like Kelly, but then they hadn't been through a war with him. For the first time, Sloane actually felt like a duke. He knew he had done nothing to earn these people's respect, but they gave it to the title anyway, or to the person who paid the bills. He sent compliments to the cook and thanked the housekeeper for a fine job.

This was how Neville Hall was always kept, the elderly woman informed him. Of course it was easier when the master and mistress were in residence, she added with a faint hint of censure. The staff did like to have their work appreciated.

Sloane was so appreciative and so comfortable and so loathe to get back on that bone-rattler, he decided to wait until the morning to visit his wife. Besides, he didn't want to frighten her, marching in at night as though he meant to claim his conjugal rights then and there.

He went to bed early and left word that he was to be awakened early, knowing from his aunt and Kelly how Lisanne could disappear for hours. Unfortunately Diablo also had a good night's sleep. He didn't want to be saddled. He didn't want to be ridden. And he definitely didn't want to take that shortcut through the woods. Since the duke didn't fancy having his head laid open by low branches or his neck broken against a tree trunk, he wisely decided to ride the long way around.

The carriage drive and grounds of Neville Hall were in the same flawless condition as the Priory's, and the house, a more modern stone edifice, was equally as well maintained. The groom who came to take Sloane's horse, however, was bent over, leaning on his stick. The fellow was never going to be able to hold the stallion, much less get him to the stable and rubbed down.

"Is there anyone else around to help?"

"Aye, Old Bill. I'm Young Bill."

If this was Young Bill, St. Sevrin marveled that Old Bill could still wield a pitchfork. He didn't much have to, the duke saw when he took Diablo around to the stable himself. Inside the vast structure were a decrepit pony nodding in its stall, two donkeys, a goat with a bandaged leg, and Old Bill, asleep on a stool in a patch of sunlight.

Diablo seemed interested in the goat, so he let Sloane get him settled in the stall next door with only one half-hearted attempt to bite the duke's hand off, and one kick that missed by feet instead of the stallion's usual inches. Sloane walked back to the house.

No one answered the front door, so he knocked again. This time the door creaked open. No, the creak was from the joints of the bewigged butler who bowed and asked his business.

"I'm St. Sevrin. I've come to see my wife."

The butler squinted at him. "No, you're not the duke. He has gray hair and a red nose."

"That was my father. I am the new duke."

The footman in the hallway had taken his hat and gloves, but didn't leave the marble entry. "What'd he say?"

"He says he's the new duke. Wants the duchess."

"Who's nude? Not Her Grace. Maybe no hat and no gloves, but she ain't never gone nude, has she, Weldon?"

Weldon had been butler at the Priory when Sloane was a boy. He should have been pensioned off then, except there was no money for a pension. He should have been dead by now. When Aunt Hattie said some of the old servants had been moved to Neville Hall, he'd thought she meant previous servants, not *old* servants.

He raised his voice: "Could you tell Her Grace that her husband is here?"

The footman pulled an antique blunderbuss from be-hind the door. "Her Grace ain't no hussy, neither."

Weldon took Sloane's hat and gloves from the table and tried to hand them back to the duke, missing him by as wide a mark as Diablo had. "Her Grace isn't receiv-ing."

"Like hell she isn't." He took the stairs two at a time, barely noticing the silk wall hangings or the gleaming wood. He did manage to register that a Turner landscape hung in the landing, and a small Vermeer at the top of the stairs. Fine, he got his rackety ancestors; she got the mas-terpieces. Then again, he got the antique furniture; she got the antique servants. Sloane thought he had the better deal.

He started opening doors and shouting until a mob-capped head stuck out of a room down the hall. It was that girl from the vicarage, done up in a gray maid's uni-form with a frilly starched apron. She bobbed him a curtsy. "Your Grace."

"Ah, Mary, is it? I was beginning to think everyone in the place was either deaf, dumb, or blind. Could you tell Her Grace that I wish to speak to her."

"I'm that sorry, Your Grace, but my lady isn't here."

She didn't sound a bit sorry to Sloane. In fact, she sounded downright hostile. It was a big house, and he didn't want to wander around for hours until he found Lisanne, so he smiled and held out a coin. "Could you tell me where I might find her?"

The maid looked at him as if he were a cat offering her a dead snake. Or a live snake. "My lady pays me fine. And, no, I can't."

Sloane put the coin back in his pocket and the steel back in his voice. Loyalty to an employer was one thing, standing in his way was another. "I am not leaving until I speak to her."

Mary crossed her arms over an ample bosom that made Sloane wonder if Kelly had obeyed any of his instructions. Then the brazen chit had the nerve to glare at him when she noticed where his eyes had strayed. "I can't tell Your Grace where my lady is because I don't know. She doesn't tell me anymore. She doesn't visit the tenants, she doesn't work in her stillroom, and she doesn't sit in the library. She never goes near the kitchen nor the dining room, neither, that's for sure. Most of the time she lays on her bed in here." Mary jerked her head to the room behind her. "Or she's gone without telling anyone where."

St. Sevrin knew where she was. They all knew where she was. The Duchess of St. Sevrin was in those blasted, bloody woods.

Chapter Twenty-one

Sevrin Woods covered over two hundred acres. That was two hundred acres of thick old growth trees, lakes, meadows, and deer tracks without one recognizable footpath or guidepost. Lisanne could be anywhere.

Before setting out, Sloane stopped in the kitchen to get some bread and cheese to carry along with him. The crone at the stove was so palsied, it was no wonder that the duchess didn't eat her cooking. Shaking hands didn't make for accurate measurements, if the ingredients got in the pot at all. The bread was fine, though, hot and crusty; and he had his choice of cheese, cold chicken, or sliced ham. He had his own flask for liquid refreshment, and there would be clear water in the streams. He didn't dare ask Methuselah's uncle at the front door to fetch something up from the wine cellar.

Sloane headed for what he thought was the clearing where he'd found Lisanne crying last spring, crying because she had to marry him or lose everything. She wasn't there, if it was even the same place, but he stayed and called her name. Then he whistled, hoping the dog could hear him and bark. Instead a flock of sparrows started chirping at him from the trees until he threw out some of the bread.

He began to see what she loved about this place. Aside from its natural beauty, the forest had absolutely nothing to do with the woes and worries of the world beyond its borders. The old oak trees were changing their colors, and a bed of orange and yellow leaves already blanketed the ground, leaving no sound but the birdsong and the scurrying of little creatures darting back and forth after his crumbs. He could be anywhere in time, anywhere in place. If there'd been an apple tree, St. Sevrin wouldn't have been surprised to see Eve peeking from behind its leaves. Druids could have chanted here, or Roman fauns presided at the Bacchanalia. The woods were ageless, unaware, and uncaring about man's petty concerns.

Although St. Sevrin felt small and young, dwarfed in size by the massive boles and soaring branches, a heartbeat in the life span of this ancient place, he also felt protected and sheltered. He couldn't understand why the locals had such fear of this expanse, but he was glad they did, for Lisanne's sake.

He wandered all morning and into the afternoon, watching the direction of the sun when he could spot it through the leaves. He never found his wife and, oddly enough, he never found the route to the Priory. He did find streams to hurdle, huge fallen logs to clamber over, and endless prickly vines to catch on his clothing. By three o'clock, according to his pocket watch, he was filthy, sweaty, and hungry, having shared his snack with squirrels, deer, and even a curious badger. He was also hoarse, having spent most of the time calling for Lisanne.

He gave it up. Even if he found her, he was in no condition or frame of mind to address his lady wife. It took Sloane two hours to find his way back to Neville Hall.

There was no need to bother the relics in the house, he decided. They'd most likely already forgotten he'd called. He headed directly for the stable to collect Diablo. Becka came charging out of the stable, growling.

"Stubble it, fleabag, I'm in no mood for your nonsense." The dog—and his wife—had likely been hiding out in the stable all day, laughing at him. St. Sevrin strode into the building. He needed a few moments for his eyes to adjust from the bright daylight before he saw her, but there she was, as heart-stoppingly beautiful as ever. She was wearing a pretty sprigged muslin gown and a silly hat on her head—and she was in Diablo's stall.

The duke reached for the pistol that should have been at his side. Hell and thunderation, of course he hadn't thought he needed a weapon to call on his own wife. No matter, he'd kill the stallion with his bare hands if the devil harmed her. Guilt washed over him that he hadn't destroyed the vicious animal weeks ago, but had brought him here, of all places.

Sloane knew not to make any sudden moves and doubted if his feet could have done so anyway, having been glued with panic to the packed dirt floor. He tried to speak, but nothing came out of his dry mouth. He swallowed stable dust and enough saliva to be able to croak out, "Come away, Duchess."

Lisanne looked up—yes, her blue eyes could still pierce him to the core with their disappointment and distrust—but she didn't move.

"Please, sweetings, please get out of there. Slowly. I should have told the grooms, but I never thought anyone would even try to get near the stallion. He's mean, Lisanne, mean and dangerous." He took a slow, desperate step closer. "Please come to me now."

"He's not mean, just lonely. I was introducing him to Nana."

St. Sevrin took another snail-step nearer to the stall, where he could see the lame goat in there with Diablo and Lisanne. Sloane didn't care if the goat ended up in the stallion's water trough or his stomach, he wanted his wife away from those metal-shod hooves and bone-crushing teeth. He held his arms open, willing her just once to do what any reasonable person would. He'd never ask anything of her again. If she wanted to stay in Devon, he'd drag the damned prince here to meet her. "Please, Duchess."

Lisanne fed Diablo the last sugar cube from her pocket and kissed the velvet patch on his nose. St. Sevrin groaned. Then she bent and kissed the goat. "Lisanne, now!"

Telling the animals that she'd be back soon, Lisanne finally turned and opened the stall door. St. Sevrin rushed over, snatched her up, and slammed the gate behind her. He ran outside with Lisanne in his arms to Old Billy's—or Young Billy's—vacant stool, where he just sat, clutching her to him, his eyes closed on the nightmare he'd see for the rest of his days. They stayed like that while his heart pounded so loudly and rapidly he thought it must be using up two years of his life. At last he managed to gasp, "Don't ever . . . do that . . . to me again."

Lisanne didn't try to struggle in his arms. She felt the hard muscle, the solid chest, and knew it would be useless, but she felt no need to break loose. Actually she was amazed. St. Sevrin might be suffocating her, he might even be breaking every bone in her body, but he really seemed to care. She freed one arm and reached up to touch his cheek. "There was no danger, truly. Animals like me."

His eyes snapped open. "Confound it, girl, I wonder you haven't been eaten alive by the wolves in Sevrin Woods with that attitude."

She flashed a quicksilver smile. "There are no wolves in England. But if there were . . ."

He shook her gently, still not letting her off his lap. "Don't tell me. I haven't recovered yet." Then he held her away a bit. "Here, let's have a look at the fearless Amazon I married." The uncertain look on her face made him add, "Perhaps not altogether fearless, then. I won't bite, you know."

Lisanne trusted animals, not men. She stared down at her gloves, soiled now with the stallion's licking. She turned her hands over, so he wouldn't see.

The duke didn't notice. He was taking inventory elsewhere. Lisanne's blond hair was bundled in some kind of net at the back of her neck, and her healthy golden glow had almost faded to insipid ivory. "You're much too pale."

"Lady Comstock said tanned skin was to be avoided at every cost. She told me to wear a hat at all times."

He untied the strings and tossed the bonnet aside. "The hell with hats. You need the sunshine. And your clothes still don't fit. What the deuce was that Frenchwoman doing anyway?"

Fingering the neckline of her gown, which did have excess material, Lisanne defended the modiste. "I've lost a bit of weight recently, that's all. The gowns Madame Delacroix made were lovely. And this one was clean this morning." She wrinkled her nose at the smudges coming from proximity to him. The earthy scent of him, all horse and sweat and soap, was fascinating, disturbing, and not to be mentioned aloud, she was sure. "I usually wear a smock when I am gardening or with the animals."

He didn't care about her clean clothes. "How could you lose anything? You never weighed more than a handful of feathers." He was undoing the net holding her hair and spreading it out with his fingers so that long golden curls fell across her shoulders. "There, that's more like it. I hardly recognized the stylish lady." Sloane pulled her skirts up an inch or two. "Too bad, shoes. They've made you into one of those uppity debutante creatures, haven't they?"

Lisanne had to smile. Truly he was outrageous. "Your aunt worked so hard at it, too."

The duke turned serious. "Not hard enough, it seems,

if you're hiding out here, not eating, not visiting your friends. Did someone insult you? Threaten you?"

She looked away. "There is nothing wrong, no problem."

"Even a dolt like me can see that something is desperately wrong. Otherwise you would have come to London with Aunt Hattie or stayed at the Priory, which has never looked better, incidentally. I thank you for your efforts there."

"Your aunt did most of it, along with the staff. They take great pride in it, you know."

"So why did you run away?"

He was going to persist until she told him, Lisanne could tell. She got up and walked away from him. It might be easier to explain if she didn't see the pity in his eyes. "I have made mice feet of everything. I made you so unhappy you wouldn't come home."

"I was giving you time to get used to the idea of marriage," he lied. "And then I had to go help my friend Trevor home from the Peninsula."

She didn't bother turning to face his excuses. "You didn't come and that made me unhappy, thinking I had stolen your comfort, your choices. You couldn't come home, and you couldn't find a wife to please you more because we were already married. And then I realized I would never know love, either. To spend the rest of my life among strangers and servants . . ."

He rose and started massaging the back of her neck. "I didn't know love was part of our bargain, sweetings. You were such a pragmatic little negotiator, I never suspected you harbored dreams of romance. As I recall, you wanted the woods and financial security. The forest is intact, every confounded inch of it, I made sure today. You're not lacking for funds, are you?"

She shook her head, no.

"We did agree on children, I remember. We'll get to that in time. And you did offer me a long tether if I didn't

182

embarrass you. You've read the *on dits* columns. I guess I've failed you there, Duchess, but not in the way you meant."

Lisanne turned to face him again, her eyes wet with unshed tears. "No, I failed you, with all that gossip. I knew you wouldn't want your wife's name a byword. I should have known that they would—"

Sloane put a finger over her lips. "Sh. There was another stipulation that I didn't fully understand at the time. You didn't want to be locked up. But what have you done here, Duchess, except make your own prison? Do you like this life you've chosen?"

"No. Do you like yours?"

"No, and I am even more responsible for my own bars and shackles. Both of us can do better."

"We can't do much worse, can we?"

He smiled, but only for a second. "I am more sorry than you can imagine that I've made you so miserable, Duchess. My only excuse is that I am not in the habit of thinking of anyone's feelings but my own. I cannot promise love, for I doubt that I am capable of the poet's emotion, but I will try to be a better friend if you'll let me. And as for no one else loving you, Aunt Hattie will have my liver and lights if I don't restore you to happiness, and Kelly will resign. Your Mary almost carved me for Christmas dinner, and my friend Trevor already swears he adores you like a sister. He tells all and sundry that you saved his life with your medicine."

"Nonsense, Lady Roehampton wrote a very pretty letter to Aunt Hattie about how you snatched her darling son from the jaws of death with your rescue ship. They were schoolgirls together, did you know?"

"Aunt Hattie went to school with every female in creation. Nevertheless, Trev has declared himself your knight-errant. We better hope Lady Roehampton doesn't get wind of his challenging anyone who sullies your name. Luckily most chaps won't accept a challenge from a one-legged man."

"And you? What kind of challenges do you accept?"

"Oh, I don't bother with duels anymore. You must have heard that by now, how I'm an uncivilized lowlife, using my fists instead of my manners. I did enough killing in the war. Now I just bounce the insulting bastards on their heads once or twice. Shuts them up quickly enough."

"I've caused you such trouble."

"And I've caused you pain. We're even. Now we have to stop hurting each other. Do you think we can?"

"You aren't just being nice so I'll go to London with you, are you?"

"I have to admit that I came here with every intention of carrying you off, willy-nilly, just to stop the damnable gossip. I won't. If you don't want to go to London, you don't have to. But I won't go without you, Duchess. Then, of course, you'll be worrying that I'm in Prinny's black books or that I'm missing the gaming hells and horse races, the clubs and balls. I won't, of course, but you won't be sure, will you?"

Lisanne scuffed her shoe in the stable-yard dirt. He was being so reasonable, so understanding. "What if I make the gossip worse by going? I could shame you even more, you know."

"Sweetheart, you are a beautiful, beautiful woman. You'll have the male half of London at your feet. The women will adore you because you are gentle and intelligent and no threat to their husband-hunting daughters, since you are already taken. Besides that, you are a duchess, a wealthy, wellborn lady in your own right, with a better pedigree than half the patronesses at Almack's. Aunt Hattie will be there to help, and Trevor, and myself. Just think of the members of the ton as yipping lapdogs and scrappy barn cats. If you can tame Diablo, you'll have those mongrels and mousers eating out of your hand."

Lisanne wondered how he saw himself, as a pampered pug or a well-fed feline. Most likely as the big bad wolf that ate unsuspecting little girls, couldn't be domesticated, and wasn't around anymore. Wolves mated for life.

She had to take the chance. "I will go."

"Good girl!" He swung her up and onto the stool so their eyes met at the same level. Lisanne was about to protest that she wasn't a girl, wasn't to be treated like a child, when he pressed a cool, soft kiss on her lips that deepened to a warm, hard embrace. He knew.

"About those sons . . ."

"I have to start packing." Lisanne jumped off the stool and ran toward the house, leaving her hat, her hair net, and her bemused husband. Her cheeks were burning with embarrassment, but her lips were burning with something else altogether.

Chapter Twenty-two

$\mathcal{I}$t wasn't the packing that slowed them down, or the second carriage necessary to carry the vast amount of trunks Mary insisted Her Grace needed to make the proper splash in London. The third carriage wasn't a problem, either, once Lisanne saw to the careful packing of her bottles and boxes and buckets of plant cuttings. St. Sevrin simply hired extra horses and drivers and outriders.

It wasn't even the dog who caused all the delays. Becka liked to ride up with the driver of her mistress's traveling carriage, her ears and jowls blowing in the breeze, when she wasn't running alongside or off on her own errands. They didn't have to wait all that long on lonely stretches of highway for Becka to return.

No, it was the goat that kept them so many extra days on the road, the lame goat that had to come in a slower wagon of her own, with ample straw and sweet rolls. The Duchess of St. Sevrin wasn't going to make a splash, the duke thought. She was going to create a tidal wave, riding into town with this particular entourage, not the least of which was his own huge roan stallion making sheep eyes at a nanny goat. It was downright humiliating, but made for an easier mount.

When he was done riding, when Diablo had been tied behind the goat's wagon to play Romeo to Nana's Juliet, St. Sevrin rode in the carriage with his wife. At first he suggested Mary exchange places outside with Becka for a while so he and Lisanne could get to know each other. That dog in the carriage, however, was not a good idea, even with the windows opened. It was easier to let Mary stay and speak of impersonal matters: the estates, his investments, what sights Lisanne might like to see, his friend Trevor Roe.

"I confess, I'm worried about Trev. It's not good for a man to have no future and nothing to do. I know. His family will support him, but I know he'd rather earn his own keep than be handed it like a remittance man." St. Sevrin was chafing enough under the yoke of his wife's fortune.

"Is he honest? Intelligent? No, I take that back. He must be if he's your friend."

"Thank you, Duchess, for thinking all my friends are paragons. May you never meet the scum I play with at cards."

"Those are not your friends." She was positive. "You wouldn't have gone to all the trouble of fetching one of them home, would you? Lieutenant Roe was obviously worth the effort, worth your worrying over him now."

"Trev is a good man and a good friend. He was a deuced good officer, with a head for details and strategy that even Old Hokey recognized. He was one of Wellesley's aides when he went down. Trev's no scholar, but he's certainly more intelligent than most of the gossoons they have working at the War Office now."

"Then why don't you make him your man of business? Mr. Mackensie won't be around forever, and you admitted yourself he doesn't keep up with the shipping ventures you're interested in." She hesitated a moment. "And if you're not to be in London all the time, you'll need someone responsible to look after your banking interests and such. Perhaps you could make him a loan so he'd be a partner instead of a mere employee. That way he'd have a share in the profits and could pay you back when he makes his own fortune."

"And I'd have an excuse for keeping him at St. Sevrin House rather than letting him go to his parents' stuffy mausoleum of a place or cheap bachelor digs with no one to watch out for him. He can have an office of his own and his own apartment. It's a brilliant idea, sweetings, thank you!" He kissed her gloved hand right there in front of Mary, who giggled.

After luncheon, the duke again rode in the carriage. "Now that you've settled Trevor so happily, my sweet, what about Kelly? He's too good a man to waste opening doors or ironing cravats."

Lisanne had it all worked out. "Oh, he's to be your estate manager when I—we—return to Devon." Lisanne wasn't sure how long before St. Sevrin's interest in the country, or his interest in her, waned. He might want her to go to London to make things more comfortable for him now, but he might forget about his promise to come home later to take up the reins of his holdings. She couldn't trust the duke yet, but she could trust Kelly. "The people like him and respect him for being a veteran, but more for being farm-bred himself. He knows a great deal and can learn more from working with the bailiff at Neville Hall. There is too much work for one man, or even two, to do it all. Even if . . . if you are there, you'll need help. And Mary will be happy."

The maid was blushing scarlet. St. Sevrin laughed. "Ah, so the wind sits in that corner, does it? I'm not surprised. It's a fine man you'd be getting, Mary, if you can bring him up to scratch."

"Oh, I aim to, Your Grace. He's already hooked. I just have to reel him in."

"Poor Kelly, he never had a chance, did he?" No more than he had, Sloane supposed. He wasn't exactly complaining. His duchess was looking charming in an apple green merino traveling costume, and another of those silly bonnets with a posy of silk roses tucked under the brim. She looked like a sprite peeking out from a garden. She was a good traveler, too, when she wasn't worried about her dog, her plants, the goat, or the drivers out in the rain. Lisanne would have ridden farther without breaks, but Sloane made sure they stopped long enough at every change of horses for her to eat something. He wasn't bringing any undernourished nymph to Town.

Sloane also stopped early enough every evening for a leisurely dinner and a good night's rest—in separate rooms. The duchess had enough in her dish now, he decided, being out in the world for the first time in her life. Hell, she'd never been out of Devon. And she was too frail. And shouldn't be breeding during the Season he meant for her to enjoy. St. Sevrin did make sure that they shared a good night kiss, though, for her to think about in her solitary chamber. He stayed down in the taproom, so he *wouldn't* think about it.

Back in the carriage, Sloane was pleased to find his wife didn't jabber on like some females he knew, but asked reasonable questions about everything she saw. St. Sevrin was looking forward to showing her the sights of London, the Opera House, Astley's Amphitheater, Hyde Park with its swans and Serpentine and Society on the strut. He was sure she'd adore the stuff he'd disdained for ages. As the cortege moved closer to Town and traffic got heavier, Sloane grew more eager, more assured of the welcome she'd receive there. Lisanne, however, grew less and less confident with every mile. She was twisting her gloves and biting her lip and not asking about the passing scenes. She wasn't doing more than crumbling her toast, either, and feeding it to whatever creature was handy.

To keep her from dwelling on tomorrow, from retreating into that quiet shell she erected, Sloane teased: "Now that you've got Trevor's future mapped out, and Kelly's, what have you planned for me, Duchess? You haven't left me much to do but sign the checks. Surely you don't intend me to become just another useless pet of Society, do you?"

"I doubt if Society would relish a bored timber wolf in its midst," she answered without thinking, and blushed when he laughed.

"They haven't in the past, sweetings. What am I to do, then, besides escort the newest comet about Town?"

"You have to make the decisions. You can't expect Kelly or Lieutenant Roe to know your mind. You can't do everything, of course. I know, for I tried. There's always a leaking roof or a blocked drain just when you're thinking about next year's crop rotations. Or there's an account that doesn't balance when you're needed to choose a new doctor for the village. Kelly and Trevor can handle the details. Besides, you'll be starting the horse-breeding farm you've always wanted. A racing stud, is it?"

"My word, woman, are you a mind reader besides? I've never mentioned that to anyone. How did you know?"

"Why else would you have bought a difficult animal like Diablo? And then, when you saw what he was, why would you keep him a stallion? I'm not a fool, Your Grace."

He kissed her hand again. "No, but you married one, Your Grace."

He wasn't such a fool, for he'd designed a room Lisanne couldn't help but adore. The walls were painted a pale yellow, but then he'd had an artist come in to paint trellises and flowers from floor to ceiling, with painted vines climbing the gauze-covered windows. Painted clusters of wildflowers adorned the white lacquered furniture, with matching live bouquets on every surface. The bed hangings and upholstered lounge and chairs were deep forest green, with make-believe birds in brilliant colors woven into the fabric.

Lisanne just kept turning in circles, trying to take it all in, together with the fact that St. Sevrin had done it for her. "It's the most beautiful room I've ever seen."

The duke was standing by the doorway, frowning. "Then why are you crying?"

"Because it's the most beautiful room I've ever seen."

The duke shrugged and went downstairs while Lisanne refreshed herself after the long journey. Mary was already bossing the line of footmen over the placement of Her Grace's trunks.

St. Sevrin waited in the library, which he'd also furnished with Lisanne in mind. Not that he'd made another garden in this wood-and-leather domain, but when Sloane had restocked the shelves of books his father had sold off, he'd considered her tastes as well as his own. The walls held all the classics, plus whole sections devoted to modern works on botany, agriculture, and medicine. He'd bought whatever he thought she might enjoy, encyclopedias and foreign dictionaries, along with current works of poetry and fiction that mightn't have come her way. Considering that he'd never seen her without a book in her pocket or nearby, even in the carriage, he thought she might like the library. He found a measure of peace there himself usually, studying the farming journals or investment guides.

His Grace would find no peace today, for Trevor found him there and demanded to know what had kept them so long. Bets were on at the clubs that St. Sevrin had decamped for parts unknown rather than presenting his wife in Town.

Instead of discussing his stallion's affection for a goat,

Sloane mentioned Lisanne's proposal to his friend. Trevor was thrilled. "Told them at Whitehall I had a head for figures. This'll be much better. Mother will have kitten fits, of course, that I'll be going into trade, but the pater will be so relieved, he'll come down heavy with my share for investing."

Trevor was still excited when Lisanne came down. "I'd get down on one knee to thank you, Your Grace, but since I only have one knee and Sherry would have to haul me up off your carpet, I'll just declare myself your devoted slave. And now I'll leave you to start my packing, so you might have your privacy."

"No," they both shouted.

"It's part of the package," Sloane told him. "You've got to be nearby to be of sufficient help. This place is surely big enough for all of us to rattle around in."

"And I'll feel better about being in London if I have familiar faces around me. Please stay."

"My lady, you are as gracious as you are beautiful. I accept, if only to have more time to convince you to leave this cad and run off with me."

"What, are you trying to give her a disgust of London already?"

Then Aunt Hattie arrived, to St. Sevrin's relief. He wasn't worried about Trev turning Lisanne's head; he was worried about getting her launched properly. He didn't know the first thing about introducing a proper female around. Sloane hardly knew any proper females, in fact, and Trev wasn't much better, having been with the army even longer. For certain they couldn't take Lisanne to their usual haunts, and neither was currently high on the invitation lists of polite hostesses. Sloane vowed to himself to keep out of low company while his wife was in Town, since it would be easier to establish her respectably if he could salvage his own reputation.

Aunt Hattie was also convinced to stay in Berkeley Square to preside over Lisanne's presentation, and Trevor was quick to enlist his mother on her behalf, too. Viscountess Roehampton was as starchy a matron as any of Almack's patronesses, but she felt a debt to the duke and his little duchess.

While the duke and his new *chargé d'affaires* got busy over their investment schemes, the two pillars of Society got busy over Lisanne's introduction to the ton. They decided not to pitchfork her into the Season, where a green girl could flounder so easily, but to ease her into the stream. In a well-orchestrated campaign, Lady St. Sevrin was carefully escorted to the theater to sit in the Roehampton box, and to the park in Lady Comstock's barouche. She was taken along on morning calls to the dowager's friends, who just happened to be the most influential women in the *belle monde*. She was introduced to small groups at select dinner parties, and slightly larger ones at musicales and card parties. The duke, meanwhile, was permitted to take his wife sightseeing when nothing more important was planned, if he swore not to let her appear blue, collect interesting weeds in her pockets, or try to rescue every overworked cart horse in London. He was expressly forbidden to take her to the Tower with its filthy, flea-ridden menagerie.

Finally Lisanne's mentors deemed her ready for her presentation to royalty. With their connections, Ladies Comstock and Roehampton managed to get their protégée a private audience with the queen and her son, instead of one of the chockablock drawing rooms. After all, Lisanne was a duchess, not a debutante, and it was the prince himself who had asked to meet her, in her mandatory hooped skirt and feathered headdress.

Prinny seemed very pleased about it, too. "Now we see why you wanted to keep this beautiful creature in the hinterlands, St. Sevrin. Glad we convinced you otherwise, what? Beauty is to be shared, St. Sevrin, that's our credo. And we hear you are back at the clubs again, too.

Good man. Next we'll be looking for you to take your rightful place in Parliament. We are well satisfied."

St. Sevrin was, too. Lisanne wasn't Prinny's type, thank goodness. He mopped his brow in relief when they were in their carriage. The meeting had gone remarkably well considering what could have happened if his bride had pulled a baby rabbit from her pocket. Sloane marveled that Lisanne hadn't seemed nervous about meeting the monarchs in the least. She only regretted that the poor king wasn't well enough to join them, which had the queen declaring her a very sweet child.

That very sweet child lit into her husband on the way home. She pulled out the ridiculous ostrich plumes that had taken an hour to place correctly in her hair and frowned across at him. "Do you mean to tell me that you don't sit in the Lords? Even my papa made sure he came for important sessions. I have been in London a sennight now, and I have seen more disease, hunger, filth, and crime than in my entire life in Devon. And you have the power to do something for the climbing boys, the child prostitutes, the unemployed veterans—and you don't?"

The duke wished he could take her in his arms and shut her mouth with a kiss, but those damnable hooped skirts were in the way. "Hold, Duchess. I've been to the stodgiest of tea parties, the most boring of musical evenings, and even a lecture on the healing properties of fungus. You and your watchdogs have dragged me to church on Sundays, by Jupiter, and to every historic cathedral betweentimes. Must I suffer another sermon after facing Prinny's? Have a heart, sweetings."

"I do. For the people you could be helping."

"Do you see your goodness in everyone? Even me?"

"I see that you aren't nearly as evil as you play at being."

If she could see what he was thinking about doing under her hooped skirts, she might reconsider. He smiled. "What makes you think I'm not all bad, Duchess?"

She smiled back. "I saw you pet the goat."

det het uitgebid scheine, and sit sit techtside. He voidnot.
"What makes you think Dayne of eight Dunkirk?"
she called back. "They were with you.

Chapter Twenty-three

*H*er Grace was officially out. His Grace was unofficially back in the prince's favor. Both their graces were in good graces with the ton. For now. Invitations came pouring in, but more from curiosity, Lisanne knew, than any sense of friendliness.

In her own quiet way, Lisanne saw much and said little. With the two voluble *grande dames* by her side, she was not required to add much to the conversation. When the dowagers weren't around, St. Sevrin and Trevor kept her entertained with their dissections of the war news, the international influences on commerce, and the state of the government—or outrageous compliments so she'd be used to having the butter boat poured over her head, they insisted.

Lisanne was hardly ever alone. A female wasn't supposed to be, it seemed. She couldn't take Becka to the locked park across the street without a footman at her heels. Heaven forfend she go to the bookstore by herself, or walk the short distance.

For now Lisanne was willing to listen to all the strictures and heed the warnings. She was here for one purpose only, and that was to see her husband's honor polished. If St. Sevrin required her to be a pattern card of conformity in order to be invited to the highest sticklers' boring parties, she would toe the mark—in shoes. If she had to be dressed to the nines to cast a good reflection on his image, she'd stand for being poked and prodded and dragged from shop to shop. She was going to make him proud of her and satisfied with this marriage, even if it killed her.

At night, alone in her bed, Lisanne had time to reflect on her situation, both the good and the bad. London was filthy, blanketed in soot, choking in poverty. It was also exciting, amusing, and informative. Just so, many of the people she was meeting were vain and empty pleasure-seekers. Why would anyone wish to be acceptable to such people? She'd be happier in the company of the carriage horses. But others, especially among the dowager's circles of wealthy, powerful women, were able to accomplish untold good with their fund-raising and endowments, pushing their husbands toward legislated reform. Lisanne arranged for Mr. Mackensie to set aside a percentage of her income for just such charitable gifts, in addition to what she handed out to every unfortunate on the streets. When St. Sevrin took his seat, she'd be able to plead her causes with him.

Meanwhile she was becoming accepted. Even the servants at St. Sevrin House were starting to turn to her for orders, not to Aunt Hattie or Kelly or His Grace. She knew they weren't comfortable with her, the aloof, polite footmen in burgundy livery and the skittery maids in their crisp aprons, but they obeyed her and catered to her wishes. Only the cook seemed actually to welcome her presence, though, especially after Lisanne provided a soothing footbath for her bunions. Mrs. Reilly also put sweetened milk out each night for the Brownies who brought the kitchen luck, so the bread would keep rising and rodents would stay out of her larder. With so many milk-mustached cats in the yard, how could the mice do else? Mrs. Reilly was happy enough to let Lisanne fill her sacks and pockets with rolls, apples, and sugar when she left for the park or the stables. The others, from the pastry cook to the potboy, looked away.

Lisanne saw those same averted glances whenever she arrived at the theater on her husband's arm or at a milliner's shop with Aunt Hattie. At formal gatherings ladies stared at her over their fans, as if she couldn't see their assessing eyes. A few gentlemen ogled her through their absurd quizzing glasses, to be chilled by St. Sevrin's frown or Lady Comstock's cut direct. Still, conversations broke off when she arrived, none of the younger females approached her on their own, and practiced hostesses tended to fumble over handing her a teacup.

She was accepted because she had to be—with the queen's nod, her illustrious sponsors, her title, and her fortune. But she wasn't approved. Gossip followed and flowed around her like a chiffon overskirt. The Findleys had brought their servants with them to Town, the same servants who had seen Addled Annie reviled all her life. Even if Uncle Alfred never spoke a bitter word, even if that rattlepate Esmé never chattered to her twenty-three bosom bows, rumors flew. St. Sevrin's cousin Humbert decided country air might be more salubrious to his health after the duke overheard him at White's, but still the scandalmongers were working overtime. Lisanne had Trevor's promise not to challenge anyone and her husband's word not to engage in fisticuffs, not if he wanted to redeem his own reputation. Therefore she wasn't upset by the gabblegrinders. Her husband was.

Everyone was waiting for her to do something outrageous. Her husband included. Lisanne was used to relatives and strangers looking at her as if she had horns growing out of her head. She wasn't used to seeing the question in her husband's dark eyes. That hurt.

While Sloane was being kind, keeping her away from the crushes, walking with Becka and Lisanne in the park, taking her to Horticultural Society lectures, he still needed a drink to face his wife. He still went out again after seeing her to the door after their evening entertainment, giving her a quick kiss for the servants' benefit. He still came home in the early hours of the morning, loud, unsteady, reeking of spirits and smoke. He still wasn't a real husband.

They'd have children sooner or later, Lisanne was confident of that. She'd seen the desire in St. Sevrin's eyes after their all too brief embraces. But how could she share such intimacy with a man who was afraid of her, afraid she'd start banging her head against the wall or start rolling her eyes and speaking in tongues? Sloane trusted her to run his households. He didn't trust her to give him normal, healthy sons, not even now when she was trying so hard to fit into the mold of propriety. Lisanne never even whistled the sparrows to her hand anymore, except here, at her own bedchamber's windowsill. Sloane didn't trust her, so she couldn't trust him not to walk out of her life the moment she displeased him.

Lisanne felt she was treading on eggshells. St. Sevrin was charming, amusing, respectful of her opinions and appreciative of her womanly charms now that her gowns fit better. She wanted his love.

If her life was going to have any meaning beyond acts of charity and the performance of her duties, Lisanne needed him to love her the way she was coming to love him. He wasn't perfect, heaven knew, and she wasn't about to accept his faults without trying her hardest to change them. Still, she could see past those shortcomings to the man underneath, and love him. Why couldn't he accept her for what she was? Why couldn't he try to love her, just a little.

Dash it, Sloane thought, why couldn't he protect her the way he'd sworn? Lisanne was being so good, so brave, enduring what no sensitive, intelligent female should have to. Confound it, his duchess could manage a huge estate. She was worth ten of Almack's simpering debs, so why did she have to suffer being inspected by every bitch and biddy on their committee? And why couldn't he scotch those blasted rumors? Blister it, Sloane couldn't fight what he couldn't see.

Findley *et fils* swore they'd kept their mummers dubbed, and Humbert was forcibly encouraged to seek greener pastures to spread his manure. Damn, the lady was stuck with St. Sevrin; she shouldn't have to be stuck with a reputation for peculiarity also. Besides, Lisanne's peculiarities were a deal more endearing than the average miss's airs and affectations. And she brewed the most effective morning-after remedy he'd ever tried.

Sloane was ready to take his wife home to Devon. She'd been seen, had been declared a diamond of the first water, and had been given the stamp of approval on an Almack's voucher. What more did anyone want? St. Sevrin wanted her happy, and he wanted her to himself. He wanted her, period. Possessive, protective, physically attracted—but it wasn't love he felt, the duke told himself. He couldn't love, couldn't be faithful to one woman. He never had been, never would be. Then again, he'd never gone so long without any woman at all, a sacrifice in his effort not to disgrace Lisanne. He'd shown her the delights of London; now he wanted to show her the delights of the marriage bed, without his best friend and his aunt looking on.

Aunt Hattie wouldn't hear of them leaving Town yet. Lisanne hadn't attended Almack's or a single rout party, to confront and confound the ton en masse. As a matter of fact, Lady Comstock declared, Lisanne ought to stay until they could throw a grand ball in her honor. Lisanne couldn't think of many things she'd like less—the plague, perhaps—and St. Sevrin knew the preparations for one of his aunt's extravaganzas could take months.

"Why can't she just share the Findley chit's come-out in two weeks?" he asked at dinner that night. "It's being held in Lisanne's own house, after all."

"Or you could move the cousin's presentation over to here," Trevor suggested. "The ballroom is larger, and you'd put out a more lavish spread than that nip-cheese Findley."

St. Sevrin put down his fork. "No, that won't do. I've forbidden the dastard my house. I don't intend to go back on my word now and have that leech trying to bleed Lisanne dry."

"If the ball is at Neville House," Aunt Hattie mused over her turbot in oyster sauce, "then by rights the two of you ought to be on the receiving line."

Lisanne was used to letting the others make such decisions. Someone was always telling her where to go or what to wear, and she really didn't mind, since they knew London ways better than she did. This time, though, she cleared her throat. Three pairs of eyes turned in her direction. The leaves were all removed from the mahogany table, so there was no vast distance between St. Sevrin at the head and Lisanne at the foot. Tonight it seemed like a mile. Lisanne felt that Sloane just wanted to see the job of introducing her around over and done, so he could pack her off to Devon and get on with his life. "I will not share Esmé's come-out."

As far as St. Sevrin was concerned, that was that. They were already asking a lot of Lisanne. If she didn't want to stand next to that gormless family, so be it. "Fine, we'll give out that the Findleys are merely renting Neville House. You wouldn't be expected to be hostess or honoree at a tenant's affair. We don't even have to attend."

Aunt Hattie almost choked on her asparagus. "What, do you want to undo all our work? The Findleys are encroaching mushrooms, but they are Lisanne's encroaching mushrooms and everyone knows that. Do you want them to think that she is not welcomed by her own family? Or"—another choke—"that she charged them for the use of her house?"

Lisanne cleared her throat again. When she had their attention, she quietly explained, "I did not say I wouldn't go, just that I wouldn't stand on the receiving line or share Esmé's limelight when she has planned for this night her entire life. I'll have many other opportunities; my cousin will not, if I know my uncle."

Trevor nodded, impressed. "Deuced generous of you, Duchess, considering."

Aunt Harriet knew better than to waste her breath arguing with her niece-by-marriage when Lisanne made one of her soft, even-toned declarations. The chit was nigh immovable when she got on her uppers. "But you'll attend?"

"Yes, I'll attend, Aunt Hattie, and hope that you will accompany me to lend your countenance to Esmé's presentation. And you, Your Grace, will please dance at least one dance with Esmé to raise her status among the other debs."

"Thank you, my sweet. That's the first time anyone has considered my dancing with a young miss to be anything less than scandalous."

"Hell," Trevor muttered into his napkin, "it's the first time I've been glad of my wooden leg."

Aunt Hattie had plans of her own for that ball at Neville House. A hint here, a reminder there, and she and Viscountess Roehampton would have every notable in Town at that party. At long last they'd all make the acquaintance of the newest reigning Toast and her reformed rake. That spotted chit's come-out would be successful beyond her mother's fondest dreams. Feckless Findley and his featherheaded wife might even get the chit fired off in one Season, when all the bucks and beaux came to ogle St. Sevrin's duchess.

Yes, they'd attend the ball at Neville House and kill off those unpleasant rumors once and for all. So content was

Aunt Hattie with her plan that she thought she might even warn the Findleys to expect a few more guests. A few hundred more. Aunt Hattie helped herself to another serving of syllabub as a reward. Yes, Sir Alfred would just love laying out his blunt for all those extra lobster patties and bottles of champagne.

Chapter Twenty-four

$\mathcal{A}$unt Harriet's excellent plan was sure to succeed except for one thing: the ball was going to be cancelled. Esmé was sick. With less than two weeks before the party, Sir Alfred was ailing, too, since he had already ordered the extra supplies. With such elevated company now expected, his wife had insisted on more flowers, a finer orchestra, and additional servants. Findley immediately dismissed the new help—and a few of the old.

When he was told the news, St. Sevrin decided the Findley chit must be suffering the green sickness because her beautiful, wealthy cousin would be making her first formal appearance at the ball. People were coming to see Lisanne, not some brash baronet's bran-faced daughter, and everyone knew it. If the brat had any honor, she'd be mortified that the ball was being held in Lisanne's house, without Lisanne's name on the invitations. Then again, if the brat had any honor, Lady Findley must have played her husband false.

He marched over to Neville House to demand the ball proceed as planned, sulky debutante or not. No one, least of all that flat, Findley, who'd caused all the difficulties in the first place, was going to steal Lisanne's chance to shine. If they weren't going to hold the party, Sloane would give the Findleys two days to pack and vacate his wife's house. Then he'd hire an army to remake the party for Lisanne. She wouldn't like it, but if they couldn't leave London until she had a ball, then a ball she would have. And it would be the finest one money—her money—could provide. If that's what it took to put to rest any notion that the Duchess of St. Sevrin was some harum-scarum hare-brain, that's what the duke would do.

Unfortunately Esmeralda truly was sick. Sloane met two doctors leaving as he entered Neville House. He knew both by reputation and couldn't discount their claims that the chit was seriously ill with blinding headaches, nausea, and fever. One of the doctors even suggested the girl might succumb to the mysterious ailment. The eminent physicians were arguing as St. Sevrin handed his hat and gloves to the butler. "I say she should be bled to relieve pressure on the brain."

"No, no, a purge is what she needs, to cleanse the system of its poisons."

"Cold baths, of course."

"Hot compresses, I insist."

When they were gone, the butler regretted that Sir Alfred was not receiving visitors. Prostrate with grief, he was, Pomfrey reported. It was more likely that Findley was in a stupor, St. Sevrin decided, knowing his only hope of maintaining this lifestyle was upstairs sick in bed. If Sir Alfred couldn't get Esmé buckled to a wealthy peer, he was up River Tick.

Nigel was not at home, not that St. Sevrin wanted to speak to that chinless clunch. From the odd word or two he'd heard about Town, Sloane concluded the sprig had most likely taken himself off to some low-rent brothel rather than be exposed to his sister's contagion. He'd rather have the pox, it seemed.

And Lady Alfred? She was suffering spasms and swoons.

Well, St. Sevrin couldn't throw them out, and he'd be damned if he'd pray for the chit's recovery, but he saw nothing else to do.

Lisanne did, of course. She told Aunt Hattie not to cancel her friend's invitations, not quite yet. She was going to Neville House to see for herself how matters stood.

St. Sevrin was adamant. "No. I forbid it. You are not putting one foot under that man's roof. A ball is one thing. Not even Findley would dare insult you in front of three hundred guests. I don't care if that coxcomb Nigel is away from home, I don't want you breathing his filthy air. Besides, we are supposed to attend Almack's tonight. Aunt worked hard enough to get you those vouchers, and the old harpies' noses get out of joint when someone refuses the invite."

He was still adamant three hours later, after he'd made the third trip back to Berkeley Square fetching books, bottles, and bundles of dried twigs and weeds from the stillroom she'd somehow found time to set up at St. Sevrin House. The Findleys' servants would never find what Lisanne needed, and she had to have Mary with her to help.

The duke didn't know what his wife was doing in Esmé's bedchamber, and he didn't want to know. He also didn't want any of Sir Alfred's staff to know. Bad enough Lisanne had tossed the two surgeons out; St. Sevrin didn't need a bunch of underpaid ignoramuses carrying tales of witchcraft and sorcery to the pubs. So he sat in a chair outside the room, or installed Kelly there when he was on an errand. Sloane even slept in the damned chair and got a crick in his neck. Heaven knew where Lisanne slept, for she refused to come away and leave Mary in charge, or the girl's mother, by George.

No, the girl's mother was less than useless with her weeping and wailing. If Lisanne hadn't dosed her with laudanum and sent the skitter-wit off to bed, Sloane would have ordered Kelly to take Lady Cherise for a soothing ride in the country. One way.

Even the food was terrible. How the devil did they think to feed the most demanding palates in London with this tripe the sulky servants fetched up? Sloane had meals brought over from St. Sevrin House to make sure Lisanne ate properly. If the Findley chit survived, they were holding that ball, and Sloane wasn't having his wife disappearing through the cracks in the floor.

The only good thing was that Sir Alfred and Nigel stayed away. Actually Sloane wished one of them would arrive and make some snide comment about Lisanne's untoward knowledge of herbs and healing. By the second day, the duke was itching for a fight. By the third, he would have strangled the Findley chit himself, to put them all out of their misery.

Then Lisanne came out of the room, looking exhausted but happy. Esmé would recover. She was out of danger and should recuperate in time for the ball. Of course Esmé had lost a deal of weight, which St. Sevrin thought might improve her figure, and she would be interestingly pale, but Esmé would be ready to dance in ten more days of careful nursing. Lisanne was willing to take turns with Mary now, so they both could get some rest. She didn't trust the Findleys' servants, and neither did the duke.

There were ten days before the ball, and nothing was being done that he could see. The chandeliers weren't being taken down for cleaning, the rugs weren't being lifted for beating. A few questions revealed that the guest rooms hadn't been aired and the silver hadn't been polished. Damn, that silver would have Sloane's wife's crest on it! The devil take it if he'd let her come to such a shabby affair.

So the duke planned the ball, with Trevor and Aunt Hattie assisting while Kelly watchdogged Lisanne and

Mary. St. Sevrin's own housekeeper came to oversee the cleaning while his own kitchens were busy preparing the menu. Trevor handled the guest lists, and Aunt Hattie selected flowers and ribbon decorations—more lavish than Sir Alfred would ever have permitted. The baronet slunk around, keeping out of the way of his nephew-by-marriage and that dangerous glint in St. Sevrin's eye.

Lady Findley dithered around, clutching a vinaigrette. She might be useless, but she was grateful.

"And I am so sorry I let those dreadful rumors make the rounds," she confessed.

"You? You were the one who tried to ruin your own niece?" St. Sevrin couldn't believe his ears, or that he was pulling this shrew's chestnuts out of the fire.

Cherise clutched her smelling salts. "Oh, dear, it wasn't that I was trying to ruin Annie, exactly."

"Her name is Lisanne, and what were you trying to do, exactly?"

"I didn't have any goal in mind, Your Grace. I . . . I was just upset. I knew what the servants were saying, of course, and then, when people started asking me about the new duchess, I simply told them what they wanted to hear."

"Do you dislike your own niece so much, then?"

"Oh, gracious no, I like her very well. But she wasn't an easy child to deal with, you know."

St. Sevrin could imagine. She wasn't an easy woman to deal with, either. He nodded for Lady Findley to go on. Guilt and gratitude made her want to explain.

"I never expected to take the place of her mother, you must understand. But Annie—Lisanne—hardly let me into her thoughts, much less her heart. And then she *would* go her own way. Sir Alfred really only wanted her to be like other children, but then he couldn't bear to be bested by a little girl. I suffered greatly from my nerves when they brangled."

What about how Lisanne suffered? St. Sevrin wanted to ask, but didn't.

"Then she grew up all of a sudden and married you. And she was beautiful and titled, smarter than both of my children combined, and wealthier than Golden Ball. Meanwhile she had left us on the brink of ruin, according to Sir Alfred. How could I not resent her good fortune?" Cherise mopped a tear from her eye. "It was so easy not to rebuke the servants for their gossip, or to recall one of Annie's odd starts for an interested ear. But I'll make it up to her, I swear. Everyone at the ball will know how good she is, how kind and wise, how hard she worked at her studies. If she hadn't spent all that time with her plants and such, and wasn't so sweet a girl to come help us, my Esmé might have perished."

The thought alone sent Lady Findley to rest on her couch, a hanky soaked in rosewater upon her furrowed brow, until she remembered that frowning caused lines.

Lady Cherise was as good as her word on the night of the ball. She replied to every guest passing through the receiving line that, yes, Esmé had made a remarkable recovery and, yes, she was in looks tonight, with all credit to her cousin. To hear her aunt, Lady St. Sevrin had snatched Esmé back from the jaws of death. An angel, she was, a saint.

Esmé added her bit about her kind and gentle cousin, who knew everything there was to know about herbal teas and tisanes. If anyone complimented Esmé on the decorations or the refreshments for the party, she was quick to heap accolades on the duke, too. Without her cousins, Esmé told everyone who would listen, there would be no ball at all. Instead the party was a success beyond everyone's expectations, except Aunt Hattie's.

Whereas the guests arrived at most of the humdrum debutante balls, greeted the hosts, sampled the refreshments, and had a drink or a dance or a hand or two of cards before moving on to the next, livelier entertainment, tonight everyone stayed at Neville House, waiting for its mistress.

Aunt Hattie had their entrance timed to the last second. The receiving line had been disbanded, the dancing had begun. Not many of the gentlemen had retired to the card rooms yet; not many of the chaperones along the walls had dozed off. Lady Comstock fussed with her turban a moment outside the ballroom until she heard the current dance set draw to a close. Then she had the butler announce them. She kicked the man halfway through, and hissed, "Louder."

Pomfrey started again. "My Lady Harriet Comstock, the Honorable Lieutenant Trevor Roe." Aunt Hattie and Trev moved off to the side to watch, Trevor using just one cane now. Hattie whispered, "Louder still," to the butler. She needn't have, for there wasn't a sound in the room as all eyes turned to the door.

"Her Grace, the Duchess of St. Sevrin and Baroness Neville, His Grace, the Duke of St. Sevrin."

Lisanne looked up at her husband inquiringly. He patted the hand resting on his arm. "You were a lady before I met you."

Pomfrey the butler nodded. He'd been one of those quick to spread tales about the odd little hoyden running wild in Devon. Tonight there was a lady, beyond the shadow of a doubt.

Lisanne was wearing a gown of azure tissue-silk, almost the color of her eyes, with a silver gauze overskirt that was strewn with star-shaped brilliants. The neckline was cut low enough that St. Sevrin wanted to take her home to bed, but high enough that Aunt Hattie wouldn't let her insert a lace filler. With the most beautiful gown she'd ever owned, Lisanne wore the fabled St. Sevrin sapphires. Instead of wearing the pendant as a necklace, however, Lisanne wore it as a headpiece woven through her pinned-up golden hair, with the magnificent central stone hanging onto her forehead. No milk-and-water miss, no ordinary young female here. Everything about her, the soft smile, the straight back, the outrageous display of gems, bespoke wealth, breeding, and confidence in her own unique character. If a flock of butterflies had taken up residence in her stomach, only St. Sevrin knew, by the trembling of her fingers. He squeezed her hand.

Esmé skipped up to them and kissed Lisanne's cheek as Lady Findley made her way to them. On cue, waiters circulated with glasses of champagne and Sir Alfred, by arrangement and under extreme duress, proposed a belated toast to the newly married pair. Every word Findley spoke might have been a drop of hemlock on his lips, but not a soul in the room could suspect that the exquisite young duchess was anything but a beloved member of the family.

As the orchestra struck a waltz, St. Sevrin took his wife's hand, but she wanted to introduce Trevor to her cousin first.

"You must be sure to rest, Esmé. I recommend Lieutenant Roe as an admirable companion to sit out the next dance."

Esmé was agreeable. She hadn't been given approval to waltz anyway, and Lieutenant Roe was tall, dark, and heroic. Besides, he was the son of a viscount. She led him to a row of gilt chairs.

"Well done, Duchess," St. Sevrin congratulated. "And now I believe it is our dance." They came together as if the room were empty, with no one else for either of them. The gliding movement, the closeness, the way their thighs touched occasionally, or their chests—oh, how St. Sevrin wished they were not in a ballroom. Lisanne could only marvel that waltzing with her dance instructor was never like this.

All too soon the set was over and the duke had to lead

Lisanne back toward his aunt and hers. The cream of Society was waiting to meet his duchess. He smiled and kissed her hand. "It's your night, sweetheart."

Chapter Twenty-five

*B*efore she was home in Devon Lisanne had a lot of miles to travel, and one more hurdle, Almack's. Aunt Hattie insisted they attend, despite Lisanne's success at Esmé's ball. Everyone near enough to get an introduction had come away from Neville House declaring the new duchess an absolute delight. The very next day some of Lisanne's admirers started coming to her with odd complaints and illnesses, until the doctors set up a cry that she was practicing medicine without a license. Now debutantes and dandies brought her their bilious bulldogs and felines with fur balls. They all stayed to tea, of course. St. Sevrin House was suddenly the place to be seen, with the most eligible *partis* hoping for a smile from the newest Toast, with the Season's debs hoping for a chance to imitate Lisanne's style.

Kelly had to find the duchess space in the stable mews for treating her upper-crust patients, in addition to the injured birds, broken-down carriage horses, and stray mongrels she seemed to acquire the way other ladies acquired new hats.

Trevor was a help and, not so coincidentally, Esmé, who had never touched a four-legged beast except with a fork before this. Lisanne was pleased at their growing friendship, but not counting her chickens until they hatched egg-shaped betrothal rings.

St. Sevrin had taken himself off to consult a ship-builder in Folkestone. It was either that or cause chaos in Lisanne's parlor by bodily ejecting all those young pups drooling at her skirts. Skirts which he, incidentally, had not been able to get near.

The night of Esmé's ball, when they were all buoyed with success and champagne, he'd decided to visit his wife's bedchamber. That poise, that gown, left no doubt of Lisanne's womanhood; Sloane was ready to prove his manhood. He was more than ready. He was eager, aching, and panting as badly as those adoring moon-calves at the very thought of making Lisanne his.

Unfortunately she was already asleep when he pushed open the connecting door to their rooms. After nursing Esmé and preparing for her first major ball, Lisanne looked exhausted in the light of his candle. Sloane could see the shadows under her eyes and didn't have the heart to waken her. The next day his house was filled with callers, his desk was hidden under stacks of invitations, and the place was turning into an infirmary for asthmatic lapdogs. Let her enjoy her success, St. Sevrin decided, as long as he didn't have to watch. He'd be back for Wednesday's crucible at Almack's. Then they were leaving, no matter what Aunt Hattie said.

According to that venerable lady, a female wasn't entirely *comme il faut* until she'd been approved by the patronesses at that bastion of propriety. A lady might be popular, acclaimed in the newspapers and journals, but she wasn't past ridicule if she didn't pass through those hallowed doors. If Lisanne didn't do it now, they'd have the whole thing to go through again next Season, or whenever the duchess came back to Town.

Lisanne would go through one more senseless ordeal then, one more humiliating rite of passage into her husband's world. She'd do it, but only for him. If St. Sevrin were ever to take his proper place in the governing of the country, he'd need a wife above reproach. For that matter, Aunt Hattie felt that Sloane needed to be seen at Almack's, satin knee breeches and all, to bolster his own reputation.

As for the duchess, she'd seen enough sights and met enough people to be convinced that she wouldn't miss this frantic bustle once she was back in Devon. Only Lisanne knew how hard it was for her to face such crowds in her own drawing room when she was used to hours—no, days—of solitude.

It might have been easier if she had her husband's support, especially since she was making herself miserable on his behalf. Sloane had been attentive at Esmé's ball, hovering nearby to make introductions and accept congratulations. He'd left her side only for the one dance with Esmé, crowning that miss's triumphal come-out. And Lisanne knew he was attracted to her: she could feel the tingling heat pass between their gloved hands during that waltz. He might have been counting the freckles on her cheeks, so intently did he stare at her. She'd hoped that night that he would . . . but he hadn't. Now he was gone, leaving her to deal with this gathering of peageese in her parlor.

Sometimes a single grain of sand can make a pearl, a thing of great beauty. In other situations, that same grain of sand can make a blister on somebody's foot. Which is to say that, over time, the smallest irritations can grow larger with constant rubbing.

Lisanne's nerves were being rubbed raw. She was dressed to the teeth again, in a gown whose cost would have fed a hundred beggars. She was wearing a tiara besides, adding the weight of guilt, at how many children could be educated with one of its diamonds, to the weight of the foolish bauble. She already had a headache.

The Almack's hostesses were adding to the pain with their subtle interrogations and sly innuendos. Sloane had said they were like sleek house cats. To Lisanne they seemed more like hunting jaguars, sniffing out new prey.

She'd been separated from her party almost instantly by Sally Jersey, who wanted her to meet Lord Alvanley, who may have been a cousin to her mother. Did Her Grace know? Her Grace knew that Lord Alvanley's eye looked grotesque through the quizzing glass he so rudely used to inspect her.

Lady Drummond-Burrell was interested in orchids, and in finding out how well-studied Lady Lisanne was on the exotic plants. Lisanne was well-studied enough to know that she could have been talking Hindustani, for all the other lady understood.

Speaking the formal French of the Russian court, Princess Lieven obviously hoped to trip the newcomer up on her schoolgirl grammar. The princess was wearing a taffeta gown with ermine borders, at least fifteen dead ermines, Lisanne calculated. She responded in Russian and moved on.

Maria Sefton might have measured the depth of Lisanne's curtsy to an inch, gauging if this interloper knew the proper degree of deference. Lisanne held her head high. She was a duchess by marriage, a baroness by birth. She would not kowtow to anyone so impolite as to make guests—paying guests at that—run this gauntlet of sharpened claws.

Lisanne caught her husband's eye across the room. St. Sevrin shrugged as if to say she was on her own now, before he returned to his conversation with the dashing redhead at his side.

Aunt Hattie had warned Lisanne how it would be, that they couldn't shield her from the tabbies tonight, not unless they wished to give rise to more questions about her competence. Aunt Hattie hadn't warned her that St. Sevrin would take the opportunity to get up a flirtation with one of the most notoriously willing widows still invited to Almack's.

Sloane was even sharing the contents of the flask in his pocket with the dazzling female, while Lisanne sipped tepid orgeat brought by some lordling produced by Sally Jersey as a suitable partner. Suitable, hah! With greasy hair and eyes that never rose above her bosom, the man wasn't suitable to walk her dog.

Well, Lisanne fumed, she was quite competent to handle this on her own if her husband chose to abandon her. She didn't like being passed around as if she were a new shipment of yard goods to be inspected or a new mix of snuff to be sampled. She didn't like not being permitted to sit with Trevor and Esmé, not being permitted to choose her own dance partners. She absolutely despised the fact that while she was suffering through Lord Higgenbotham's lumbago and Sir Sheldon's sweaty palms and fetid breath, St. Sevrin was having a high old time peering down the widow's low neckline. Any lower and the collar would be a belt around her waist.

My, how that grain of resentment rankled.

Lisanne was walking through this genteel fire for St. Sevrin, damn his roving eyes, to establish him as a gentleman of stature and honor. He, meanwhile, was taking the first opportunity to confirm his reputation as a rake. He even looked the part in his elegant black and white formal wear with a single ruby in his cravat highlighting the reddish glints to his hair. No other gentleman present had such broad shoulders or well-muscled legs. No other gentleman present interested Lisanne in the least. In fact, she was sick and tired of the whole business of being presented, being approved, being accepted. St. Sevrin hadn't even accepted her as his wife, by Jupiter. Her chin rose. She'd been accepted down paths where these fools couldn't hope to tread. How dare they sit in judgment of her. How dare he dally with that deep-chested demirep.

Lisanne wanted to go home, not to Berkeley Square,

but to Devon. Now. Lisanne had proved she was a lady, now she'd prove she was what they had all believed anyway, St. Sevrin most of all. He kept waiting for her to do something outlandish, didn't he? She wasn't going to disappoint him again, the way she'd done in their marriage.

She watched as Sloane escorted his new friend out of the ballroom proper. They'd already had two dances. One more and the widow may as well be standing on the corner of Covent Garden, so they must be headed for the card room. At least Almack's did not tend toward secluded corners and private chambers. St. Sevrin never played for the chicken stakes permitted here, though, so likely there was a higher ante, such as the woman's favors. The redhead would win when pigs flew.

Lisanne sent her latest partner, a clumsy dancer and a clumsier conversationalist, off to the refreshment room for another tasteless drink while she took up a position next to a potted plant at the edge of the dance floor. The palm tree looked as parched and brittle as Lisanne felt.

"How do you do, sir?" she asked. Getting no response except a startled look from the two chaperones nearby, Lisanne went on: "It's a terrible crush here, isn't it? I'm finding it hard to breathe myself, with all these perfumed bodies, so it's no wonder your fronds are drooping." One of the chaperones had scurried away to whisper in a different ear. The other stayed, fascinated, her mouth open, as Lisanne continued her one-sided chat. "I suppose we should be happy they use perfume, my dear, for I understand some of the guests see water as rarely as you appear to."

Out of the corner of her eye she could see a wave of motion travel across the room like a breeze blowing through a field of wheat. Not quite every eye in the room was turned in her direction, but almost. Sticking her gloved fingers into the pot, Lisanne scrabbled around until she had a sample of the dirt in her previously immaculate hand. Then she sniffed at the dirt and went so far as to stick her tongue out near it, pretending to taste the soil. That may have been too far, for the thud she heard could only be Aunt Cherise's limp body hitting the floor.

Aunt Hattie was across the room, trying desperately to extricate herself from an old court card in a bagwig who kept shouting, "What's that they're saying? They're awarding a palm?"

Esmé and Trevor were arguing over what to do. Trevor won and limped off to get the duke.

Lisanne had a moment before all of them, plus a few of Almack's outraged hostesses, converged on her. So she recommended that her friend ask for some ground fish bones, or tea made from well-rotted manure. "Perhaps that's what they are serving here. The stuff tastes like—"

Esmé got to her first. "My, what a sense of humor my cousin has," she commented to the room at large. "So witty, so amusing. Why, she kept us all in stitches back in Devon."

Aunt Hattie was out of breath, but she managed to wheeze, "My dear duchess, I am the one in the family who is supposed to be eccentric. You're much too young to affect quirks to be interesting, isn't that so, Lionel? I mean Sloane, of course."

St. Sevrin's mouth was smiling. His eyes were shooting daggers. "I believe my bride was trying to get my attention, ladies, that's all. I admit to being derelict in my attentions this evening. I'm still not used to leg-shackles, don't you know."

A few nearby gentlemen laughed in commiseration. A new bride was a deuced nuisance, and that flame-haired widow could make any man forget his own wife, even if the wife was a tiny golden-haired beauty. More than one of the men wished he'd been quick enough to console St. Sevrin's bride.

"You see me a chastened man, Duchess," the duke was

claiming for the spectators' benefit. "I swear not to leave your side again tonight."

With that he bowed to their audience and led Lisanne onto the dancing area. Actually the grip on her forearm was more like a vice clamp, cutting off circulation. "Smile, damn you," he whispered.

Lisanne pasted a smile on her face that matched his for insincerity, and they got through the set. Without stopping to speak to anyone, St. Sevrin led her off the dance floor and out the door to the entry hall, where Aunt Hattie and Trevor were already waiting with their wraps. The carriage was at the curb.

Trevor looked from the duke to the duchess and suggested that he and Lady Comstock take a hackney home.

St. Sevrin was already helping his aunt into the coach. "No, for if you're not along, I might strangle her."

Ordinarily the carriage was spacious enough for the four of them. Not tonight. Ordinarily they'd have been chatting about the evening's entertainment. Not tonight.

"Hell and damnation," the duke finally ground out. "Why the deuce did you have to pull this stunt tonight?"

"Those women were being hateful, and I am tired of being scrutinized like an insect under a microscope. I decided that since you never cared what anyone said about you, I wouldn't care, either."

His voice was as sharp as a knife. "I may have been careless with my own reputation, Duchess, but I do believe that you knew how very much I cared about yours. That's what this whole time in London has been about. All of Aunt Hattie's efforts, all those boring teas and dinner parties, were to make your peers respect you. Now it's all wasted, damn it."

"I just gave them what they expected."

"You gave me a kick in the—The devil take it, you don't even talk to your own potted plants."

"Yes, I do."

"You do not."

"I do."

"You don't."

"Children!" Aunt Hattie had her hands over her ears. "Stop this instant, or I'll faint like that ninnyhammer Findley woman, I swear."

Lisanne folded her hands in her lap and with utmost reserve stated, "I always sing while I am working in the garden. Or I hum. The plants like it."

The duke snorted. "Then I suppose we should consider ourselves lucky this one didn't request an operatic aria."

Trevor chuckled, which rewarded him with a kick from Aunt Hattie. Since it was his wooden leg she kicked, Trev didn't notice, but Aunt Hattie gasped.

"You see, now you've given my aunt a spasm with your idiotic behavior."

"My behavior? My behavior? I wasn't the one ogling some female's bosom all night!"

"Aha! I was right all along. You were jealous, that's what. You were bitten by the green-eyed monster and tried to bite me back." The idea didn't seem to bother Sloane as much as he thought it should.

"Why should I be jealous? We had an agreement and . . . and I don't care what you do."

"You were jealous, admit it."

"I was not!"

He folded his arms over his chest and winked at Trevor, who was grinning by now. "She likes me, you know."

"I do not."

Sloane smiled. "Then give me another explanation for this night's debacle."

First there was silence. Then a low murmur: "I want to go home."

Chapter Twenty-six

Spun sugar and steel were an unlikely mixture, but that was St. Sevrin's duchess. They couldn't stay in London—who knew what she'd do next to get her way?—and Sloane wouldn't cave in and take her home. A man had to have some pride left, some sense of mastery. Besides, in Devon Lisanne would disappear into the estate books or the library or those blasted woods. St. Sevrin had a better idea. He gave her one day to pack, one day to make whatever arrangements she needed. They were going on their honeymoon.

The yacht was waiting in Bristol, back from another trip to pick up injured officers from the Peninsula. They'd sail to Ireland, to Liam McCardle's horse farm. If there was one thing St. Sevrin knew, it was gambling. He had some of his own money put by, winnings and earnings on his investments, and now he was going to start that racing stud. He had to do it soon, before winter set in and they couldn't travel to Ireland, where Liam, another retired army officer, was breeding the finest Thoroughbred mares. Somewhere in Portugal they had discovered that Liam was a distant relative of Sloane's own Irish mother Fiona, although Lady Comstock repudiated the connection. McCardle had written back to Sloane's request with an invitation to come at any time. The house was not up to ducal standards, but it was always open to Sherry, especially if his pocketbook was open for horse-trading.

That was the first part of Sloane's plan. The second was to carry his impossible wife on board the yacht and not let her out of their cabin until she was breeding. If she were enceinte, that nonsense at Almack's would be chalked up to the well-known vagaries of incipient motherhood and forgiven in a minute.

His third intention was to make her enjoy it. With no maid, no dog, no duties, no one to care about her behavior or his, Sloane meant to show Lisanne how much he cared, how little other women appealed to him. The gist of the strategy was that he wanted his wife, and was deuced tired of waiting.

While Lisanne was leaving instructions with an appalled Kelly about the dog and the other invalids now placed in his care—made bearable only because Mary was being left behind to help him transport the menagerie back to Devon—the duke was stocking the yacht's master cabin. Loaded aboard were champagne and oysters, wine and cheese, baskets of flowers.

Lisanne was charmed by his preparations despite herself and Sloane's high-handed ways. Maybe they could have a real marriage after all, and maybe she'd learn to be satisfied with whatever he could give. For now she was eager and anxious, excited and aquiver about their long-delayed wedding night and her first boat ride.

It might be her last ride anywhere, Lisanne was so sick. All of St. Sevrin's grand schemes were going overboard, along with the champagne and oysters, the wine and cheese. He never thought for an instant that his intrepid wife might get seasick! He never thought to bring peppermint, ginger, or any of the usual remedies. He never thought he'd be spending his honeymoon holding a basin and a damp face cloth. At least he'd proven his devotion, although Lisanne was too miserable to care. Somewhere between Swansea and the Irish Sea, St. Sevrin vowed to stop drinking if only she'd recover.

By the time they docked in Ireland, Lisanne had to be carried off the boat, begging Sloane to promise that they'd walk home.

Liam was delighted to welcome Sherry and his new wife, although privately he considered the duchess too wan and weak for a man of St. Sevrin's iron. With apologies for his bachelor quarters, Liam placed Lisanne in his housekeeper's care and took Sherry off for a taste of home-brewed Irish whiskey. When the duke stuck to one glass of ale and hurried back to make sure his lady was sleeping peacefully, Liam reassessed his opinion. Perhaps there was more to Her Grace than met the eye.

By the next morning, Lisanne was recovered enough to join the men at the paddock, having already visited the barns, made friends with the head groom's children, and helped cook breakfast.

"I see you are feeling much better, Your Grace," Liam offered, while Sherry helped her to a seat on the fence railing.

Lisanne threw off her bonnet, letting her unpinned hair fall to her shoulders. She laughed out loud, the happiest sound Sloane had ever heard from her. She opened her arms to include the rolling green hills, the clear, clean air, the beautiful horses in the field. "How could I not feel wonderful in this enchanted land? It's just too bad that it's an island."

Soon it was time to get to the serious business of selecting a mare to breed St. Sevrin's future champions. Stable boys led the horses past them while Liam recounted their ancestry and racing history. Every one of the mares was a winner.

Lisanne pointed to a pretty bay with a star on her forehead. "That's the one you should buy."

"What, on a look?" Sloane scoffed. "I'll need to see

them run, study the stud books, check them for sound-ness. It's not as easy as picking a bonnet, sweetings."

Lisanne just laughed. She pulled her carved flute out of the pocket of her red wool cape, along with some string, papers, a handful of clover wrapped in a handker-chief, and an apple. She played a few notes and, sure enough, the bay mare trotted right over to the fence and daintily accepted the apple from her hand.

"Can you play some more, Your Grace?" Liam asked, thinking, like Sloane, that it was pure coincidence. "Maybe the other mares will like your music, too."

So Lisanne played a tune, like nothing St. Sevrin had ever heard. He thought he recognized birdcalls and the running notes of rippling streams and the song butterflies might sing, if they could. The other horses pricked their ears, but the bay mare stayed by the fence near Lisanne's boot, swaying to the music.

There were tears in the eyes of the old grooms, and clapping from the young ones. Liam was stunned. "No wonder you like it here, lassie. There must be a bit of the old country in you." He slapped his friend's back as a blushing Lisanne climbed down and ran off. "Your wife is magnificent, Sherry."

St. Sevrin turned to watch as Lisanne skipped away with the groom's children laughing behind her, like some Pied Piper. The oldest boy yelled back that they were go-ing to show the duchess where a dragon lay buried, and a real true fairy ring. "You don't think she is . . . different?"

"Different? I'll say she is. She's one in a million, you lucky dog. If every woman was like your duchess, there'd never be a bachelor left in the world." With that Liam left St. Sevrin at the gate, most likely to follow Lisanne, too.

Damn, Sloane thought while pretending to study the field of horses, Lisanne just wasn't like other women. "I'll never understand her," he muttered to himself.

"Seems to me, boyo, ye don't have to understand the lassie to love her."

There was no one nearby. St. Sevrin shook himself. He'd known that giving up drinking was going to wreak havoc with his system. He'd expected shaking hands and sweaty skin—not hearing voices. He tried to get his attention back on the mares, ignoring Lisanne's bay, for what did his wife know of race horses? "Now, which one of you is going to bring me the luck of the Irish?"

The same voice, with a shade more impatience, spoke again: "Seems to me ye've already got all the luck ye need, ye blitherer, and the good advice."

St. Sevrin looked around, then down. Far down. At about ankle height, he spotted a tiny gentleman in a green suit. St. Sevrin reached for the flask that had always been in his pocket until today when he needed it. Since giving up demon drink was obviously too hard, Sloane switched his vow to giving up wenches. That was easy; his wife was the only woman he desired. Seeing Lisanne in his dreams was one thing, seeing leprechauns in broad daylight was another. "What am I supposed to do now?" Sloane asked his hallucination, "catch you and make you tell me where you've hidden your gold?"

The little man wagged his finger at the duke. "Ye've already found the pot o'gold, spalpeen, ye're just too clottish to recognize it."

That touched a sensitive nerve. "I didn't marry her just for the money."

"I know that, ye noddy Englishman. Does she?"

Either he was suffering from the lack of drink, or else he was going crazy. As crazy as his wife.

St. Sevrin decided to buy two mares, the one with the best record and breeding, and the one Lisanne picked. Liam was willing to take the yacht as payment for one of them. The duke hustled his wife through quick good-byes and onto a blessedly short, smooth ferry crossing. He hired a carriage to take them the rest of the way home to Devon.

At the first inn, St. Sevrin waited until after dinner and tea, and then fifteen minutes, no more, before he knocked on his wife's door. She was sitting at a dressing table braiding her hair for the night, wearing a lacy nightgown that made the breath catch in his throat.

"You're not sick?" he asked. "Not tired? You have no injured bird to tend or the innkeeper's children to read a story?"

She shook her head, smiling, hoping. She knew he wasn't drinking, for her, just as she knew he'd bought the bay mare for her.

Encouraged, Sloane went on with the speech he'd prepared over the last two days. "Lisanne, I want to be the best husband I can, the husband you deserve. But I need you to show me how."

"In London?" she asked, troubled.

He stood behind her and unbraided her hair, then reached for the brush on the dresser and started feathering the blond curls down her back. "I don't want to go back to London, not without you. But I don't want to be in your way if you don't wish me in Devon, either. I never want to see you hidden away like a hermit. I think we can have a good life together. Will you let me try?"

"I think I would like that very much." She already liked how her toes were tingling at his touch, but it wasn't enough. "I know it wasn't in our agreement, but do you think you could come to love me?"

"I don't know." He stopped brushing and Lisanne lowered her chin so he wouldn't see the tears forming in her eyes in the mirror's reflection. She'd taken his crumbs, like the birds in her hand. Maybe she could love enough for the both of them.

Sloane moved to stand in front of her, then crouched so their eyes met. He cupped her chin in his hand, one finger brushing at a crystal teardrop. "I don't know what love is, sweetings. You're the one with the wisdom of the ages, it seems. You tell me. If you are on my mind every minute,

227

waking or sleeping, if I would gladly lay down my life to make you happy, and if I want you with me for the next century at least—what do you call that?"

"I'd call that love." Now tears of joy fell unashamed. "But . . . but are you sure you're not afraid I'm insane?"

"Precious, I'm only afraid you're too sane to love me back."

Later, deep in his embrace, with nothing between them but satisfied desire, Lisanne whispered, "Now that is something you never have to worry about."

"Are you sure the children are safe playing in the woods by themselves, Lisanne? I know you trust Buck to look after them, but shouldn't they have someone besides a dog, even if he is Becka's son?"

"Stop worrying, darling. They don't need the dog. They'll be fine."

St. Sevrin wasn't satisfied. "The boys are one thing, but even little Fiona? Are you sure?"

"I am certain, my love, as certain as I am that I love you."

"Well, in that case, let's go upstairs. We might as well take advantage of the peace and quiet for once."